COMATOSE

THE BOOK OF MALADIES VOLUME 5

D.K. HOLMBERG

.

THE FIRST VICTIM

Alec paced through the ward at the university, scanning the beds. There weren't as many occupied as there often were, with fewer people having come to the university. Alec wasn't sure whether that was something to be excited about or whether he should be concerned. He hadn't been in his position long enough to know what the typical trends for the university were, and not long enough to know whether the absence of illness was something to worry about.

"You're walking too fast," Beckah said.

Alec glanced over to his friend. She had her hair pulled up, and it was twisted into something almost like a braid, giving her a more elegant appearance than she normally had. "I need to walk fast," he said. "Now that I'm a physicker—"

"Now that you're a physicker, you can slow down and take your time. Gods, you're walking faster than the junior physickers. They have no trouble taking their time as they make their way through the wards."

Alec shook his head. It had only been a few weeks since he had been promoted to full physicker. A few weeks since he had demanded testing, taking advantage of an old tradition that had been rarely used in the university's history, and only a few weeks since he was granted equal stead with many of the people he had long admired at the university. He didn't have the same cachet as the master physickers, but he was only one step below them in rank now.

"I still feel as if I have to prove myself," he said, lowering his voice. Even though he had been promoted, it was still difficult for him to feel comfortable with his position. Since his promotion, he had spent even more time in the library studying, and even more time in the wards working with the people who came for healing.

There was something peaceful about his time in the wards. It was familiar and throwing himself into his work was satisfying in a way that spending time in the library reading through books was not.

"You already proved yourself. That's how you got here," Beckah said. They paused in front of a cot where a young woman lay sleeping. She had dark hair much like Beckah's, and an olive complexion. Her features were delicate. Though she was reclining, making it hard to tell, she looked short, maybe only a little taller than his friend Sam. Alec had examined this woman before, trying to determine what was wrong with her, but she was one of the true mysteries in the ward. She was one of several in the ward. People with ailments whose sources the master physickers weren't able to uncover, and Alec was drawn to those most of all. If he could uncover the secret of what was wrong with them, he thought he could gain even more respect.

It would be easy enough to restore her, he thought, and all it would take would be using easar paper and his and Sam's blood, but that felt like a cheat. He would do it if not for the fact that his supply of easar paper was limited.

"You know what's wrong with her?" Beckah asked.

"I'm supposed to be asking you the questions now," Alec said, smiling over at her.

Beckah made a face and shook her head. "I think we both know that you have no intention of testing me."

"Is that right? I *am* a full physicker."

"And as I suspected, now you're impossible."

Alec grinned. "I thought you would like the fact that I was promoted."

"I like the idea that you have access that we didn't have before. I'm optimistic that your access will allow you to get closer to those Scribes who are a part of the university," she said.

"It hasn't, not yet," Alec told her.

He studied the woman as he spoke. Had her complexion changed? He didn't think so. Her breathing was regular, and every time he assessed her heartbeat, it was steady. There were no signs of fever. There was nothing outwardly wrong with her. She simply wouldn't wake up.

Alec had tried various treatments that would help with sedation, thinking that perhaps she had been poisoned. He had been exposed to plenty of substances that would lead to an ongoing sedation such as this, but nothing seemed to work. Nothing about her changed, leaving him to conclude that it wasn't an illness like that. Whatever it was, he remained unable to make the diagnosis.

It pained him to have to admit that.

"What about Master Eckerd?"

"Master Eckerd is difficult to find. When he is around, he is often unavailable, taking time to work with the students."

"I seem to recall that you were once one of his students."

Alec nodded. He had hoped that with his promotion to physicker he could continue his studies with Master Eckerd, but that didn't seem to be the case. The master physickers rarely took on physickers as mentees. Now that he was promoted, he was on his own quite a bit more than he had been before.

"It's different," Alec said.

"What about your father? What has he said?"

"My father was pleased, though I sensed he was slightly surprised," he told her. When he had gone to his father's shop, Alec remembered the look on his father's face when he told him that he been promoted to full physicker. It matched the surprise when he shared with his father that he'd demanded testing.

"Now that you're a physicker, have you thought about trying to get him to come back?"

Alec shrugged. That had been on his mind. His father

was a master physicker. He had abandoned the university after Alec was born, around the same time he lost his wife —Alec's mother. Knowing what his father knew of healing, his departure was a significant loss to the university. Having his father's knowledge would have been valuable. How many would benefit from it?

Then again, how many had benefited because his father had spent time outside of the university and had continued to heal, not demanding payment for his services? He had probably helped far more there than he would have been able to help at the university.

Yet had he stayed at the university, he would've been able to train future physickers, and they would have been able to help others. Perhaps his father could have convinced the other masters there was no need to charge for services. Maybe he could have had a different sort of influence.

Instead, he had influenced Alec, and he was the only one who benefited from his father's knowledge and training.

"Alec?"

He looked up. Beckah smiled at him, and she hesitantly touched him on the arm.

"You seem distracted."

He smiled. "I have all these things working through my head. It's not just my father, and it's not just trying to come to terms with my new position and what that means for me, but it's also…"

"It's Sam."

He nodded. "It's always Sam, isn't it?"

"She's on your mind much of the time," Beckah said.

"I've gotten used to knowing that when you disappear like that, you're thinking about her."

"I keep waiting"—he leaned toward her, lowering his voice, not wanting any of the junior physickers to hear him talking—"knowing that she's going to go after the Thelns, knowing that she needs to go after Tray, but when? I worry that she will run off without asking me for help."

"Do you really think she would do that? She needs your help."

He hoped she did, and hoped Sam recognized there was value in their partnership, but the more she learned about her abilities as a Kaver, the more she didn't need him. He had seen the way that she could fight even without her augmentations, and the way that she now was able to use her staff, fighting with it in a way that he still could barely comprehend. Was it something of her Kaver ability that granted her such skill or was it simply training?

Alec wasn't sure, and maybe he didn't need to know. Maybe he wasn't meant to know. He could be impressed by her ability without knowing and could simply marvel at the person that she had become. She was so different from the woman he had met all that time ago, and even then, she had been impressive.

"I had thought she might have gone before now," he said.

"Isn't it better that she hasn't? If she had, and had she asked you to join her, you would have been pulled away just after your promotion. Don't you think that would've raised even more questions?"

"It might've raised questions, but I think that some of the other Scribes would've been able to minimize those. If nothing else, Master Eckerd and Helen might have been able to help with that."

"It still would've raised questions. Think about everything you've gone through since your promotion. Think about the reaction that everyone has had since then. If you hadn't been here for that, it would've raised different questions."

Alec knew she was right, and he also knew that it probably didn't matter. In the scheme of things, he was Sam's Scribe, and he needed to assist her with everything that she did. Even if that meant that he had to sacrifice his own training."

"I might not have been disappointed to miss all of that," Alec said.

"No? You haven't enjoyed the looks that you've been getting?"

"I think some of the looks have been more than I would prefer."

"What about Master Carl?"

Alec looked around the room. There were no master physickers here, not yet, but in time, they would arrive, bringing their students with them. Alec had made a point to avoid Master Carl when he came to the wards. He had agreed to Alec's promotion, but that didn't mean they now got along, and it didn't mean that Master Carl even knew anything about Alec's role as a Scribe.

"Master Carl has given me space."

"Is it because he has chosen to give you space, or because you have created it?"

"Does it matter?"

"I don't know. I think you need to own the fact that you were promoted. Gods, few are ballsy enough to demand promotion and pull it off. I know how I would be if that were me. I might be flaunting it to everybody who came through."

"Which is why I wouldn't vote for your promotion," Alec said, smiling.

"You don't get a vote. You're only a physicker. It's only the *master* physickers who get to vote."

Alec grinned and turned his attention back to the woman. He grabbed the record hanging near the end of the bed and started flipping through the pages. She had come to the university already sedated. He skimmed over the various treatments that had been attempted but didn't find anything that was useful. Alec had an entire page of his own, though there were other junior physickers who had attempted various things. That had surprised him. He thought the junior physickers would defer to the full physickers, and maybe it was the fact that it was Alec that they didn't, but it seemed they were muddying the potential treatment by all of them having a shot at helping her.

"Is it because she's pretty?" Beckah asked.

Alec blinked and looked up. "What?"

"Is that the reason you're so fixated on helping her?"

"It's not because she's pretty," Alec said.

"So, you do think she's pretty?"

"Stop."

"I'm just trying to figure out what motivates the great Alec Stross to choose his subjects for healing. I mean, if it were me lying here, would you be so inclined to work with me?"

Alec shook his head as he glared at her. "This young woman's appearance has no bearing on my attempt to heal her."

"Now she's a young woman? See? I knew it was her appearance that motivated you."

"I might make sure that you're assigned extra responsibilities," Alec said. "I seem to recall that physickers are allowed to assign punishments."

"You wouldn't."

"Maybe I wouldn't if you didn't harass me. Stefan doesn't harass me in that way."

"Only because he's still angry. He thinks we're keeping something from him."

"Because we are," Alec said.

As he scanned the page, trying to think about what he might offer this woman next, the doors to the ward opened. A cart rolled in, and Alec saw that an older man was lying on it.

"You can go over there," Beckah said. "You don't have to wait on me."

"It's supposed to be the junior physickers who are given first attempts at healing."

"Just because that's the way it's supposed to be doesn't mean you have to follow those traditions. If you followed traditions, you wouldn't be in your position now, would you?"

Alec looked around. None of the junior physickers had moved away from the people they were working on, practically ignoring the students who had rolled in the new person. There wasn't anything he could offer this woman, and he would need more information—maybe from a family member, if one could be found—to find out what might have happened to her before she arrived. He might even consider going to his father. He didn't have a master physicker here that he could work with, but that didn't mean that he didn't have access to a master physicker. His father could still serve as a mentor for him.

Alec made his way over to the cart. The two students were arranging the sheets overtop the patient, and as he approached, they looked over. One of them was Stefan. Alec didn't like the sense of separation between them, but he hoped that he could ease it. The other was Andrew—a student that he had never gotten along well with.

Andrew frowned. "Physicker Stross," he said.

Alec didn't love the distinction that was now between him and those he had once studied with but hearing it from Andrew was fine.

"What do we know about this person?" Alec asked, not yet initiating his own examination. He would take the assessment from the students as was expected of him.

"He… he was brought in unresponsive. We haven't been able to determine anything other than that he seems stable," Stefan said.

It was much like the young woman, though that was probably only a strange coincidence.

"Do we have anything from the person who brought him in?"

"Physicker Stross?" Andrew asked. Discomfort in his tone—or maybe it was pure resentment.

"What is it?"

Andrew didn't answer, but Stefan did. "Physicker Stross—*Alec*—look."

Alec looked down, and when he did, he realized why there had been strangeness.

The person they had brought in was his father.

BACK HOME FOR ANSWERS

Alec searched the grounds of the university, looking for Mrs. Rubbles. He assumed that she had been the one who brought his father in, but wouldn't she have stayed? Beckah trailed along next to him, and he was thankful for her presence. It wasn't uncommon for physickers to have students with them, and he thought he could deflect most of the comments about Beckah's presence, but his mind wasn't on that at all.

What had happened to his father?

"She should be over here," Stefan said.

"That's all you know?" Alec asked.

He looked over at Stefan. He was taller than Alec, and incredibly thin, and he gripped the bottom of his short gray student jacket. "She wasn't able to give us much information. She told us his name, who he was, and told us to look for you."

Alec nodded. Mrs. Rubbles would have sent them after Alec, especially as she knew Alec was here. It still didn't make sense that something would've happened to his father. His mind raced as he tried to think of the possibilities. Had his father been collecting something that could have poisoned him? Many of the things he collected for his healings had dangerous effects, so it wouldn't surprise Alec to learn that he had, but his father was also careful, and incredibly well-versed in the effects of everything that he worked with. The idea of poison didn't strike Alec as likely.

"He'll be okay," Beckah said.

"I don't know that he will." Alec had done a brief examination of his father before going in search of Mrs. Rubbles and had found that Stefan and Andrew's assessment was accurate. He was stable. His heart rate was regular. His breathing was steady. He didn't have any localized findings. He simply was unresponsive.

It was like the other woman.

Alec had a good memory, and he traced through all of the things that had been attempted on the woman, thinking of what he might try on his father, but he couldn't shake the idea that they had to be unrelated. It made no sense for the two of them to present with a similar type of illness.

He would need to try some antidotes to various compounds his father had at the shop, but first, he would need to examine what his father might have been working with. Once he identified that, then he could try to figure out what might best counter those effects.

They continued their sweep of the entrance to the university. It was early in the day, and there was a line of people waiting to be granted entrance, hoping to be healed. Alec had once been in that line—it seemed almost a lifetime ago. That was when he discovered there was a significant barrier to entry—and healing. Money. In order to be granted access, one needed to have coin on hand and be willing to pay whatever was asked. It was a barrier that essentially ensured that only those with money were allowed access to the healers. His father had railed against that belief system. Alec hoped that when—or if—he ever reached the level of master physicker, he could attempt to change it.

Alec surveyed the people in line, but there was no sign of Mrs. Rubbles.

He hurried across the bridge, Stefan and Beckah close behind. There were guards on the bridge, but their purpose was simply to prevent fighting, not to prevent access, especially at this time of day when many sought access to the university.

"You can't think to go and solve this yourself," Beckah said.

"Why not? I know my father better than anyone." Alec looked around at the people they passed on the bridge. The line stretched across the entirety of the canal. It was surprising that there were so many people here and the ward was as empty as it was. Maybe it meant that most people were healed before they reached the ward, but if that were the case, why wouldn't there have been a summons for assistance? "Besides, I want to find Mrs. Rubbles to see what she might know."

"She said she didn't know anything," Stefan said.

He had been quiet for the most part since they had gone in search, and as they left the university section, he looked around. Alec hadn't brought Stefan to his section of the city before, and as they crossed the second bridge, his friend began to stare around him. They were still in one of the inner sections—places that Sam would have referred to as highborn—so there shouldn't have been any trigger related to the wealth available.

"She might not have known what answers she actually knew," Alec said. "It's possible that she knows more than she realizes."

Stefan looked over at Alec and shrugged. "I'm just telling you what she told me," he said.

Alec glanced at Beckah, and she only shrugged. There had to be a way to reach Stefan, to get through the strangeness that was there between them, but if there was, he didn't know how to do it.

Instead, he stayed silent as they hurried through the city, crossing through one section after another. Alec had been this way often enough that he knew the shortest route. It wasn't quite as quick as going with Sam, who simply jumped the canals when she needed to cross, rather than taking the bridges, but there was a fairly direct pathway to the Arrend section.

When they reached it, Alec breathed out. There was something familiar and peaceful about being back in his section. It was home. Before heading to the university, it was the only place he'd ever lived, other than the short time when he had stayed with Sam to work on what their connection meant.

"This is your section?" Stefan asked.

"This is," Alec said.

"It's so… nice."

Alec looked over. "Did you think that I lived in one of the outer sections?"

There were many people in the central sections who believed the outer sections were for lowborns. There was a certain amount of poverty as well as crime present in those outer sections, but the people were good, much like the people anywhere were good. Even the criminals were often better people than some that Alec had met. He thought of Bastan, and the way that he had looked out for Sam over the years. Without someone like him, Alec wasn't sure what would have happened to her. Sam certainly seemed to believe that without Bastan and his concern for her she would have ended up in a much different situation.

"I knew you lived outside of the main part of the city," he said.

"This is still part of the city." Beckah shot Stefan a strange look. "Wait... Have you never been this far into the city?"

Stefan paled. "Most of my time has been spent in one of the inner sections. You know my grandmother..."

"I think we're quite well aware of Master Helen," Beckah said. "And I thought she might be more favorable toward us because of you, but she hasn't been."

"She wants me to make my own way."

"It's because she made her own way," Alec said. "She was the only one before me who demanded testing and was promoted."

"She *what?*" Stefan asked, stopping in the middle of the street.

Alec glanced over at Beckah. He'd shared that detail

with her, but suddenly realized that he probably hadn't shared that with Stefan. Had they only spent more time together, he might have.

"Your grandmother was the only person in the records of promotion who had ever demanded testing—until I did. The records weren't clear whether that person had been successful or not, but when I was tested, she told me she had."

"I never knew," Stefan said softly. "She doesn't talk about her days as a student very much."

Beckah laughed. "Probably because she wasn't a student for very long. If she demanded testing, think about our friend Alec. He had been a student for much less than a year, and now he's a full physicker."

Stefan looked over at Alec, and something in his expression changed, softening. "Grandmother kept us together, and we lived near the university. I was never in the same section as the university, but I grew up with it in sight. I don't think I had much of a choice about whether or not I would attempt to attend. If I hadn't, I suspect my grandmother would have been angry."

"How many grandchildren does she have?"

"Grandmother Helen only had a single son, and I'm his only son."

Alec's breath caught. Having expectations like that might be even harder than what his father had demanded of him. His father had wanted Alec to learn what it was like to serve as an apothecary, and had trained him, but there had been no expectation that he would attend the university. Alec had thought that was beyond his grasp, and had wanted it for himself, but not because of any desire on his father's part, at least not that he'd been aware of before now.

"So, when you came to the university—"

"It was the first time that I left my section," Stefan said.

"Gods," Beckah said. "I didn't realize you'd never been outside the inner portion of the city."

"And you had been?" Alec asked with a smirk.

"More than what it seems Stefan has been. I at least have visited a few of the other sections, though not quite as many as you. I mean, I haven't been to the edge of the city the same way that you have." She watched him, the smirk on her face mirroring the one that he had given her.

Alec suppressed a laugh. He hadn't been outside of his section much before meeting Sam, either. When she had come into his life, all of a sudden, he was dragged all over the city, sneaking into sections that he never would have visited before, and had experienced places that he once would have considered as dangerous as Stefan likely thought that Arrend was.

It was all about perspective and experience. Before, Alec had had no experience. It was much like the way Sam had perceived what she called highborns. She had no experience with those who lived in some of the central sections, thinking them related to the royal family. And now—ironically—she was in a position where she was closer to the royal family than any of the so-called highborns.

"Let me show you my section," Alec said.

He pointed to familiar shops as they wandered the streets. There was the baker—Ms. Smithson—a woman who had been very maternal to Alec. Many of the women in this section had been maternal to him. Likely, they felt bad for him, thinking that spending all of his time with his father had been detrimental. He pointed to a tailor and thought about his time going there for clothing, and the welcome that Mr. Jones would give him each time he entered his shop. He was a kind man and had an easy-going nature, quick to make jokes. At each shop, Alec pointed out who ran the shop, knowing everyone by name. It wasn't anything he'd thought about before, but now he realized what a close community it was.

They reached Mrs. Rubbles' store, and he checked the door, half afraid that it might be locked. If it had been, would he turn away? He could always go to his father's shop to see what he might have been working with prior to succumbing to whatever illness he had, and he would do that, anyway, but he wanted a chance to speak to Mrs. Rubbles, to see what she knew about his father.

The door was unlocked.

Alec entered. There was a certain odor to her store, and it was one that Alec always attributed to the parchment that she sold. That and the inks. Those all had a very particular smell. It wasn't unpleasant, only distinctive.

She had a bell over her door that was like the one over his father's, and she emerged from the back room. Her hair was in a bun on top of her head, and she wore a black and white floral dress.

"Alec, thank the gods," she breathed when she saw him. She glanced at the others with him and nodded politely. "Do you know what's wrong with him?"

"I don't, Mrs. Rubbles. What can you tell me about what happened?"

She took another deep breath before answering. "I found him in his shop. He was slumped over the table. I assume you've gone there to see?"

"I'm going there next," Alec said. "I thought that I would come to you to hear what you knew."

"I should have stayed at the university, but I thought… I thought that you would know. Your father said that you had been promoted." She glanced at him, taking in the thigh-length gray jacket that Alec now wore, a marker of his status as full physicker. Junior physickers had a shorter jacket, and student wore an even shorter jacket. "I can see that you have, but perhaps even more than I was led to believe. Not that I'm surprised. I've always said that you take after your father, and I've always said that he knows just as much as any of the physickers at the university."

Alec swallowed. He had always felt the same way, and it had taken him studying at the university to realize just how much his father had known. "I don't know what's wrong with him," he said. "I… I want to do everything I can to help him, but I can only do that if I know a little bit more about what you saw when you came across him."

She nodded and leaned on the counter. She picked up one of the dozens of pens that lay there—all for sale—and started tapping it on the counter. "I thought he was asleep at first. He works so hard, your father, and I thought that perhaps he had drifted off there at the table. It wouldn't have been the first time I found Aelus sleeping in a strange position. When I went to wake him, he didn't come around. That's when I knew something was wrong. I tried using some of his herbs," she said with a flush. "He has shown me ones that can help with alertness, but they didn't do anything. I figured it was time to take him to you."

"To me? Not the university?"

"I figured taking him to the university would essentially get him to you," she said.

"How did you carry him all that way?"

Mrs. Rubbles twisted her hands together. "I'm not the only one in this section who owes your father for what he's done for us over the years. Jerad helped me."

Jerad was a tailor whose shop was at the end of the street. Alec and his father had helped see him through a particularly bad injury when he'd cut into his thigh a few years ago. "I'll have to thank him too."

"We care for your father, Alec. All of us do."

Alec smiled at her. "You did well, Mrs. Rubbles."

"Do you think you can figure out what happened?" she asked.

"I will do everything I can. If you think of anything that might be helpful, let me know."

"Such as what?"

"Such as anyone he might have been working with, anything that might have seemed off, anything that might explain where—or who—my father might've been working with. Really, anything would be helpful."

She nodded. "I will try to think of anything. I don't recall anyone unusual around. If there had been, your father would have kept them away."

Alec smiled to himself. His father would likely *not* have

kept anyone away. If there was someone who was needing help, his father would've invited them in and done whatever he could to help them. That was just the way of his father.

"Thank you, Mrs. Rubbles."

He motioned to his friends, and they headed out.

When they were back out in the street, Beckah looked around. "It's strange," she said.

"Mrs. Rubbles means well," Alec said.

"That's not it. I can tell that she means well. I think she cares about your father."

"Why would you say that?"

"Just the way she talks about him."

"She has known him a long time. I think they respect each other."

Then again, Alec had thought the same. He had noticed that there seemed to be a connection between his father and Mrs. Rubbles, and though his father would never admit it, he thought Mrs. Rubbles probably helped keep his father from being as lonely as he had been.

"Let's go see if we can figure anything out from his shop."

Alec was quieter as they made their way along the street. It was familiar here, the distance between Mrs. Rubbles' store and the apothecary were only a short distance. When he reached the apothecary, he found the door unlocked. He frowned at that. Mrs. Rubbles should have locked it, though it was likely that she was too agitated to have done so. If she was worried about his father, she might have not taken the time, thinking that she would come back to it later.

Once inside, Alec looked around. It was dark, and very little light drifted through the windows in the front of the shop. He hurried to the pair of lanterns and lit them.

When he did, Stefan gasped. "All of this is your father's shop?"

Alec looked around. The rows of shelves were so familiar to him that he barely noticed them anymore. On each shelf, there were jars upon jars of various leaves and roots and oils, all of which his father had painstakingly collected, or had found a place to purchase. It wasn't only his father's knowledge that was impressive, it was his ability to find sources for medicines, sources that rivaled even what the university was able to acquire.

"All of this is his shop," Alec said.

"He's not just a simple apothecary," Stefan said.

"He's never been a simple anything," Alec said. He decided not to share with Stefan that his father was a master physicker. Beckah knew, but then Beckah knew much more about him than Stefan did. Until he had a better handle on Stefan, and what type of reaction he might have, Alec wasn't about to share too much with him.

"I knew he had supplies. I remember you talking about what you could find, but I was thinking there would be just a few cabinets. This is more than what you can get in certain parts of the university."

"The university has a well-stocked supply cabinet," Alec said. "Now that I've been promoted, I have visited it more than once."

"The university keeps quantity. But this is such an extensive breadth of various compounds, I don't know that even the university would have everything here, Alec."

He smiled to himself, at least pleased that Stefan was referring to him by first name again. He was tired of the Physicker Stross comments, at least from those he had known as a fellow student.

"I'm going to see if I can figure out if there's anything here that would explain what happened to my father."

Alec made his way to the back of the shop to the table where Mrs. Rubbles had found his father. The chair was against the wall, likely pulled back when Mrs. Rubbles and Jerad had managed to get him from here. He pulled himself up to the table, searching for evidence of what his father might have been working on, but found nothing. The table was empty except for a stack of papers.

Pulling the papers toward him, he began scanning them. Beckah watched him, but she said nothing. They were his father's records, the notes that he made about each person that he healed, the same sort of notes that he had trained Alec to make. There was nothing unusual, and in fact, they were fairly straightforward illnesses that his father had been treating. The medicines that he had used were also quite common, nothing that would lead to any sort of complication from his own exposure.

"Do you see anything?" Beckah asked.

"I don't see anything that would explain what happened to him. He was busy. I can see that from the pages here. There had to have been multiple people who came through here over the last few days, and most of them appeared to have been from the Arrend section."

"Was that common?"

"We had people come through here from all sections. Well, at least from all of the outer sections. When they heard that my father was willing to heal and treat without regard for costs, it appealed to many people."

Alec pushed the papers back to where they'd been and leaned forward, placing himself in a position that would have been like the way his father had been discovered. How would he have been resting?

He set his head down on the table, thinking of what his father would have been doing. It was possible that his father *had* been simply resting. Alec had found him in a similar position many times before. His father often worked late into the night, and often made sure to complete every part of what he considered his tasks before retiring. That would include taking the notes that he thought were necessary so that he could complete his documentation. His father didn't like to end his day without everything being finished.

But, if that was what he'd been doing last night, where was the ink?

For that matter, where was his pen. Would his father have finished and put them away?

Had Mrs. Rubbles not been in such a frantic state, he could have seen her putting those things away, but she'd not even remembered to lock the door.

Glancing around, he saw a bottle of ink behind the stack of papers he'd looked through. He hadn't noticed it when he'd pulled the papers forward to review. Alec lifted it and shook it, and then brought it to his nose, sniffing. It didn't smell like anything he recognized, and he didn't recognize the color. It was purple, not a color that his father typically used, and it wasn't used on any of the pages he'd looked through.

"What is it?" Beckah asked.

"Just a few strange things," he said.

"You're looking at the ink. Is it…" She held her hand out and nodded to her palm.

Alec shook his head. "Not like that. I don't know why he would have this color of ink, and I don't see any pages written in it."

Alec stood from the chair and stepped over to a cabinet that contained some of his father's most sensitive items. This was where he had stored the eel venom, and there were other compounds that were equally dangerous.

Could somebody have attacked his father for these items?

That seemed unlikely. There wouldn't be many people who would even have known that his father had them.

When he pulled the cabinet open, he was surprised to find it empty.

Beckah stepped up beside him. "You look worried."

"Only because I know what was here before."

"And what was that?"

He lowered his voice before answering. "A way to face the Thelns."

Could there be anything to that?

Maybe his father had given everything that he had to Bastan, knowing the man was intent on defeating the Thelns. Or maybe there was another reason. Had Bastan been here, he would have drawn attention. At least, Alec thought that he would. Then again, Bastan had many people who worked for him, and he could just as easily have sent one of them here.

"I think I need to go to the Caster section."

Stefan looked over. "You can't be serious."

"Why not?"

"I may never have been out of my section, but I at least know the sections of the city. I know that Caster is one of the outer sections, and it's supposed to be incredibly dangerous."

"And our Alec has spent considerable time there," Beckah said.

"You have?"

"I don't know that I would say considerable time, but I have spent time in Caster. And to get the answers I need, I think I need to go there. But I don't want to go by myself."

"I can go with you," Beckah said.

"You could, but I'm not sure that you should."

"I want to find him too," she said with a whisper.

Alec frowned. As much as it might upset Sam, Beckah was right. She had every reason to be searching for Tray, the same as Sam. She needed to find out more about what it meant for her to be his Scribe. And since they weren't entirely sure what it meant for Tray to be both Theln and Kaver, Beckah's connection to him might be dangerous. But she should be allowed to understand.

"Just… Just try not to antagonize her."

Stefan watched, and Alec hated that he couldn't tell him anything, and hated that if he tried, Stefan probably wouldn't understand.

"Let's return to the university. I want to check on him first."

3

TO BE A PHYSICKER

The hospital ward was nearly empty of staff. Alec arrived late in the day, late enough that most of the junior physickers weren't even there, having long ago gone for food. There would be a single physicker responsible for ensuring the welfare of everyone in the ward, and even that person was not here.

Having been out in the city, Alec was more aware of the astringent odor in the air. The ward had a medicinal stink to it, and he was surprised that he didn't notice it more often. As he took several deep breaths, he was able to pick out the smell of a few different medicines that he recognized. Several of them were ones that he had been using lately. Could it be his fault that the ward smelled the way that it did?

Alec went to his father's cot and looked down at him. It was strange seeing him this way, and strange for him to not be able to speak to him. Whenever he'd faced a mystery with healing, his father had always been the one who he went to for answers.

"I need to know what happened," he said in a whisper. Alec took his father's hand and found the skin still warm. It wasn't sweaty or clammy, just warm. It was as though his father was simply sleeping and should wake up and talk to him—only he didn't.

He completed an examination, going from head to toe, looking for anything that he might've overlooked before. There was nothing. His father was well, other than the fact that he did not respond.

He looked around and pulled a slip of easar paper out of his pocket. He had a single vial of his and Sam's blood, and he pulled it out, preparing to write.

"I wouldn't do that," a voice said.

Alec looked up, quickly slipping the easar paper into his pocket. A flush washed over him, and he feared that it was one of the master physickers who shouldn't see the paper.

Master Helen eyed him, then looked down at his father. She wore a heavy brown robe, and Alec wondered if she had been traveling outside of the university. He had seen her at the palace before, and still didn't know what role she had there, though didn't expect Master Helen to ever share that with him. Her long, graying hair was brushed out and pooled in the folds of the hood of her robe. She sighed deeply for a moment.

"I haven't seen him in a long time," she said.

Alec ignored the first thought that came to mind. "Why shouldn't I use the paper?"

Master Helen looked back at him and frowned. "Doing

so without knowing the underlying cause of the illness runs the risk of unwanted effects."

"I attempted a healing on the princess without knowing what had happened to her."

"You did. And such a healing was more dangerous than you know."

Alec frowned. He hadn't considered that there might be a reason that he shouldn't attempt healing. It was something that he still didn't know about his role as a Scribe.

"He's completely well, other than the fact that he won't wake up."

"And what would you attempt?"

"I would work on alertness and perhaps focus on bringing him around so that he could tell me what happened."

"And what if your attempt at increasing the patient's alertness only causes his illness to accelerate?"

"Why would it do that? Bringing him back around would only help me understand what happened to him."

Master Helen stood at the end of the cot and placed her hands near his father's shoulders. "There are many causes for decreased alertness, Physicker Stross. If you target the wrong one, you run the risk of causing injury. This is a dangerous type of illness without knowing the possible causes to it."

"Is this related to the other woman?"

She frowned. "Other woman?"

Alec took her over to the other young woman, his gaze lingering on his father for a moment before he finally pulled his attention away. "She came in a week ago. I've tried countless different concoctions, all of which should help bring her around, but nothing has worked."

Master Helen grabbed the record at the end of the bed, and quickly flipped the pages, her eyes scanning each page more rapidly than what Alec thought he would be able to do. He might have been the first person to be promoted directly to full physicker, but he still suspected that Master Helen was the brighter of the two of them. The only reason he was able to be successful was because his father had trained him the entirety of his life. Without that knowledge, Alec wouldn't have been promoted nearly as quickly as he had.

"Yes. I see that you have tried many things. Most of these would only cause a brief awakening."

"A brief awakening was all I was aiming for. Without knowing the underlying source, I was trying a lower potency treatment. Anything with more significant potency might have been dangerous."

She looked up at him, an accusation burning in her eyes. "Exactly. You're willing to be cautious with this young woman, but not with Aelus?"

Alec flushed. He should know better. She was right. He had learned that his connection to the blood magic was tied to his knowledge, and if his knowledge was inadequate, he wouldn't be able to heal using it.

"I see what you're trying to say."

"Good, Physicker Stross."

"Have you seen anything like this before?"

"I have not, and that troubles me. Everything that you've tried should have been effective. The fact that it was not is disconcerting."

Master Helen proceeded to perform her own evaluation, working her way along the woman, checking her heart, her lungs, her stomach, before moving on to lifting her eyelids and looking into her mouth, as well as examining her throat. She had a very similar technique to his father's, one that Alec hadn't seen from any of the other master physickers.

"You knew my father when he was here, didn't you?"

"I knew him. Many of us knew him."

Alec watched as she continued with her evaluation. "He was one of your students."

She looked over and nodded curtly. "He was one of my students. When he left the university, I was angry with him. Many of us were."

"Why?"

"Your father has a brilliant mind. I'm sure you're aware of that."

"Is that why I was treated the way that I was?"

She sniffed. "It's unfortunate the way that you were treated, Physicker Stross. Many of the full physickers as well as junior physickers saw you as little more than an apothecary. None of them understood who your father was, or the breadth of what he knew, which was to their detriment. I think that was why they were surprised by how much you already knew. Those of us who knew your father were not surprised." She looked back down at the young woman. "Oh, I suppose some of us were surprised that your father had taught you as much as he had. I think we all expected him to have worked with you, but he trained you as if you were one of his students."

"He always let me work with him."

"Because of that, you are in a much better position than many of your colleagues. It is the reason that I supported your request for testing."

"What do you mean that you supported it?"

"A request such as you made could have been refused." She glanced up, studying him, and a small hint of a smile quirked the corners of her mouth. "You didn't realize that?"

"I didn't."

"Can you imagine what would happen if all of our students began to demand testing? How many of the students do you think believe they know more than the junior physickers?"

"I thought I knew more than the junior physickers."

"Because you do. Your father saw to that. I think had he never left the university, you could have been brought in as a junior physicker, not even needing to serve as a student."

"I don't think my father would've wanted me to have things quite so easy."

"No. I doubt that he would."

Master Helen replaced the record at the end of the bed and turned to leave. "Master Helen?"

"Yes?"

"If these are related, why would that be? What do you think caused my father's illness and this young lady's illness?"

"I told you that I don't know."

Alec looked around, but the room was still empty. "Could it be related to the Book?"

Her eyes narrowed. "I pray that it is not."

"You pray?"

"Only at times like this." She glanced over to his father's cot. "Don't attempt to save him without knowing more about what happened."

She started away, and Alec called out to her again. She paused and turned back toward him. There was annoyance on her face, but Alec ignored it. "I need someone who can help me understand what it means to be a Scribe," he said.

"I think you're managing well enough on your own."

"I don't know that I am. I understand some of my abilities, but I don't know nearly as much as I think I need to in order for me to help Sam."

"You believe that it's all about helping her?"

"Isn't it?"

She frowned. "It is not a one-sided relationship." She made her way over to him, getting close enough that she didn't have to speak too loudly. "It is not all about the Kaver. The Scribe has an equally important role. If you don't know that—and if you don't believe that—then there is very little I will be able to tell you that will be of use."

"What is it then? If it's supposed to be a partnership," he started, uncertain how that would work, especially since Sam seemed to be the one who gained the most benefit from their pairing. "What can I do to better understand what my role means?"

"You are doing it."

"What? Learning what it means to be a physicker?"

She shook her head. "You already know enough about

what it means to be a physicker. You wouldn't wear that jacket if you did not. It's the asking of questions."

"That's it?"

"That's not it. That's the beginning."

"How can I learn more if I don't have someone willing to work with me?"

Master Helen sighed. Had he upset her? He had thought the master physickers who were Scribes would want to work with him, and that they would want to help him understand what it meant for him to do the things that he did, but so far, none of them had expressed any interest; no one seemed willing to train him.

"You must be patient, Physicker Stross. Your understanding will come in time, but unfortunately, when it comes to learning what it means to be a Scribe, it requires that you observe, and that you document, the same techniques that your father has taught you."

"Why can't you simply tell me?"

"If I were to simply tell you, you wouldn't understand. There are things you can learn through telling. There are things you can learn by reading. And there are some things that you can only learn by questioning and discovering them on your own."

She turned away from him then and left the ward.

Alec breathed out and returned to his father, looking once again to see if there was anything he could discover, but there wasn't. Whatever had happened to him remained a mystery. It was a mystery that he would have to solve, but it wouldn't be one that would be solved through his use of easar paper.

Thankfully, his father was stable, which meant that he had time.

Hopefully, Sam would respond to his request, and hopefully, she would be willing to go with him to the Caster section, but even if he didn't hear from her, he would have to go. Bastan might not know what happened to his father, but he was a man who knew many things, and Alec would have to see if there was anything he could learn from him.

4

AN UNCOMFORTABLE ALLY

The Caster section made Alec somewhat uncomfortable. He tried to hide the fact that he felt that way, but there was no concealing that he felt as if he shouldn't be here. It was almost as if the section of the city wanted to push him out, to prevent him from spending any time here. When he'd first come here, Sam had been the one to guide him, and having her with him—someone who belonged—had made it tolerable. Without her, he acutely felt like an outsider.

It didn't help that he was dressed the way he was. He had discarded his university jacket, leaving it behind when he and Beckah made their way to this section, but he still knew that he was overdressed, especially compared to others who were here.

"You could've waited until we found her," Beckah said.

"I could have, but I don't know how long she'll be gone. Her training often takes her away for long stretches of time."

"She leaves the city?"

He knew she went to the swamp, but not more than that. "Maybe she doesn't leave the city, but her training takes her throughout the city."

"I still think we could have waited for her."

Alec wasn't sure whether Beckah was right. Sam would be upset if she learned that he had come to Caster without her, especially if she discovered that he had come to meet with Bastan without her, but he wanted to know if there was anything he could discover about his father.

"I don't know how much time my father has."

"You said he was stable."

"He was stable. He *is* stable. But I'm not sure whether he will remain stable."

It would have been better had Master Helen known something. When she had appeared in the ward, Alec had hoped that she might be able to provide answers, but she had not.

He had chosen to come in the early evening. It was better to come into Caster with light, rather than to attempt walking through this section in the darkness when he would draw notice—and not the kind of notice that he wanted. He would be a target, and Alec knew enough about Caster to know that someone like himselfwho came through here would be the kind of target that drew dangerous people.

Beckah looked around as they walked, her eyes looking at everything. "I still can't get over this part of the city."

"You don't have to get over it. These are people."

"Thieves."

"There are some."

"Including the man that we're going to visit."

"He's helped Sam on many occasions over the years." But that wasn't the reason Alec was coming to him. It was because he knew his father had helped Bastan in the past. They finally arrived at the tavern and went inside. It was mostly quiet, though there was a minstrel playing in one corner. A fire burned brightly in the hearth, casting a warm glow to the room. Food smelled fantastic, not surprising considering Bastan seemed to take pride in the quality of his kitchen.

"This is it?" Beckah asked.

"This is where we start."

Alec took a seat at a table, waiting for a familiar face to appear. Bastan used many of the kitchen staff to serve him, and they worked in both reputable as well as disreputable positions.

One of the men came out, and Alec tried to catch his attention. "

"Him?" Beckah asked. "He looks like…"

"He looks like Kevin," he said. Kevin had dark hair and a prominent forehead, and he was muscular, far more muscular than anyone working in a kitchen should be. Alec had seen that he was quick with knives, and—most importantly—Sam liked him.

Kevin weaved toward him and crossed his arms as he stared at the table. "You bring another woman in here?"

"She's a friend. Sam knows her."

His posture relaxed only a little. "If you're looking for Sam, I don't know where she is. I haven't seen her in quite a while."

"I'm looking for Bastan."

"You? Without her?" He glanced at Beckah. "And with *her*?"

"It's not like that," Alec said.

"It better not be. We all have something of an opinion about Sam here, and it's all good. If you hurt her, well, let's just say that you coming to Caster isn't going to be something you're going to want to do."

"Why would I hurt Sam? You've see me with her."

"I haven't seen you with her in quite a while. Could be that she's decided she's done with you. Not that I blame her. Man like you seems a little—soft—if you ask me."

Beckah grinned at Kevin. "Alec is a little soft."

"Thanks," he said.

"I'm just trying to be helpful. You told me that I needed to keep quiet while we were out on the streets. You didn't say anything about me having to keep my mouth shut once we got here."

"I told you to be quiet when we were talking to Bastan. But I'm amending that. You need to be quiet around Kevin too."

"What if I told him that Sam is angry with you because you broke her heart? Just think of the way she would feel knowing about our growing love, think about the way that she would feel knowing the way you look at me, the way you hold me, the way you…"

Alec glared at her, but Kevin began laughing.

"She's a bit like Sam, isn't she?"

"If you mean that she's nothing but trouble, then you're probably right."

"I mean that she's got spirit. I'm a little surprised to see it from a highborn, but you know, I respect it when I do. It's not common that we get highborns here, though more than we used to. Bastan sure has taken a liking to their money."

"What do you mean by that?"

"You know I can't tell you. You are welcome enough here, but you aren't part of the crew. Gods, even Sam isn't a part of the crew, not any longer. Not since she started spending time with you. You practically turned her into a highborn."

"I didn't turn her into anything. Sam is the same person she was when she used to be here all the time."

He wondered what Sam would say if she learned that he was talking about her in that way. Maybe she wouldn't be upset, but he had a feeling that she would. Sam took pride in being fierce and strong as well she should. She *was* fierce and strong, and she intimidated Alec with those traits.

"If you're looking for Bastan, I'll give word."

"We can't go back and speak with him?"

Kevin smirked at him. "You? Nah, I don't think he'd be too thrilled if I let you go back to his office. He's a little particular about who he lets back there, and a man like you, with a girl like that, well, let's just say you wouldn't be welcome there."

Alec decided not to tell Kevin that he had already been back to Bastan's office, and that he had a better understanding of Bastan than what Kevin might even know. Instead, he just nodded thanks. If Kevin was going to give word to Bastan that they were here, that was all that Alec could do.

A waiter appeared and set two mugs of ale in front of them.

Beckah looked at Alec, and it took a moment for him to realize that she was waiting for him to pay.

He shook his head and fished a couple of coins out of his pocket, handing them over to the man.

"You get into the university and get promoted to physicker, and you already start to forget how to treat a woman," Beckah said. "I might have to hold that against you."

"Thanks for that, by the way."

She laughed. "I thought it would be entertaining. You seem so tense here, that I thought it would lighten the mood."

"I'm not certain this is the kind of place where you want to lighten the mood. You don't know Bastan and what he's capable of."

"If he's the kind of man who spends significant time in Caster, I think I have a reasonable idea about who he is and what he's capable of." She tipped back her drink, and her face screwed up as she took a sip. "It's a little more bitter than I was expecting."

"Don't tell Bastan that. Like I said, he takes pride in his kitchen, which includes the ale that he serves."

"I wasn't saying that it was bad. Bitter doesn't mean bad. Bitter means bitter. What if I said you were bitter? I don't think you're bad."

"Sometimes, you don't make a lot of sense. I think that maybe I will need to have you do some sort of penance."

"If you try that, Alec Stross, I will make sure that is the

last thing you do as physicker." She took another sip, and her nose wrinkled again. "It really is bitter."

Alec decided to take a sip, and as he did, he noticed the door to the back office open and Bastan appeared. He was an imposing man, despite the fact that he was probably twenty years Alec's senior. It was something about the confident way that he scanned the tavern, or maybe it had to do with the fact that he had taken on the Thelns on his own, armed only with a crossbow. That was something Alec didn't think he would've even tried.

When Bastan saw him, he shook his head and headed his direction. He stopped at their table and glanced at Beckah for a long moment, an appraising look on his face. "Is she one of you?"

"A physicker?"

Bastan gave him a hard-eyed stare. "You know what I mean, Physicker Stross." ·

Alec blinked. Bastan knew about his promotion. He shouldn't be surprised, but he still was. Bastan shouldn't have any ties to the university, no way for him to know… Unless Sam had told him. But why would Sam still be out here working with Bastan?

Unless Bastan had his own sources. If he did, that meant that he was keeping tabs on Alec, and Alec didn't like the idea that Bastan was keeping tabs on him.

"She is," he said.

Beckah made a face at Alec. Bastan only chuckled. "Physicker Stross knows that I mean him no ill will. Besides, it isn't that difficult to discover that there's a new physicker. All it takes is for someone to keep their resources directed at the university. The university doesn't attempt nearly so much privacy as places like, say the palace would."

"I don't know where Sam is. I tried to get her to come with me, but I couldn't find her."

"I haven't been able to find her, either. I was hopeful that you coming here meant that Sam was returning to me, thinking that she might want another job."

"I think the only thing Sam wants right now is to find Tray."

"Finding Tray means that she would have to travel someplace I don't think she should," Bastan said.

He took a seat across from Alec, pushing Beckah to the side on the bench. She flashed a smile at him, but Alec could see the nervousness in her eyes. If he could see it, he suspected Bastan could as well.

"Why are you here, Physicker Stross?"

Alec took a deep breath. "Something happened to my father."

Bastan smiled and leaned forward. "I will tell you this only one time. I'm not responsible for what happened to your father."

"I didn't think that you were."

"Then why have you come here if you aren't here to accuse me of something happening to your father?"

"Because I know what he acquired for you."

"We agreed not to discuss that, *Physicker Stross*."

"Fine, but did he provide you with the entirety of his collection?"

Bastan frowned. "Why are you asking?"

"Only because whatever happened to my father, now his more… delicate… collection is missing."

"Delicate?"

"The same type of delicate collection he had acquired for you."

Bastan stared at him for a moment before leaning back. "I will put out the word that I would be interested in information about what happened to the apothecary."

"Which means that you don't know anything at this time."

"I don't know anything at this time," Bastan said.

"If there's anything that you learn, would you send word?"

Bastan watched him for a moment, and Alec resisted the urge to shift in his seat. There was something about the way Bastan looked at him that made him feel a little uncomfortable. The man had a dark intensity to his stare, and Alec didn't care for the way he looked at him.

"I will send word if you commit to having Samara visit."

"You know that I can't make Sam do anything."

"I didn't ask you to *make* her do anything?"

"You asked me to have Sam commit to visit. That suggests that I have some way of forcing her to come."

"I would never ask you to force Samara to do anything, Physicker Stross. What I would suggest is that you see if there's anything you might be able to do to remind Samara that we have a shared interest."

"And if she's already gone?"

"If she's already gone, then I fear that I may not have any information for you."

Bastan tapped the table and then stood, glancing back at them for a moment before he retreated to his office.

"He is quite intimidating, isn't he?" Beckah asked.

"He is that indeed."

"Do you think he knows something?"

"It's possible, but I think if he did, he would've shared it."

"Why do you think that?" Beckah glanced back toward where Bastan had disappeared. "What would he gain by sharing anything with you?"

"He cares about Sam. I don't know the details about it, only that he harbors real affection for her. If anyone were to do something to help her, it would be Bastan."

"It makes me uncomfortable."

"What? Being in Caster?"

"No, relying on someone like that. That's what makes me uncomfortable." She tipped her mug of ale back and took a long drink. When she was done, she set the empty glass back on the table and motioned to Alec. "If we're done here, we should get going."

"I want to take a little longer," he said.

"Alec—"

Alec only shrugged. "When we return to the university, I become Physicker Stross again."

"Didn't you want to be Physicker Stross?"

"I did, but only because I wanted to help Sam identify Marin's Scribe. Otherwise, I don't know that I would have challenged for testing. It's almost easier to go unnoticed."

"Trust me, Alec, you have never gone unnoticed."

"I know that, but I had sort of hoped that I wouldn't be quite as well noticed. It's not as if I want to draw attention to myself. And now that I'm a physicker, that's all I have done."

Beckah laughed softly. "You know how many people wish they had the ability to do what you managed to? Do you know how many people who study at the university wish they had the knowledge that you have? I think of all of the students there, most would love to be in your position. You've studied for a year or less at the university and look at you now."

"Look at me now. I have junior physickers angry that I jumped past them in rank. I have students who look at me and wonder why I was able to challenge and be raised to physicker. And even those who are supposed to be my friends wonder."

"Stefan will get over it," she said. "Besides, it's not that they're jealous of you, not in the way that you think. Do you even know how long it takes to be raised to junior physicker?"

Alec hadn't given it much thought. There had never been a reason to. When he had come to the university, he had been placed based on knowledge that he already had, and he assumed that meant that he had quite a while to go. There were others at the university who didn't have the same knowledge as he, and some who he suspected would never get there. Just because they were allowed to enroll in the university didn't mean that they were guaranteed to be promoted to physicker.

"How long?"

"I studied for three years before you came."

"Three years?"

She nodded. "Three years. Before that, just to be allowed the option to be tested, I studied for two years. That's simply to be granted an opportunity to gain entry.

It was the same for Stefan. He was at the university when I came, and we both were promoted quickly, but neither of us was promoted anywhere nearly as quickly as you."

Alec hadn't considered that. "I'm sorry."

"Sorry? I don't want you to be sorry. I want you to recognize that what you have done is impressive. I'm still probably a year or more away from reaching the level of junior physicker, and then from there, it'll take me another few years to be promoted to full physicker. By the time I reach that level, you'll likely have already been promoted to master physicker." She leaned toward him. "All of that is basically to tell you that you need to be thankful for what you've accomplished. You should be proud of it. Don't be ashamed of your intelligence and the fact that your father taught you before you came to the university. There's no reason to feel that way. The only thing you should feel is an obligation to continue to work at it. Well, that and a desire to help your friends out."

"You mean my friends who are still students? I'm not sure I can do that. I think I might have to get new friends."

She glared at him. "If you even think like that, I will…"

"You'll what?"

Beckah looked around, and then with a devious smile, she shrugged. "I'll return to Bastan, and maybe I will share how you mistreated me—and Samara."

"That wouldn't be very kind of you."

"Whoever said I was kind?"

5

THE SWAMP

There was pressure against the canal staff, the kind of pressure that left Sam's heart racing. She hopped, pushing off with the staff to vault slightly out of the water, enough that she could clear whatever might be attempting to bite at the staff. She knew better than to believe that the swamp was devoid of ominous creatures. She had already seen eels swirling beneath her, and she feared that they were following her, trailing after her as she made her way across the swamp.

This was a mistake.

How long had she been out here?

Half a day, maybe less. But long enough that she wasn't sure whether she would be able to get back. She could take pressure off of her arms by wrapping her legs around the staff, and she had balanced on the staff, having learned the technique well enough to manage, though she wasn't nearly as skilled as some of the other Kavers.

Again, she felt pressure against the staff, and a soft splash sent water spraying up toward her.

Sam swore under her breath. She wasn't about to fall and risk encountering the eels. For that matter, she knew better than to risk coming here without letting anyone know. Alec will be furious if he learns that she came without telling him, but she needed to try this without his help.

Elaine had told her that she had made the swamp crossing many times without augmentations. If Sam was going after her brother, she would have to do it without augmentations—at least she would have to be prepared to do so.

She jumped, switching directions and heading back toward the city. It wasn't even visible from here. There was nothing more than a vague sense of the city in the distance, and she breathed out a heavy sigh, pausing again to station herself higher up on her staff—high enough that an eel would have a difficult time of trying to take a bite out of her leg, were it to jump free of the water.

Despite the disgusting fetid odor of the swamp, there was something calming about it. Maybe it was the fact that there was no one around her. Sam enjoyed the solitude. She always had, which was why she made such a skilled thief before she had learned about her Kaver abilities. She didn't mind being out in the dark or being alone, though were she honest with herself, she did prefer to have someone else with her. And she missed Tray watching over her, providing a look out and offering his massive protection.

Though she had always been the provider for them while growing up, he had always been the protector. His massive size and strength coming in handy over the years. Now, it was her turn to look out for him, though she would need to get to him in order to do so.

There was another splash, this time farther out.

Sam looked down and saw one of the eels swirling around the end of her staff.

How many of the stupid creatures were out here?

More than enough to devour her if she slipped and fell in.

She gathered herself, taking a deep breath, and started back. It had taken her the better part of the morning to get this deep into the swamp, and she wasn't about to linger when she was barely able to cling to the staff. She had enough experience to know what would happen were her strength to fade, and she had no hope that Alec might attempt to place an augmentation. She hadn't been gone long enough for him to do that.

That meant it was up to her.

Kyza!

How was it that she had already failed?

She hated the fact that she couldn't make the crossing, much as she hated the fact that she still didn't know how Elaine managed it. She had to make sure her mother didn't find out that she had attempted this. Sam could only imagine what she would do if she knew. Already, she kept Sam from learning more about her abilities. If she found out that Sam was preparing for a crossing, would she do something to thwart her progress? Would she try to impede Sam's efforts to learn more about what it would take to chase after Tray?

And he was long gone. Tray didn't have the same restrictions as Sam did. He had stolen a barge and was using that to make his way toward the Theln territory. More than that, Tray had a high-ranking Theln with him —a Theln who they now know is Tray's real father. So if they were caught, Ralun would likely guide him to safety.

Sam continued flipping her way back to shore. She angled in such a way as to draw the least amount of attention. It wouldn't do for someone on shore to see her coming and going so often, though it was possible she would be detected, regardless. As far as she knew, Elaine had the entire shore monitored, which meant she would know the moment Sam attempted to leave.

It was nearly evening by the time she made it back.

Sam tapped the water from her staff, examining the length of wood, searching for signs of bite marks, but there were none. For a moment, she doubted herself. Maybe there hadn't been any eels. Maybe she was letting her imagination get away from her. But if not eels, what else had been slamming into her staff as she made her way back to the city?

If she were braver, she would risk jumping into the water to see if it were eels there, though Sam didn't think she was that brave. No one was that brave.

When she had her staff secured beneath her cloak, she started back into the city. She thought about returning to the palace, but it was still early enough that she didn't want to do that. She could go to the university—and it had been a while since she'd seen Alec, so she probably should, but something drew her away.

She'd left to try and get her head straight, but even that hadn't worked. It didn't help that Marin had escaped from custody—somehow breaking free from all the guards who had been sent for her—after Sam had thought she was captured. Now she was free, roaming the city, and potentially a threat at any time.

Sam hadn't had the heart to tell Alec. Yet.

He needed to know, especially since he had been a part of what had happened before, but not until she knew more. At least this time, it didn't seem as if Elaine intended to keep her from the pursuit.

A part of Sam wondered if Marin would even *try* to attack her. She was interested in the princess, not in Sam, but maybe she still thought she could find Tray. What would she do if she learned Tray had left, gone to Ralun?

As the sun fell and she crawled along the rooftops, Sam felt a certain peace in the city. It was the same peace she felt while out in the swamp, the peace that came from solitude. Maybe she wasn't meant to experience anything other than solitude. Had she never learned that she was a Kaver, she would have remained a thief. Whether or not she served Bastan was of little consequence, though she suspected he felt otherwise. But solitude came with the territory, regardless.

Thinking of Bastan drew her to the Caster section.

It was easy enough to make the crossing, and no longer did she fear falling into the canals. As she flipped from one section to the next, she didn't worry about the width of the canal, not as she once had. She didn't bother concealing herself, either. Were she captured, she had a ring that would grant her free passage with the guards. She could flash that ring to the guards and cross the bridges, but where was the fun in that? Besides, Elaine would have wanted her to practice. At least, that was what Sam told herself.

Night had fallen in full by the time she reached Caster.

She remained in the shadows, engulfed by the darkness, her cloak wrapped around her. The swamp was a distant memory, though the trembling in her arms told her that the effect of the swamp was not a distant memory. She needed to be stronger, especially if she intended to make the crossing all the way to the other side of the swamp. There had to be some way for her to get strong enough—and quickly. But without augmentations, Sam wasn't sure how she was going to manage it.

Maybe that was the point. Maybe that was why Elaine was so adamant that she continue to train.

Sam hated the idea that she wasn't strong enough. She hated even more leaving her brother to venture off into a dangerous place with questions about himself. She had her own questions, and so far, she had failed to find the answers.

Maybe Tray would be more successful than she had been.

She noticed two men rushing through the city and decided to follow. Could they be Bastan's men? They weren't anyone that Sam recognized, though Bastan had lost a few men in the last attack. It was possible that he was recruiting.

The man reached the edge of Caster and headed toward the bridge.

Sam jumped off the street, using the staff to launch herself onto a nearby rooftop. The street ran along the edge of the canal before coming up to the bridge that crossed over and into another section. She followed more closely now, not worried about them catching her. It would be difficult for them to notice her following from the rooftops.

As the streets intersected, Sam noticed a third figure appear. The first two seemed unperturbed by the sudden appearance of a third person, something that should be more alarming at this time of night.

"Did you find it?" the newcomer asked.

"He didn't have it," one of the others said.

"He had to have had it. We have word that it was effective."

"You can't trust them."

"You can with what *he's* paying."

"How do you know that he's offering more than Bastan?"

Sam leaned over the edge of the roof, trying to get close enough to hear better. These weren't Bastan's men, and from the sound of it, they were working against him. These were the kinds of men that Bastan would want to know about.

It was surprising because there weren't too many people in the city who were willing to risk themselves against Bastan. Most feared offending him and risking his ire. It was one of the reasons Sam had always been impressed with Marin. She had never feared Bastan.

"We know what he's paying. You think he's the only one with contacts throughout this section?"

"He's been here long enough that he is the only one with contacts *here*."

"And that will change."

"You'll need to be careful. I heard that Bastan was willing to—"

The newcomer raised a finger, silencing him. "Not here. We can't have conversations here, or he'll learn about them."

"You can't believe he is that well-connected."

"I can, and I do. I've seen the way he seems to know things. Come on. Let's cross over and get a few sections away. Then we can talk."

The men disappeared into the darkness.

Sam decided to follow. She threw herself from the roof and jumped across the nearest canal, ducking back into the darkness to observe where the men went. They moved from Caster over into Dolav, one of the neighboring sections. Sam knew Dolav nearly as well as she knew Caster, though it didn't have quite the same flavor as Caster. There was a little more repeatability to Caster than she would find here. The men disappeared along the street, and Sam flipped up to one of the rooftops, racing along the top to see where they might have gone, but came up empty.

Who would be working against Bastan? And who would be paying more than he would for whatever they were after?

Both important questions.

Without answers, she wasn't sure that she should even

go to Bastan, though knowing him, he would want to know, regardless.

Sam slipped into the shadows and headed back to Caster.

When she crossed the canal, she saw movement—and the sound of a fight. When she got near, she groaned to herself as she realized Bastan was involved and quickly joined in the battle.

6

HELPING A FRIEND

Fighting with the staff was easy—at least easy enough now that Sam had all the training she'd been given by her mother. When she thought back to how she'd used it to fight with before, she realized how little she'd known then. Elaine had taught her to not only balance on the canal staff, but how to use it more effectively as a weapon. Sam sent it spinning toward the brawl, a twirling barricade that prevented anyone from getting too close to her.

The first man went down, his sword clattering to the cobblestones.

Who fought with swords in this section of the city?

Getting caught with the blade was a sure way to end up in the prison, and most people were smart enough to know that they shouldn't risk that, especially not here. But she didn't recognize this man, so maybe he wasn't smart enough to know what he should have in the section.

As she turned to the next attacker, she wondered whether there was another reason. Maybe a sword wasn't forbidden for him to possess the way it was for so many others.

If that was the case—and if he worked at the palace—that meant these men would be guards.

As she knocked the next one down, she glanced briefly for any sigil that would indicate this was one of the palace guards, but she saw nothing.

"I had this," Bastan said.

Sam got closer to him, practically shoulder to shoulder, and smacked the next attacker with her staff. He went spinning away, spiraling to the ground where he flopped forward. She smacked him once more with her staff just for good measure. It was better to keep him from moving and getting up to come after her.

"Five against one? Bastan, I think even you needed some help."

Bastan punched the nearest attacker, moving past his sword, somehow managing to strike the man before he was able to react. Sam lunged forward, slamming her staff down on him to complete it.

That left one attacker.

She spun around, looking for where he went, but the street was quiet.

There were only the motionless attackers, now lying bleeding and broken on the cobblestones.

"You could say thanks," Sam said. She looked over at Bastan. His silver hair was slicked back, and a sheen of sweat dripped down his cheek. A small gash had been opened below one eye.

"As I said, I had this."

"There were five attackers, and only one of you. I

know you're skilled"—she didn't know how skilled a fighter Bastan was, but knew that he had to have been fairly talented, especially considering the fact that he had survived in his position as long as he had—"but even you have limits."

"As do you, Samara."

Bastan knelt before one of the men and began rifling through his pockets. He pulled a few coins free and tossed them on the cobbles. Sam quickly grab them up, ignoring Bastan's soft grunt as she did. He might have enough coin, but she didn't always, and she wouldn't pass up an opportunity to have more. She never knew when her fortunes would change, and she would suddenly become dependent on what she was able to save.

"What are you looking for?"

"I'm looking to see why these men would risk carrying swords."

"Your men risk carrying swords."

"Not openly."

Sam realized what he implied. Three of the men had scabbards strapped to their waists, and none of them wore cloaks that would conceal them. They would have been openly carrying swords.

"They're not guards. They don't have the sigil."

"No. I didn't think they were guards. They haven't sent anyone against me in quite some time."

"They? As in the Anders family?"

Bastan stood and dusted his hands on his pants. There was a single cut along his pant leg, as well, this one fairly deep. It bled and soaked the fabric.

"We need to get you to someone who can help you with that," she said, nodding to his leg.

"I will manage just fine, Samara."

"Kyza take you, Bastan. All I want to do is help."

"And you have. Trust me, Samara, you have helped."

"And still no thanks," she muttered.

She leaned over the remaining men and went through their pockets, grabbing the handfuls of coins that she could find. Bastan watched, amusement on his face as she did. "What?"

"Only that you don't have the same need of coin you once did, and yet you still pilfer as if you are the street thief I raised."

"I was more than a street thief."

"Yes, you are much more than a street thief. And I don't say that as a way to insult you, Samara. Far from it. I have the utmost respect for your abilities."

"What was this about? Between this and the men that I saw—"

The smile faded from his face abruptly. "What men?"

"There were men. I don't know. I came here for…" Sam didn't know why she had come to Caster, other than its familiarity. She should have returned to the palace, and she should have avoided coming here where it was all too easy to get embroiled in such minor conflicts when there was something much larger that she needed to resolve. "Whatever. I came here for some reason and overheard these men. They were talking about you."

"Tell me about them," Bastan said.

Sam described the men to him and what she'd overheard, and as she did, Bastan's brow furrowed. "What is it? Who are they?"

"Nothing more than a rival."

Sam arched a brow, watching Bastan with amusement. "A rival. I didn't think you had any rivals."

"Not in Caster, but there are dozens of other sections to this city, Samara. I don't have the same control of them as I do of Caster."

"I don't think you have complete control of Caster, either."

"No? And if not me, then who?"

Sam waved way the question. She didn't need to get into an argument with Bastan, especially not about something like this. "Who is this rival?"

"It doesn't matter. I will take care of it."

"It does matter, especially if they intend to attack you."

Bastan glanced over at her. He had been studying something on the ground, and Sam nudged close to him, forcing him to take a step out of the way. There were shards of glass on the ground, though she couldn't see why that was important. Maybe it wasn't, or maybe there was something that Bastan knew and wasn't telling her. She reached for one of the shards, and Bastan grabbed her shoulders and pushed her back.

"What's that about?"

"That's about their way of attempting to attack me."

"Other than coming at you with swords?"

"They knew the swords would be ineffective. This attack was something else."

If Sam thought that Bastan might explain more, she

was mistaken. She shrugged and turned away from him, looking along the street. "You know I can help," she said.

"Can you? After everything that you've done and become, are you allowed to help someone like me?"

"Why wouldn't I be?"

"Only because you serve a very different master now than you did when you worked with me."

"I think you're mistaking the phrasing. It's not that I worked *with* you so much as you made me work *for* you."

Bastan started down the street, and Sam trailed along. When he turned the corner, two massive men appeared. For a moment, Sam thought they might attack, but Bastan leaned close to them and whispered something. Without saying a word, they hurried off, disappearing along the street in the direction that she and Bastan had come from.

His men.

She wondered briefly what he would do with the attackers, before deciding that it didn't matter. She had struck two of them with her staff hard enough to break bones. Without reaching a physicker, they weren't going to recover very easily or quickly. Knowing Bastan, they would be tormented for information. She wasn't naïve enough to be offended by that.

"Something's going on, Bastan. Something more than what you're telling me."

"There is nothing more going on," he said. "Do you think this is the first time that I've faced a challenger?"

"I don't know. I've never been around you when you've been attacked like this."

"Then let me tell you that it's not. And you have been

around me when I've been attacked. You were there when my tavern was destroyed."

"That was different. That was—"

"Yes. The Thelns. I seem to recall encountering them."

Sam glanced back to the street. In this section of Caster, all of the buildings were made of stone, and most of them had parts of their faces crumbling. Attempts at maintenance had been done over the years, but the masons who created these buildings had a much different skill set than those who had attempted to restore them. There was simply no comparison to the original work.

Wind gusted through, and it carried with it the smells from the canal. Sam suspected she stank of the canal, as well, though there was little to be done for it now. As likely as not, she wasn't nearly as obscured as she had thought. How much had her stench carried?

"I am surprised to see you still in the city, Samara."

"Why, because you thought I would go after Tray?"

"I thought that had always been your intent."

She shrugged, but she couldn't shake the irritation. "That has been my intent, but—"

"But something is keeping you from going after him. If it's access, I may be of some assistance."

Sam shook her head. If she asked that of Bastan, she knew that she would be tied to him much more than she wanted to be. She had been tied to him enough and was tired of it. It was time for her to manage on her own, though every time she tried, it seemed she always ended up needing help.

"I'm not sure how much help you could be," she said.

"Perhaps not as much as I would like," Bastan said. He

stopped at an intersection. In one direction, Sam could see the front of the tavern. Down another was a narrow alley that would lead to a back entrance to the tavern and Bastan's office. "You are always welcome here. And you know that I will do anything I can to offer my protection," Bastan said.

She watched him. There was something almost endearing about the way that he said it. Why, then, did it annoy her? "Anything? Even if it means that you have to give up part of your reach?"

Bastan watched her for a moment. "It was good to see you, Samara. Now, if you don't mind, I have a few tasks that will need my attention."

Bastan strode along the alleyway and back toward his tavern.

"You could have said thanks," she muttered again.

She started off and decided to return to the location where Bastan had been attacked. When she got there, she wasn't surprised to see that the bodies of the men were gone. What did surprise her was that the glass fragments were also gone.

Whatever had happened here was important enough to Bastan to ensure that it was all cleaned up. What was he trying to hide? And who was he trying to hide it from?

As much as she wanted to stay to figure out what Bastan was hiding from her, she didn't think that she could—or that she should. It was late, and she'd been gone for most of the day. She needed to get back before there were too many questions, the kind that she already would face. When Elaine discovered that she'd been gone, she would question her, and how would Sam answer? Would there be anything she could say that would convince Elaine that she wasn't plotting out a way to cross the swamp?

Each jump across the canals brought her closer to the palace. It was late enough that she didn't think she could stop to visit Alec at the university, though there were questions she thought only he would be able to answer. And she needed to get to him, to find some way of getting those answers, but now wasn't the right time. Especially now that he had been promoted to full physicker. He needed to be left to his studies, so regardless of what she wanted to know, there were things that Alec needed from her. And right now, one of those things was space.

She approached the palace, glancing over to the bridge and the pair of guards that were there. Without staring too long, she jumped the canal.

When she splashed into the water, Sam swore to herself, flipping herself back out and to the shore. She had broken her concentration. She knew better, but she was tired from everything that she'd been through today, and that had been without any augmentations. How tired would she have been had she bothered to attempt an augmentation? Though it gave her the strength she needed, it always left her weakened.

Regardless, her supply of easar paper was dwindling, and though she had a few vials of blood ink, she didn't dare to use it without having Alec in her presence. If she did, and needed it later, she worried that she would waste the supplies.

Dripping wet, she made her way back into the palace, already preparing for what Elaine might say to her.

7

THE PRINCESS EXPLAINS

Sam stormed through the palace hallway. She made no effort to muffle her passing, not caring whether she drew anyone's notice. She was annoyed. Then again, she was often annoyed, especially since having come here. Training wasn't quite what she had been promised, and for the third day in a row, no one had been there for her, so what was the purpose of her even staying here? She had practiced on her own, spending time in the courtyard working on her balancing, watching the university in the distance, thinking of what Alec might be doing. And with each passing day, she was no closer to getting to her brother.

Worse, she was no closer to understanding what Marin had intended for her.

The woman was still missing. Maybe that was what she should have set Bastan on. If nothing else, he could go looking for Marin. As far as Sam knew, she had headed south, leaving the city by boat, but there were only so many places that she would have been able to go. How extensive was the Kavers' reach? How much would Elaine be able to determine about where Marin had gone?

She reached the princess's room and knocked.

Sam knew she should be more cautious. This was the princess, but she also was Elaine's Scribe, so Sam had something of a different relationship with her than what she once would have believed likely with the princess.

The door opened, and Lyasanna glanced out. "Samara? To what do I owe this honor?"

"Honor? I'm trying to find Elaine, but she's been gone."

"You've seen that Elaine is gone many days. Why is today any different?"

It wasn't—not really. Elaine was often gone many days, and Sam had seen that she would disappear for long stretches, likely on assignment for whatever Lyasanna asked of her. And maybe on assignment for things that the rest of the Anders family required, but Sam had reached a point where she wished that she knew what Elaine was doing and where she was going. Couldn't she help? With everything that she had learned, wasn't she able to assist? She was a Kaver, after all.

"She was to be training me," Sam said.

"There are other Kavers who can participate in your training."

"And they have," Sam said. Reyelle had taught her the most about balancing on her staff, though even that was more a demonstration of what was possible than any actual teaching. What she needed now was someone to spend time with her, to actually teach her what it meant

If anyone should sympathize with Sam and her desire to go after Tray, it would be the princess, wouldn't it?

"I'm not sure there's anything we can do for Tray," she said. Her voice caught, and Sam understood the reason.

The princess struggled with the loss of Tray, almost as much as Sam did. She had needed to hide her connection to him—that he was her son, and Sam understood, given that a Theln was his father and the family had never known of the pregnancy at all. But what she didn't understand was why the princess continued to conceal her connection to Tray. And Sam continued to wonder why Marin had established and maintained a contrived connection to Tray for as long as she had. There was more to everything that was taking place than what Sam knew—and what she was allowed to know. It grated on her.

"I'm going to go after him. He needs my help whether he knows it or not."

"We know so little about the Theln lands," Lyasanna said.

"Can you help me?"

Lyasanna stared at her. After a while, she let out a heavy sigh. "I'm not sure there's anything I can do to help with this, Samara. Elaine intends to find out what she can about Tray, but even she doesn't have much hope of discovering what the Thelns plan for him."

Sam swallowed the lump in her throat. As she often

did when talking about Tray, she thought about everything they had been through when they were younger, and when Tray had served as her look out. They had been all that the other had for so long.

She looked past the princess into the room and found it empty. "Can I come in?"

Lyasanna nodded and Sam stepped all the way into the massive sitting room, closing the door behind her. The princess's rooms were much more ornate than Sam's, but she'd gotten used to that aspect of the palace overall since coming here. The chairs were covered in lovely fabrics and rugs were clearly of high quality. Probably imported. She had two large wardrobes and Sam imagined the formal clothing hanging inside them. As likely as not, they were filled with gowns. Several shelves had stacks of books placed haphazardly on them. Another doorway led back to the princess's sleeping quarters, where Sam imagined an enormous bed occupying much of the space. It was probably much more comfortable than the one Sam was given.

Lyasanna signaled for Sam to take a seat in one of the chairs in front of the fireplace. Sam did so, and stared straight ahead, trying to organize her thoughts.

"Why didn't you ever go after him?" Sam asked.

"Tray?" Lyasanna said.

Sam breathed out heavily. "You knew about him, and it seems as if you care about him, so I can't figure out why you wouldn't have gone for him."

"Because I thought he was gone."

"Gone?"

"When Ralun is involved in anything, there is no middle ground. I was led to believe that Tray was gone."

"Gone where? Did someone take him?" When the princess simply stared, Sam nodded. "Marin. I see. Why would she hide from you the fact that Tray still lived?"

Lyasanna sighed deeply. "I… I struggled to escape from Voldin." When Sam arched a brow, Lyasanna said, "That is the outer city in Theln where we met. It took many lives to get me free, and that was just me. Others were tasked with bringing Tray, but in hindsight, I should have known better."

Sam shook her head. "Marin pretended that he was lost getting him out of the Theln lands?"

"Marin has deceived us for a long time," Lyasanna said.

"I still don't understand. I don't understand why you allowed yourself to be seduced by Ralun."

"You're still young, Samara, so it's unlikely that you can understand. There is simply something about a man like Ralun. In Voldin, he was not the violent and dangerous Theln he has shown himself to be here. There, he was simply Prince Ralun."

Sam's eyes widened. "Prince?"

"It's not quite like it seems. There are many princes in their lands. But Ralun was the most impressive. He had a certain confidence to him."

"Confidence? You mean arrogance."

"At the time, I thought it was nothing more than confidence. In hindsight, now I see it as arrogance, which is probably what I should have seen at the time. And then, there is the power of their Book."

"You've experienced the Book before."

"I have. And because I'm a Scribe, they thought they could seduce me, that they could offer me promises of power and access to knowledge that I wouldn't have otherwise. It was compelling, but only for a moment."

Sam struggled to understand what would have compelled Lyasanna to act in the way she had. Ralun's actions made much more sense, which troubled her to admit.

"And now Tray is off with Ralun, and we have no way of knowing what they might do."

"We don't." Lyasanna sat in silence for a long moment.

"Will we ever understand Marin's motivation?"

"It's possible that we won't," Lyasanna said.

"But why did she use the Book to steal my memories? Why would she use it to forge a connection between Tray and me? Why would she—"

"Because she is Marin."

"Everybody says that, but I don't really understand what that means."

"Marin was one of the most skilled Kavers in the city. She was the one who was in charge of my protection when we went to the Theln lands."

"Not Elaine?"

"Elaine was still learning. I was still learning. At the time, I didn't fully understand what it meant for the two of us to have the connection that we did. It's not common for my family to carry the Scribe connection."

"You normally have the Kaver connection?" That was news to Sam.

"Most in the Anders family have the Kaver ability," Lyasanna said. "Which is why the university exists. It was always supposed to be a training facility for Scribes, but it had an added benefit. The physickers were able to help others within the city, and together, we have always done everything that we can to provide protection to those who live here."

"How many of your family have been Scribes before?"

"As far as I know, I am the first."

"But you don't train at the university…" As she said it, understanding finally hit her. "That's why she's been here, isn't it?"

Sam thought of the master physicker—Master Helen—and realized that must be the reason that she was here. "Have you been getting private education?"

"I couldn't very well spend time at the university. Doing so would only raise questions. As much as I want to understand my Scribe abilities, there are images to maintain, and we have been very careful about ensuring that the perception of the Anders family is intact."

Sam frowned to herself. "It's more than that, isn't it? It's more than maintaing perceptions about your family. You don't want the Thelns to know that you're a Scribe."

Lyasanna smiled tightly. "They can't know."

"But they know about Kavers."

"They don't know that many of the Kavers come from my family. As far as the Thelns know, we're served by the Kavers and they offer us protection, not anything more than that."

"But Tray knows about you."

"He does?"

Sam thought about what she had uncovered and tried to think about exactly what Tray might know but struggled. He knew she was his mother. Ralun had obviously told him that, but maybe he didn't know about Lyasanna being a Scribe. Which hopefully meant Ralun didn't know either.

"I don't know exactly what he knows, but I think he knows something."

"That would be a challenge."

"Which is why you should let me go after him. I'm the only one who can get through to him. If something happens, and the attack goes wrong, he might only respond to me."

"I suspect that you're right, which is why I've asked Elaine to train you with even greater urgency. You will be needed, Samara. Your connection to Tray is critical in what is to come."

"And what is to come?"

"I don't know, not entirely. All I know is that Tray has opened up an age-old conflict."

"It seems as if the conflict was open long before Tray."

"It's not his disappearance that opened the conflict, or his reappearance. It's who he is—*what* he is—that has created the conflict."

"I don't understand."

"The Thelns have a different kind of power than you or your mother have, but they are not unrelated. The Thelns would use the power of the Scribes, and they offered them a different reward as they temped them to create the Book."

"Scribes are responsible for the Book of Maladies?"

"Scribes—what you know as Scribes—are responsible for a great many things. And the war that you have just begun to experience has long been about power, but a different kind of power then you probably expected."

"What kind of power, then?"

"The power of knowledge. And I'm afraid that losing Tray has shifted the tide of power away from us and to the Thelns."

8

AN UNUSUAL CASE

The inside of the intake room had a certain odor to it. Alec hadn't spent too much time here, his transition from student to full physicker had prevented him from having the same amount of time in this place as many of the other physickers did. There was a sense of chaos here, and Alec tried not to let it get to him, but there was also such a need for help here.

He made his way to the row of chairs. It was here that he'd had his first experience with the university, and this is where he had come when trying to gain access so that he could help Sam as they fought to find answers about the princess, but it wasn't a place that students were allowed to spend much time, despite what Alec had thought then. Typically, junior physickers were here, and they were the ones to make the initial assessment, and they were the ones to assess the fees. Once they determined what was needed, treatments were confirmed with a full physicker or a master physicker, whichever was available.

It wasn't Alec's turn to be here, but he felt compelled, especially after seeing the line waiting to get into the university.

"What ailment brought you here?" he asked a young girl. She was maybe fifteen or so and was accompanied by an older gentleman, who stirred awake at Alec's approach. How long must they have been waiting?

"It's… It's my eyes," she said.

"What happened to your eyes?" Alec asked.

"They're blurred."

"Blurred vision isn't something you would need to come to the university for," Alec said gently. "There are many opticians within the city who could help, and I suspect could do so at a cheaper rate than what you must've paid for entry to the university."

The girl glanced over at her grandfather—at least, that was what Alec presumed the man to be. "We have tried opticians, physicker," she said.

Opticians. That meant they had been to more than one. "And what did they tell you?"

"That there is nothing their lenses would be able to fix. As much as they wanted to be able to help, they didn't have anything to offer."

That surprised Alec. Opticians were nearly as bad as the university when it came to collecting fees, but the opticians were known for accepting payments for treatments that weren't always effective. Too often, they would claim money for lenses before they were even made, and from what he had seen, they did nothing to ensure the quality of the lenses. It was frustrating to him, and it was likely frustrating to those who were involved.

"Come with me," he said.

Alec offered the older man his hand, but he shook him off, preferring to cling to the his granddaughter's arm. They made their way to an empty intake booth, the same sort of place that Alec had gone with Sam. One of the junior physickers caught his eye and frowned. Was he upsetting them with his presence? He suspected they could take it one of several ways. They could either appreciate the help, or take offense to his presence, presuming he thought himself better than they. But the real reason for his presence was something much simpler. All he wanted was the opportunity to know what it was like to be on this side of healing. He had spent quite a bit of time in the wards, but there were certain things that he couldn't see and experience within the wards, some of which required him to come to the intake and work as he once had with his father.

Inside the intake booth, he helped the older man to sit down. He turned to the young girl. "Tell me about your vision difficulty."

"It started slowly," she said, her voice taking on a note that indicated she had told her story more than a few times. "At first, it was nothing more than a little blurriness. We thought that maybe I was tired, or perhaps that I needed to visit one of the opticians. I wouldn't be the first person in my family to need lenses, but they are so expensive…"

Alec sat with his hands resting on his lap, listening. There was no need for notes, at least, not yet.

"Over time, the blurriness got worse. It got to the point where I couldn't see to perform day-to-day tasks."

"What sort of tasks?"

"I am apprenticed to a seamstress."

That was a highly desired apprenticeship, Alec knew. And involved tasks that would require clear vision, especially when attempting to thread needles. There were certain tasks that seamstresses did that would've been nearly impossible with blurred vision. "How long have you been unable to maintain your apprenticeship?"

"It's only been a few days, physicker, but I don't dare wait any longer. Especially knowing that if I'm not able to maintain my apprenticeship, it will pass to someone else."

Alec sighed and nodded. "I understand. Let's see what we can do."

He grabbed a lantern off the wall and brought it close to the girl's face. With the extra light, he examined her eyes. The pupils reacted quickly, so he knew that her eyes were working to draw in the light. He decided to attempt a different sort of test and pulled out a slip of paper from his pocket and scratched a few words on the page.

"Are you able to read?"

The girl nodded. "Been able to read since I was a little girl. My grandfather taught me." She turned and gave him a gentle smile.

"Why hasn't he said anything," Alec asked.

"He can't speak."

"Why? Has he always been a mute?"

"No, something happened years ago. An illness. It took away his ability to speak."

"Why didn't he come for help?"

"We weren't able to afford help at the time. Even coming here has taken more than we have to spare, physicker. You understand that the cost is a burden."

Alec sighed. "Yes, I do understand."

"And we have enough. Please don't choose not to help me because of concern about my ability to pay. If you can help me, if you can preserve my vision, I will be of benefit to the city. I'm learning a valuable trade."

It pained Alec that there were people like this girl who struggled with their ability to pay, and who felt as if they had to justify to the physickers why they should be granted healing. "I'm not concerned," Alec said. He tapped on the page. "Now, can you read this?"

"I can see the outline of the letters, but… it's blurry. I can't make out what you wrote."

Alec glanced at the paper. He'd written in large letters, large enough that he would be able to see them from across the room. For her to see nothing but blurred letters meant that whatever was happening had advanced beyond some simple problem.

"Let me try this," he said. He moved his fingers on either side, and waited for her to turn toward them, but she didn't. There was no reaction. "Do you see the movement?"

"What sort of movement?"

"Maybe this wasn't the right sort of test," Alec said.

He decided to try a different approach. He moved behind her and began waving his hands at her sides, waiting for her to notice them, but it wasn't until his hands were directly in front of her face that she seemed to see anything.

How bad had her vision gotten?

"And you were able to see well before this began to happen?"

"Before this happened, my vision was normal."

"Have you had any fevers?" She shook her head. "Have you injured yourself in any way?" She shook her head again. "Have you been sick in any other way?"

"No, physicker. I've been well up until this happened. I need to keep my position with the seamstress. If I can't…" Her gaze drifted to her grandfather, and Alec thought he understood. There was a reason they hadn't been able to afford healing before, but could now. It was because of her apprenticeship. Without her income, the old man would likely suffer.

Alec leaned close to her and brought the light up even closer to her eyes. As he did, he stared into them, studying what might be there. He brought the lantern up, almost close enough to burn her, but he kept it away from her face so that it didn't. As he stared, he noticed a sort of milkiness in her eyes.

Alec leaned back. He had seen something similar in others, but only in the very old. That was strange.

"Have you worked with any chemicals recently?"

"No chemicals."

"How long have you been apprenticed?"

"I've been at my position for the better part of a year."

"Has anything changed with your apprenticeship?"

The girl shook her head.

Alec tapped his lip, trying to think through what else it could be. "I will need to look into this more. I don't have an answer for you at this time, but I promise that I will find an answer and get back to you."

"We won't have money to make a return visit," she said.

And if she had to return, she ran the risk of losing her apprenticeship. There was another option, but Alec worried it wouldn't be viewed as a serious enough injury.

"Then you will stay here until I have an answer," Alec said.

"Here? In this room?" She looked around, and her gaze drifted to her grandfather.

"Not here. The university has a healing ward, and that's where I would have you stay."

"What of my grandfather?"

"I'm afraid he won't be able to stay, so I hope there is someone who can help take care of him."

The girl breathed out in a sigh. "I suppose that Nestor can stay with you, Grandfather."

He nodded and reached toward her, grabbing her hands and squeezing them.

To Alec, the message was clear. He wanted her to do whatever it took to get better.

"I will do all that I can to help her," he said to the old man.

The man turned toward him and smiled. When he did, Alec realized why he was unable to speak. A portion of his tongue was missing.

What had happened to him? What kind of torment must he have been subjected to for him to miss a chunk of his tongue?

And yet, that wasn't why they were here. They were

here for the girl, but even if they had come for her grandfather, there wasn't anything Alec could do for him. There were limits to healing, short of his attempting to use easar paper, and he wasn't even sure whether easar paper would make a difference when it came to someone who had lost a portion of their tongue.

Yet... it might be valuable for him to know. What would happen if something like that happened to Sam? Would he be able to assist her in any way, or would she be left with an injury, forever maimed?

"What is your grandfather's name?"

"Why?"

"In case I need to send word to him," he said.

She looked over to her grandfather before turning her attention back to Alec, almost with a suspicious glance. "His name is Rynance Vold. Most who know him call him Ryn."

"What section of the city are you in?"

"We're in the Hosd section."

That was an outer section, though not quite as far out as Caster, still it was one of the sections that was known as lowborn. More than ever, Alec wanted to help this girl and her grandfather. He suspected Sam would approve of him attempting to use easar paper in such a way, even if it meant they'd have less paper for their own needs. Eventually, he would need to find more paper, but so far, he didn't know where to start. Their supply had been pilfered from the university, so he wasn't even sure if there would be more paper available for them. Those were more questions for him to ask of Master Eckerd when he had a chance to do so.

"If anything changes with her status, I will send word to you, Rynance," Alec said.

The old man nodded. He looked over at the girl and smiled. It was likely he believed that Alec would be able to help, and he was determined to try. He would find a way to restore her vision, even if it meant using easar paper on her.

He guided them back out and led the old man to the entrance of the intake room, where he offered him a chair, before turning to address the young girl. "I will have someone send word to your section and to Nestor that he is here and waiting."

The girl nodded. "Thank you."

Alec patted the man on the arm, giving him a warm, encouraging smile, then guided the young girl toward the ward. He found an empty cot and motioned for her to lie down. While she got settled, he made notes in the blank record, placing her name, age, and a few other details about her, but omitting the name of her section. If there were any junior physickers who believed too much in the highborn versus lowborn philosophy of healing, he wasn't about to limit her opportunity to receive treatment.

As he was making his last notes on the record, he saw that there was a master physicker in the ward. Alec wasn't entirely surprised to see Master Harrison here, but he was surprised to see him alone, without his usual cadre of students. He nodded toward Alec and began to make his way over to him. Alec hurriedly finished his notes, wanting to keep the girl here, and worried that Master Harrison might find some reason for her to be dismissed.

"Physicker Stross."

"Master Harrison, I have admitted a young woman with an abrupt visual change—"

"You may admit whoever you feel is appropriate," Master Harrison said. "We require that the junior physickers get the permission of a full physicker or higher before admitting someone, but we don't require the same for you. As you have been promoted to full physicker, you do not require anyone's permission."

Master Harrison grabbed the record and quickly scanned it. As he did, he looked up at Alec. "This will be a difficult treatment."

"Because of the rapidity of her symptoms?"

"Because visual symptoms are difficult to treat," Master Harrison said. "There are few treatments that are very effective."

Alec noticed the girl watching, and he guided Master Harrison away, keeping her from overhearing the rest of their conversation. "That's my fear, but I was hopeful there might be something that could be done to assist her, though I'm not entirely sure what that might be. I'll admit that I don't have much experience with changes in vision."

"I would say that few master physickers have much experience with that, either. It's reasonable that you would like to investigate more, but I caution you that you will likely not be as successful as you would hope in restoring her eyesight."

Alec sighed. It was one more thing to search the library for. Not only did he have to find some way to help the people like his father and the young woman in a similar state, but now he would need to search for something to help this young girl? At least with her eyesight, he thought there might be an easy restoration if he dared use it.

"How much was she willing to pay for this healing?" Master Harrison asked.

"I didn't contract for payment," Alec said.

"You understand the reasoning behind charging what we do," Master Harrison said. "I was under the impression that you have had that conversation with Master Carl."

"We have had that conversation, but there are certain times when I think we need to have compassion."

"All of us have compassion, Physicker Stross."

Alec glanced back, thinking of the young girl and everything that she had been through, and thinking about how her family depended on her as well as depending on her apprenticeship. Without her apprenticeship, what would become of that family? Would they be forced into something less than reputable? Would they be forced to work with someone like Bastan? The girl deserved better. Her family deserved better. And if Alec had anything to do with it, he would ensure that they were able to afford something better.

"Of course, Master Harrison. I meant no offense, it's just that I recognize there are times when some who aren't able to pay might present conditions that could be of interest to the physickers and teaching the students. Thus admitting them to our care shows our compassion and interest in their care while also providing us with valuable documentation for future cases. In this case, I don't have much experience treating visual problems, and I thought that having a case to learn from would be of benefit to me so that I can see what impact I might have on restoring her vision."

"Ah. Yes, well there are times when physickers must make exceptions so they can continue to learn and become the best physickers they are able to be." Master Harrison looked around the room. "I have not yet congratulated you on your promotion. I can't say that I'm all that surprised. You have done well from the moment you arrived, so there are few of us who have spent any time working with you who expected anything less. Perhaps we didn't expect it quite so quickly, but we are all pleased that you have joined our ranks."

Alec wasn't certain that all of the physickers were so pleased, but it was nice of Master Harrison to make that claim.

He went back to the cot and smiled at the young girl. "I will keep you here. You will be provided with food and water, but your time will be incredibly boring. I will see what I can find about what happened to you, and I will restore your eyesight as quickly as I can."

"Thank you, physicker," she said.

"Don't thank me until I've succeeded," he said.

9

FAILURE

Failure was frustrating Alec. He continued to struggle with how to help his father and the other injured woman, but so far hadn't come up with any ideas. There had to be some answer, something that would explain what happened to them, but so far, he'd found nothing.

He pushed the books away from him and sat up, rubbing his eyes. The library was dark at this time of day, other than the light from his lantern. The librarians had long ago left, and he seemed to be the only one remaining. He had become accustomed to that role. Over the last few days, he'd spent as much time as he could studying in the library, searching for answers that he had not yet found. Alec was convinced that they would come—eventually. For his father's sake, he needed to find those answers.

The door to the library opened, and Alec glanced up before returning his attention to the next book. He was focusing on those that detailed changes in level of alertness. All of these were previous records of illness, and he had stacks of them to work through. He was searching for patterns, anything that would help him find a way to help both his father and the other woman, and so far, he had found some similarities in past cases, but none of the cases spoke of conditions where the person simply seemed in a permanent state of sleep.

"Alec?"

He looked up to see the tall, slender form of Stefan. "You don't have to be afraid to join me, Stefan."

His friend sighed. "It's been difficult."

"I can see that," Alec said. "It doesn't need to be, but I can see that it is."

"I haven't known what to make of the fact that you are a full physicker."

"To be honest, I haven't known what to make of it, either."

Stefan chuckled. "I've been waiting for you in your room, but you haven't returned."

His quarters were quite a bit nicer now than what they had been when he was a student. They were nicer than the junior physickers had, and those were quite a bit nicer than the students' quarters. They didn't feel quite right, not feeling quite like they were his, but he did his best to make them his own. At least now, he had a way of locking his door and was able to prevent those who might think to break in from gaining access to his room. That hadn't really been an issue before, other than with Beckah. And Alec wasn't sure he could stop Beckah entirely this way. It was possible she would find some way in, regardless.

"I'm determined to figure out some way to help my father," he said.

"If anyone can find it, it will be you," Stefan said.

"I tried talking to your grandmother about him," Alec said.

"You did? What did she say?"

"She hadn't seen an illness like this before. She wasn't able to help."

"Oh. She's seen everything," Stefan said.

That was what Alec feared. If Master Helen hadn't seen it, and if she had no way of helping, there might not be anyone who could help. She was the most capable master that Alec knew. Between her and Master Eckerd, there was a significant amount of knowledge. He hadn't approached Master Eckerd, but if Master Helen didn't know, Alec didn't have great hope that Master Eckerd would. Besides, Master Eckerd continued to work with the students, and he would have been aware that Aelus was lying sick in the university.

"So, I'm now searching through centuries of records, all of them with some similarity."

"What did you use to search?"

"The level of alertness. Librarians have been helping, and they've given me a stack." He motioned to the pile of records on the end of the table, and then there were two more nearly as high as the table resting on the floor. "I figure at this pace, it will only take me the better part of a year to go through all of them."

And he didn't think that his father—or the young woman—had that much time. They were feeding them, but at what point would their conditions become permanent? At what point would he lose his father because of this illness?

"It's a strange condition, isn't it?" Stefan said.

"It is. With my father, I thought that maybe there was something he was exposed to, but I haven't been able to determine anything. I've tried various treatment options, but none of them has been effective." He had been careful in doing that. He hadn't wanted to attempt anything that might put his father in danger, but at the same time, he needed to try something. Each of them had been small tests. He was gauging response, thinking that if he could discover whether there was the slightest change, he might be able to use the easar paper. Ultimately, he feared that he would need to use the easar paper regardless of Master Helen's warning. He was prepared to try it if nothing else worked. He owed his father that much.

"Can I help you?" Stefan asked.

He glanced up at his friend, relieved. "I would like that."

Stefan grabbed a book and pulled it open. "What am I looking for?"

"You're looking for anything where the patient was mostly well but unresponsive. There are quite a few where they're unresponsiveness is tied to infection or to something going on inside their head, and quite a few where blood loss led to their condition, but this is different from those. If you find anything, I will take a look to see if I can find a pattern." With treatment, especially with difficult treatments, it was the pattern that was the most helpful. That was what he needed to find. If he could discover a pattern, he would be able to help—he was certain of it.

They fell into a rhythm, and Alec appreciated that Stefan was there, working with him. It was nice having his friend, even if they weren't saying anything. He lost track of time as he sorted through the records, setting aside those that were completely wrong. That stack much taller than the short stack that had cases with any similarities to what his father was going through. His despair was growing.

After a while, the door opened, and he looked up. It had been quite late when Stefan had come, though his friend had been looking for him. It was even later now as a young student—one Alec didn't know—poked his head around the stack of books. "Physicker Stross?"

Alec nodded. "What is it?"

"I was sent to get you," he said. "You have a visitor outside."

Alec glanced over at Stefan who waved at him. He was deep in one of the records, and his own stack of discarded records was growing nearly as quickly as Alec's. "You don't have to keep at this without me," Alec said.

"No. Let me help. Besides, consider it my way of working with a physicker," Stefan said with a smile.

Alec patted him on the shoulder as he passed by and followed the student through the hallways. The halls were quiet, given the hour. They didn't pass anyone on their way. A few lanterns provided light, but not much. The halls of the university were stark. Stone floors and walls of a white marble rising on either side. There were a few paintings hanging on the walls, but not many.

The student guided him to the main entrance. Could Sam have come for him? But wouldn't she have snuck in as she usually did. She knew where his new quarters were, and she would have been able to reach him without sending a messenger to him. If not Sam, who?

"Did they tell you who they were?"

The student shook his head. "I didn't ask. At this time of night, I thought speed was more important than asking a lot of questions."

Alec sighed. This was a young student, someone new to the university, who likely thought students weren't supposed to ask questions.

When they reached the door, Alec stepped out into the night.

But it wasn't Sam.

"What are you doing here?" he asked Bastan.

"Come on."

"Bastan, it's late."

Bastan glanced at the student and waved his hand. "You can go. I have need of Physicker Stross."

The student looked over at Alec for a moment and waited for him to give him a nod of permission.

Bastan chuckled. "You *have* risen quickly."

"You know what happened."

"Only some of it. Sounds like quite the story."

"Maybe not quite as exciting as what you think. We did it hoping we could find a master physicker we suspected was tied to Marin."

"And you still let them get away."

"I didn't let them get away."

"No? I imagine that Samara would have been able to catch Marin."

"If Elaine couldn't catch Marin, then Samara wouldn't have been able to. If she had tried to, especially if Marin had her Scribe, she would have been placing herself in danger."

"I think you underestimate the relationship between Marin and Samara."

Bastan guided him down the stairs leading away from the university. There was a wide path lined with tall shrubbery that they walked along. "Marin cares more than she lets on."

"Sort of like you?"

"I'm not unwilling to reveal that I care."

"You're only unwilling to reveal why you care."

"You don't think that I should care about my best thief? Samara was the most skilled person I had working with me. Were it not for you, she would still be working with me."

"I don't think I'm the reason she's not working with you. She was looking for a way out from under your thumb even before I met her."

"Only because she didn't know."

"Know what?"

Bastan shook his head. "It doesn't matter."

"Where are you taking me?"

"You came looking for word of your father."

"You found something?"

"I don't know what to make of it, but there was something."

Alec followed Bastan as they crossed the bridge leading away from the university. It felt strange doing so at this time of night, with a sliver of moon shining down, and doing so without Sam. Alec had wandered the streets of the city late at night before, but he'd always done so with his Kaver connection with him.

There was a quiet that hung over everything, an almost somber sense that he enjoyed. There was something peaceful about the city when he walked through it this late at night. Eventually, people would awaken; there would be the sounds of the morning activity and the steady din of thousands of voices all mixing together to create a murmuring sort of noise. At night, there was only silence.

"Keep moving," Bastan said.

"I was only enjoying—"

"I know what you are enjoying. It's the same reason I like to pull my jobs at night."

"I thought you pulled your jobs at night because doing so kept you from notice."

"That's part of it, but sometimes, working at night adds to the difficulty. Depending on where you go, there might be people that you want to avoid. If you go during the daytime, it's a greater likelihood that you will avoid those people. At night, you get to enjoy this." He held his hands out and turned slowly. "There's almost something magical about the night. Certainly, at night, you can almost feel the presence of the gods."

"I didn't know you were so religious."

"A man doesn't have to be religious to recognize that there are higher powers. I think of you and Sam and all of those Thelns that we've been facing. You are all different from the rest of us, even if I am not sure quite how or what to make of that difference."

Bastan stopped at a section several over from the university. He moved slowly now, and one of his hands drifted into his pocket, and Alec was left nervous. Was there something dangerous here?

He motioned but said nothing as they turned a corner, heading down an alleyway. Alec wasn't scared—not really—and that was only partly because he had some experience out at night. Having Bastan with him was reassuring in a different way. He had seen how confident and competent Bastan was, and though he doubted there would be Thelns attacking at this time of night, he felt somewhat safer knowing that Bastan was with him.

"They should be here, somewhere," he mumbled softly.

Alec looked around the street. There was nothing other than the darkened shape of buildings on either side of the alley, and strange shadows rippled toward the middle of the street. Was that all from moonlight?

Near the end of the street, he saw two people crouched. "Bastan?"

"Don't worry, Physicker Stross. That's where we're heading."

Alec trailed after Bastan, and they reached the two men crouched at the end of the street, and Alec realized there was a body lying between them.

Not a body, but a man. And it was someone Alec recognized. "Kevin? What happened to him?" he asked, looking over to Bastan.

"That's why I came for you."

"Is he dead?"

"Not dead. He still has a pulse." When Alec arched a brow, Bastan shrugged. "A man has to learn a few things in order to remain in my position. Anyway, he's not dead. We found him like this."

"And you just left him here?"

"I thought that if there's anything you need to discover from the area, it might help to leave him where we found him. It's not as if he's suffering."

Alec nodded. Bastan had a bright mind and had done basically what Alec would have requested. Had he taken the man from here, he might not have been able to learn much of anything.

He started forward and briefly studied Kevin. There was no sign of injury. He checked his pulse and found it regular. His breathing was normal. A cursory evaluation for evidence of internal pain or bleeding showed none.

Whatever happened to Kevin was the same as what happened to his father. And the woman. Alec was certain of it.

"Can you tell me what he'd been doing?"

"He had been looking into the apothecary."

Alec glanced at the other two men and then nodded. Was that Bastan's way of telling him that these men didn't know who he was? "Was there anything particular about this section of the city that you think might be important for me to know?"

"Only that Kevin had heard there was movement here, something about a particularly dangerous poison. He thought, given what we had discussed about delicate treatments, that he should look into it."

"It's okay to move him. I can take him back with me to the university."

"He's not going to the university," Bastan said.

"Until we figure out what is happening, he'll need to be fed. Can you do that at your tavern?"

"For Kevin? You're damned right I can do it. I'm not sending him to the university to have him poked and prodded by students there. I know what kinds of things happen at the university."

"*I'll* be at the university."

"Not all the time. And not if you're going to figure out what happened, you're not. I'm not about to leave Kevin someplace where there'll be someone who's not invested in his well-being."

Alec looked over at Bastan and shrugged. He was surprised by Bastan's reaction, but he was mostly surprised that Bastan cared this much. His people meant something to him, which told Alec that it had to hurt him when he lost people too. In the line of work Bastan was in, he *had* lost people, Alec had seen it.

"Fine, take him back to your tavern, but make sure that you're grinding up food and getting it down his throat into his stomach."

"It wouldn't be the first time we had to do that for a man," Bastan said. He motioned to the others, and they lifted Kevin and carried him away. Once they were gone, Bastan crouched down next to Alec. "Now would you care to tell me what is going on?"

"I don't know. This is the same way they found my father."

"You found him?"

"I didn't find him, but this is the same way he was found. That's why I came to you asking about the delicate items."

"Kevin wouldn't have been in contact with them. He would only have been chasing someone who might have heard something."

"Can you at least share with me what you heard? If we know where we're looking, maybe we can figure out if there're some similarities."

"He was following a lead."

"What kind of lead?"

"The kind that would give me more information about where to find poison that shouldn't be readily available."

"The eel venom."

Bastan didn't say anything.

"My father and Kevin aren't the only two suffering like this. There is a third person, a woman, who is at the university, though she's been there longer than my father. She's in about the same condition, but I don't know what happened to her or anything more about her than I do about the others."

Bastan frowned to himself. "Your father had the eel venom, and Kevin was looking into it. What if this other person is connected to it?"

"Then we would at least have identified a connection, but we still wouldn't know what happened to them."

"Nope. No way of knowing, but it's a start."

Bastan stood and reached his hand out to help Alec up. After he pulled him up, he breathed out heavily. "I need to see this third person."

"She's at the university."

"And I need to see her."

"Why?"

"Because if she's tied to this, it might be that I'll recognize her. Are you going to take me to her, or am I going to have to break in?"

SNEAKING WITH A THIEF

There was something uncomfortable about sneaking Bastan into the university. Alec was not certain he should do it, especially given his recent promotion. But he needed to know whether there was anything that Bastan could help him with, especially if it could lead to information about what happened to his father and these others.

"It's been a long time since I've been to the university," Bastan said.

"When were you last here?"

Bastan shot him an amused expression. "A long time ago."

Alec shook his head, determined not to let Bastan bother him. He knew the man took joy in challenging Sam, but he wasn't going to let Bastan get into his head.

They moved quickly through the university gates. It was late, and there were few enough people out at this time of night that Alec needed to avoid attention; he couldn't risk being observed with someone like Bastan.

The man had something of a reputation that Alec had to be concerned with, especially if one of the master physickers appeared, and if they recognized Bastan.

Once inside, he found the halls empty, and they were able to make their way through the university without anyone noticing them.

"What do you know about this illness?" Bastan asked.

"Probably the same as you," Alec said. "Both my father and this woman arrived unresponsive. They are otherwise well, and we have struggled to figure out the cause of their illness."

"Do you suspect some sort of poison?"

"It could be," Alec said. "There are a few different poisons that could induce this state, but everything that I've tried to counter them as been ineffective."

"What sorts of poisons would do that?"

Alec glanced over at Bastan. He studied the man for a moment before shaking his head. "I don't know that I feel comfortable revealing that to you."

"Do you really think I would use it in some way?"

"I think you would use any information that you could to maintain your power," Alec said.

"That would be true, but if you think keeping knowledge like that from me is going to prevent me from discovering it on my own, you underestimate me."

Alec glanced over. As he did, he thought about what he knew of Bastan. This was a man who had known enough to get Aelus involved when it came to finding something that would work against the Thelns. He had known enough to convince his father to help him, so if nothing else, Alec should trust the fact that his father was a good judge of character and had been restrictive about with whom he shared some of the secrets of his knowledge.

"It could be sleaph toxin or Heller's compound or a mixture of jandran root with bostich berries or—"

Bastan chuckled. "It wasn't a test, Alec. I believe you know what you're doing." He eyed Alec for a moment. "You've tried healing all of those things?"

Alec nodded. "Tried all of them and a few others have had no effect."

"Then I guess it doesn't matter."

"What doesn't matter?"

"It doesn't matter if I have my healer attempt the same."

"You have a healer?"

"I have someone I can call on when needed," Bastan said. He frowned at Alec. "Did you think I wouldn't?"

Alec laughed to himself. He shouldn't be surprised that Bastan would have somebody. Especially knowing the kind of work that he did. "Did your healer already test these things?"

"Before calling you, yes. I thought I would try a simpler route."

"Simpler?"

"Fine. Someone who wouldn't attract quite as many questions. Do you think I like coming to the university and being subjected to the types of questions I am sure to face?"

Alec shook his head. "I don't know what you like," he said.

"I don't like the idea of putting Sam at risk. Me

coming here, and revealing my connection to her, puts her at risk. Drawing attention to myself here puts her at risk."

Alec had always known that Bastan cared for Sam, but Bastan tried to conceal that fact, though Alec didn't know why. Why would he care about hiding his connection to Sam?

Maybe it was more about protecting himself. Because of what Sam was, and the connections she now had, they put Bastan in a more difficult situation. Alec could imagine that Bastan was more concerned about protecting himself that way than anything else.

They stopped in front of the doors to the ward, and Alec glanced over at Bastan. "If we're stopped, I'm going to claim you're her husband."

"Is that right?"

"Would you rather be her brother?"

Bastan chuckled. "No, I think husband is a more effective answer."

"It's not always about what's most effective, it's about what will attract the fewest questions. I don't want you to draw the wrong kind of attention here."

"Trust me, Alec, I don't want that, either."

Alec pushed the doors open, and they hurried into the room. As expected given the hour, he found no staff. There would be a junior physicker available, and that person would periodically come through, but wouldn't be here all the time. He wondered if they ever came at all. They were supposed to be the night watch, there in the event of an emergency should one arise. But did they shirk their responsibilities during these late hours, since it was likely they'd not be caught? Something else that he might look into once he became a master.

"I never thought I would see this place," Bastan said.

"If you're sick enough, anyone can come here for healing."

Bastan glanced over at him. "It's not a matter of sickness, Alec. You know that."

"It's not always about money, either. The master physickers have committed to attempting to heal anyone, regardless of whether they can pay."

"It doesn't sound like the physickers that I know."

"Well, they haven't committed to heal everyone. It's just that they have agreed that they wouldn't use ability to pay as the only criteria."

Bastan chuckled. "It doesn't sound as if anything has changed at all."

Alec looked around. The ward had been emptier than usual lately, and that in spite of the fact that there was such a line to gain access to physickers. Nothing really had changed, had it?

"It's something I will keep working on," Alec said.

He guided Bastan to the cot holding the woman. Bastan looked at her, and his eyes widened slightly. "This is her?"

"This is the woman I was talking about," Alec said. "Why?"

"Because I know her."

Alec's breath caught. "You know her? I need to know everything you can tell me about her. She was brought here without any additional information."

"There won't be any."

"Why not?"

"Because there's no one who knows anything more about her."

"Why? What happened to her family?"

"There is no family."

Alec looked over at Bastan, watching him for a long moment. "What do you know about her?"

"Only that she is skilled in ways that remind me of Samara." Bastan frowned, and he scanned the inside of the ward. "Where's your father?"

Alec guided him away from the young woman and over to his father. His coloring had not changed at all. He seemed no different from before, but could his breathing be a little more labored than before? Alec hoped that wasn't the case, but it was possible that his father's breathing had changed, becoming more ragged.

"Do you know how long he's been like this?"

"It's been the better part of a week," Alec said.

"And what about Kara?"

"I presume the young woman is Kara?"

"She is."

"She arrived a few days before my father."

"How long do they have?"

"I don't know. We can continue feeding them, but I don't know if there's anything else taking place."

Bastan looked up at him, and he had a question in his eyes. "What more do you think might be taking place?"

"I don't know. It's possible that something is happening internally that we don't know about."

"What of your other abilities?"

Alec licked his lips. "I've been advised to refrain from

attempting to use them. If I do, and I don't know enough about what else might be taking place, I run the risk of harming them."

"That's awfully convenient," Bastan said.

"How is it convenient? If there was anything I could do, I would try to do it."

"Oh, I don't doubt that you would try, only that it's convenient that there is nothing that can be safely done." He looked around the room. "I presume there are others with your similar ability here."

"There are. It was one of them who warned me against attempting anything."

Bastan frowned. "Could they have another reason to stop you? Might they have a desire to see certain people silenced?"

"Why? There doesn't seem to be any connection between them. I mean, think about what happened with Kevin."

"Kevin was investigating your father. I don't know what he might have come across."

"And what about Kara?"

"That will be up to you to learn."

"If you want me to help Kevin, I need to have as much information as I can. That might involve you helping me with this."

Bastan looked over with a smile on his face. "Is that right?"

Alec shifted his feet and resisted the urge to look away from Bastan. He knew better than to show weakness to this man. Any sign of weakness would be dangerous, especially with Bastan.

"I am new to my position. I can't be disappearing for long stretches of time and maintain that same connection. I'm going to need help from people outside of the university."

"And you think to employ me in such a fashion?" Now, there was obvious amusement in his voice, and his eyes practically sparkled with it.

"I don't intend to employ you at all," Alec said. There was a promise in the idea that he would employ Bastan, and he had no interest in subjecting himself to something like that. Already by asking this of Bastan, he placed himself in the other man's debt. Knowing Bastan, there would be a price to pay. "I'm only asking you to help."

"What of Samara?"

"Sam can help, but…"

"She intends to go after Tray."

"Eventually. I think she will hold off for now, but there will come a time when she will go after him, so I need to be ready and able to react when she does."

Bastan studied him for a long moment before nodding. "For Kevin, I will look into this. I don't make any promises about what I will discover, and I may require more from you depending on what I find."

"I'm aware of that."

"Just as long as we're on the same page," Bastan said.

Alec looked around. There was sound near the back of the room, and he motioned to Bastan. It was time for them to go. When they reached the door, Alec glanced back. He thought he saw Master Carl but couldn't be certain. If it was Master Carl, there *would* be other questions, and he had no interest in trying to answer them.

The other man didn't care for Alec, and though he had allowed him to be promoted to full physicker, it didn't change the fact that they weren't on the best of terms.

When he escorted Bastan back outside and returned to the ward to check on his father again, he saw that he had been right. It was Master Carl.

"Physicker Stross," he said, clasping his hands behind his back and thrusting out his enormous belly. His hair had been slicked back, and his cheeks were ruddy even in the faint light of the lanterns. "It's awfully late for you to be visiting the ward."

Alec looked around. "It is, but with my father here, I thought I would check on him."

"Do you believe that the junior physickers are incapable of alerting you if there's a problem with him?"

"It's not that they are incapable," Alec said. "It's more a matter of me wanting to know the moment something changes."

Master Carl watched him briefly before his gaze flickered to the door. He had seen Alec, which meant that he might have seen Bastan, which meant that there would be questions.

"You must be careful not to extend yourself too much. The temptation for many full physickers is to overextend themselves, and you wouldn't be the first physicker to find yourself struggling with your role."

"Thank you, Master Carl. I will take your advice to heart."

"I doubt that."

Master Carl glanced around the room, his gaze lingering on Aelus and then drifting to the young woman, before he turned his attention back to Alec. He pressed his lips together in a tight frown, and Alec thought that he might say something more, but he didn't. Rather he strode off, keeping his hands clasped behind him. When he was gone, Alec breathed out. There wasn't anything for him to do, and antagonizing Master Carl wouldn't help. Besides, there was something that Bastan had said that left him troubled.

Could there be a connection between these illnesses? And if there was, what did it mean for his father? What did it mean for Kara? And would others come to the university with the similar symptoms?

FIRST ASSIGNMENT

The canal staff jutted out of the water, and Sam perched on top of it, trying to remain motionless. It was difficult to hold the posture, but if she didn't, she would do more than simply fall into the water, she would fail at this task. She was determined not to fail.

Water swirled around her. Every so often, she could swear she felt pressure on the canal staff and tried to tell herself that it was only imagined. There was no way the eels were harassing her, chomping at her staff.

She had lost track of how long she had been here, though it had been morning when she started, and it had to be noon at this point. The sun was well up in the sky, and her stomach rumbling told her that it had been long enough. When would Elaine come for her?

She was tired of all the stupid training. Did she think that forcing Sam through training like this would prevent her from going after Tray? Once she had made her preparations, she fully intended to go after him.

It wasn't as if she didn't know where he was heading. Theln territory. Sam needed to learn more about it before making her way and possibly risking herself.

"How are you feeling?"

She opened her eyes and saw Elaine standing on the shore. From here, situated this far into the swamp, she was small. "I feel fine. But I'm hungry. It's time to eat."

"You need to learn to suppress those urges."

"Suppress the urge to eat? After sitting here on this Kyza-forsaken staff, I don't know that I can suppress anything."

"Then you will never be able to cross the swamp."

Sam jumped, flipping toward the shore, balancing on her staff as she went. The balancing gave her increased control over the flipping, so that each movement was easier. It was much easier than when she first learned to use the staff in this way.

"I don't understand why I have to cross the swamp using the staff," she said as she landed on shore. "The stupid barges do well enough."

"Those stupid barges aren't always available. And often, you can't find a captain willing to pole you all the way across the swamp. You need to find your own way, and it's likely that once you cross, you're going to need help returning."

Sam suppressed her irritation. It was just Elaine trying to prevent her from chasing after Tray. Why would she refuse to let her go after him? The princess would want her to chase Tray, especially now that Sam knew that he was the princess's son.

"I can't cross the swamp on my staff. Not if my Scribe is coming with me."

"Your Scribe cannot go with you," Elaine said.

"Why not? If I go without him—"

"Trust me that your Scribe can't go. If the Thelns manage to capture him, they will have more power than they already do."

"What does that mean?"

"It means that the Thelns would love to grab a Scribe, especially one who is connected to one of their own."

"Tray is not one of their own."

"He's close enough for them. Most of them would view him as one of their own, which is why you need to view him the same way."

Sam couldn't view Tray as a Theln. That wasn't who he was to her.

But should it be?

"Your Scribe needs to stay at the university for his protection as much as anything," Elaine went on. "Why else do you think Marin's Scribe remained at the university?"

Sam hadn't given that much thought. Alec believed he had stayed behind mostly to uncover secrets that might be found, but she wasn't sure. Maybe there was a different reason. Maybe it was as Elaine said, that the Scribes put themselves in danger when they left the university.

"You're just saying that so I don't bring Alec with me when I go after Tray."

"I am. Because I know what could happen if you take him along. If you go, and if they capture him, he will be used against you. He will be used against us."

"Alec wouldn't do that."

"Others have said the same. And others have failed to resist the temptation."

"Temptation?"

"There is a certain appeal the Thelns have that allows them to use a Scribe against you."

Sam couldn't imagine Alec working against her. They were more than Scribe and Kaver. They were friends, and if the shared connection meant anything, it was possible they would be more than friends. With all of the training they had been going through, Sam hadn't had time to think about it, and she suspected Alec hadn't, either, especially as his training was equally rigorous, if only in a different way.

Then again, maybe there would never be a good time.

"Then I have to go after Tray myself," Sam said.

"You're not ready."

"What happens to my brother then?"

Elaine watched her for a long moment before speaking. "I'm not sure what will happen with Tray. All I know is that if he's gone to the Thelns, he won't be the same person you have known. It's possible that he's not even Tray anymore."

"He's still Tray."

"But is he still your brother?"

Sam sighed and looked out over the swamp. She was tired of trying to understand everything that had happened with her brother, and tired of wondering whether he was the same person she had known growing up. To her, he would always be her brother, regardless of what connection actually existed between them. How could he not be?

"He's still my brother," Sam said softly.

"I hope so. For all of our sakes, I hope that he is."

"Did you come here just to harass me about Tray?"

"No. I came because I need your help. I think you might be the best person to assist me with my next task."

"And what is that?"

"Finding Marin. There was a sighting."

"A sighting?" Sam laughed softly. "I thought you said she left the city."

"As far as we knew, she had. Now, we're getting word that maybe she hasn't, and maybe she's here. If that's the case, we need to discover why."

"There's got to be something she wants."

"Or there's a reason she can't go," Elaine said.

"What reason would that be?"

"There are probably many reasons, but most likely it's because she realized the danger her Scribe would be in if he went with her."

"She would've known that already, wouldn't she?"

"She would have, but knowing Marin, I imagine she thought she would be able to keep them safe from capture. If she chose to remain in the city, it was probably because she was threatened somehow."

"Are you saying the Thelns have remained in the city?"

"No. I doubt they would have stayed."

Sam looked around the swamp. The air had a foulness to it, and it was humid, unpleasantly so. Sweat soaked through her clothing, leaving her saturated. "Where are we going?"

"Out of the city."

Sam turned her attention northward, and beyond the borders of the swamp.

"Not that way," Elaine said.

"You're only doing this to keep me from going after Tray."

"No. You're a Kaver, and I am asking you as a Kaver to assist in this task. Are you telling me that you have no interest in helping?"

"You know that I am willing to help."

"Then why are you arguing with me?"

"Will Alec be allowed to come?"

"This is not a task for your Scribe."

"I thought you were only concerned about the Thelns."

"It's not that I fear for his safety, not where we're heading, it's just that there are places he may not be able to reach."

"Great," Sam said.

"And what does that mean?"

"It means that you intend for me to use the stinking staff to hop across some stupid distance, don't you?"

"You're a Kaver, Samara. What else would I ask of you?"

OUT INTO THE STEAM

The southern edge of the city loomed before them. Sam had rarely been to this side of the city. Most of the southern edge was a shallow rock shelf that let out into the sea, making it difficult without having a barge or some other transport. To the west were the steam fields, a wide expanse of emptiness that ran along the entire western side of the city. It wasn't quite like the swamp, but the land was nearly impassable, nothing more than jagged rock that stretched farther and farther before eventually leading to the mountainous volcanic peak in the far distance.

The landscape was inhospitable, covered by fields of steam, and anyone who had tried to navigate through them usually failed. Caster was close to the steam fields, and she had seen people attempt to cross often enough. Whether it was from the heat or the occasional steam bed, crossing beyond the western border of the city was a death sentence.

"You want us to go there?"

Elaine nodded. "That is where Marin went."

"Then she can go. It's not as if she can get very far, especially not over that," Sam said, motioning to a pocket of steam that suddenly erupted with a loud hiss. She shivered, despite the heat from the steam drifting toward them.

"You would be mistaken. Marin is far more resourceful than you give her credit for."

"I give Marin plenty of credit. I'm just saying that I have no interest in risking myself going after her. Besides, I still think my time would be better spent going after Tray."

"And how do you think to do that?" Elaine said.

"Well, you've taught me to stabilize myself on my staff, so I anticipated just crossing the swamp that way."

"How far have you tried going out into the swamp?" Elaine asked, glancing over.

Kyza. Elaine knew. Sam should know better than to try to be deceptive with her. Elaine had proven that she was far cleverer than Sam gave her credit for, and she had proven that she was more capable than Sam, especially when it came to using her Kaver abilities.

Then again, Elaine had been captured by Ralun. That was something that Sam had over her. At least when Sam had been captured, she'd escaped. But truth be told, it was only thanks to Alec's augmentation. So maybe she couldn't claim that.

"I might have tried seeing how far I could go."

"And how far were you able to make it?"

"Maybe a half a day," she said. She would've gone farther, but her arms had begun trembling, and without any augmentations, she feared she would end up dropping into the swamp.

"A half a day is only part of the distance. To cross the swamp, you will need to be able to maintain your balance for at least an entire day, likely more, especially if you don't know where to take your breaks."

"How many islands are there within the swamp?"

"Not enough. There are maps, as you can imagine." Sam *hadn't* imagined and hadn't thought to look for such maps, but now that she knew of them, she would figure out a way to find them. "But even with the maps, it's difficult to navigate through the swamp safely. Most who attempt to do so aren't successful."

"But you said you have done it."

"I've done it many times."

"Without augmentations."

"As I've told you, if you become too reliant on augmentations, you will only struggle when you don't have them."

Sam stared at Elaine for a long moment. "How? I mean, *how*?" With as much as she'd trained, Sam still wasn't able to go very far. She could see herself improving, getting stronger and going farther, but getting all the way across? That began to border on an incredibly high degree of difficulty.

"I've told you that you need to practice," Elaine said.

She started off, taking a meandering pace across the rough ground. Sam followed, and as she did, she was all too aware of the heat radiating beneath her, pressing through her boots and making her uncomfortable. Every so often, Elaine would lean on her staff and elevate her feet.

Sam began doing the same thing and decided that this crossing would be far more difficult than anything she had tried before.

"Marin couldn't have come this way."

Elaine glanced over at her. She hung in the air on her staff, her body propped up slightly, and she looked casual —almost comfortable—as she was suspended there.

"And why not?"

"Because her Scribe wouldn't have been able to come this way."

"Are you certain? I suspect that her Scribe had a supply of easar paper, and between that and Marin's natural cleverness, they figured out a way to make their way across here."

Elaine took off, continuing across the rocky terrain. She moved with a fluidity that Sam wasn't sure she'd be able to mimic, at least not yet. How much training would it take for her to rival what Elaine was capable of doing?

Maybe that was the point.

Elaine brought her with her with an intent. She must have wanted Sam to know just how hard it would be for Sam to keep up with her, though Sam wasn't sure she needed that reminder. She had seen Elaine in action before and had sparred with her enough times to know that while Sam had skill—and she was continuing to get better—Elaine was a master.

"How well do you know Bastan?" Sam asked as she

caught up to Elaine. She elected to walk as much as she hopped on the staff, preferring to conserve her arm strength for when she might need it more. The rocks were hot but didn't melt her shoes, at least not yet. There might come a time when she had no choice but to remain balanced on her staff, but if that happened, she would worry almost as much about the integrity of her staff as she would about her boots.

"Why are you asking me about Bastan?"

"Only because you seem to have a familiarity with him."

"Why would you say that?"

"I've seen the two of you together. There is something of a comfort level." Sam didn't know how to explain it any better than that. When they had faced the Thelns—when Bastan had fought Ralun—there had been something of a familiarity between Elaine and Bastan.

"I don't know that I can claim to know Bastan nearly as well as you," Elaine said. She perched atop her staff, her legs pinching the top of it as she peered out over the landscape. "I know of him, probably more than I know him."

"What do you mean by that?"

"Bastan hasn't necessarily kept his presence a secret. He has been well-known throughout the city for his role as someone who searches to acquire power, though he does it in a different way than many."

Sam frowned. That wasn't quite what she was thinking. There was something more to it than what Elaine was admitting, though Sam wasn't sure that it mattered. "Do you know if he has any rivals?"

Elaine looked down at her from her perch, and a wry

smile came to her face. "You lived in the Caster section for how long and you question whether Bastan has rivals?" She turned her attention back in front of her. "Given the nature of his business, it's a guarantee that he would have rivals."

"It's not just business rivals," Sam said. She jumped up on her staff and mimicked Elaine's posture, perching next to her. As she looked in the direction of Elaine's gaze and took in the rocky landscape that stretched out toward the lowest level of the mountain. She was trying to see what Elaine might be looking at. She saw nothing but rough, volcanic rock, and pockets of steam rising in places. Sam swiveled, looking behind her, and saw other pockets of steam rising behind them. She understood then what Elaine had been doing. She perched here so that she could choose their course. There would be no maps of this area. It was all steam and fire and danger. "Bastan was attacked, and I intervened."

"You shouldn't intervene. Anything you do in the city only raises suspicion."

"I'm not going to let Bastan get brutalized by nearly a half-dozen men."

"Bastan can manage on his own. And I'm sure he was not in danger of brutality. From what I know of Bastan, I would suspect he had plenty of men keeping an eye on him."

Sam frowned, following the direction of Elaine's gaze as she stared out over the pockets of steam bursting from the ground. At any given time, another pocket erupted. How were they going to cross this? Sam had thought crossing the swamp was impossible, but crossing something like this seemed even worse. At least with the swamp, she only had to worry about falling in the water and eels devouring her. Here, she had to worry more about the steam and what it might do to her. One misstep, and she could have half her body burned.

"That's just it. Bastan didn't have anyone watching him. A couple of his men joined him later, and I think they cleaned up the mess, but they weren't there when he was attacked."

Elaine glanced over and smiled. "Have you thought about why that might be?"

"I doubt that Bastan would allow himself to be attacked intentionally."

"I don't know about that. Bastan is clever, so it's possible that he would have used himself as bait to draw out potential attackers."

Sam shook her head. "He said there was a rival within the city."

"There are many outer sections that don't have the same lawfulness that many of the inner sections have."

"Yes. I'm well aware of what we lowborns have in the city."

Elaine glanced over. "I said nothing about lowborns. You have a tendency to make up many things about your position. Haven't you seen that you are more than where you call home?"

"Maybe," Sam said. She knew that she sounded petulant, but she didn't care. She had been isolated at the palace, and there was something about her status that she still wasn't comfortable with. She might not truly be lowborn, but she certainly wasn't a highborn.

"The outer sections are more difficult to patrol. The Anders only have so many resources, and they are supplemented by the merchants in the inner sections." Elaine glanced back down. "Yes, wealth does buy protection, but it's not protection that's offered by the crown. It's protection offered by those who have the ability to afford it, which is not that much different from what Bastan does, I would say. Bastan has his own means of protection, and he offers his services to those in his employ, which I seem to recall included you."

"Are you trying to tell me that you agree with it?"

Elaine shrugged. "There is only so much that can be done."

"That doesn't mean it's right."

"No, but you're not asking the right question."

"And what's the right question?"

"You have asked why the Anders don't have resources to protect some of the sections within the city."

Elaine leapt off of her staff and ran forward, flipping into the air as she went before coming back down.

Sam had been following long enough to know that she needed to follow quickly and hurried after Elaine. She caught up to her and kept pace, staying right behind her. If she didn't, she knew that another pocket of steam might burst, risking injury.

"Why don't the Anders have enough resources to protect everyone in the city?"

"What do you think the Kavers do?" Elaine asked.

"Apparently, we fight the Thelns," Sam said.

"Do you think that's all we do?"

"No. I've seen that you make a point of harassing me almost as much as you do anything else."

Elaine shook her head and vaulted into the air before coming back down on the other side of a large crater. Sam followed, uncertain whether she was making a mistake in doing so. As she landed, steam burst from the crater, and she staggered forward, not wanting to get caught by it.

Elaine grabbed her and helped her back up. "What you see as harassing, I see differently. I'm working to train you, though I will admit that you are one of the more difficult people I have attempted to work with."

"Thanks. I think that I'll take that as a compliment. Besides, Bastan would tell you that I'm nothing if not wonderfully difficult."

"Don't worry, I have asked him."

Sam frowned, but Elaine jumped off, vaulting into the air once more. When she landed, a massive pocket of steam started simmering. Sam couldn't go over it, not without getting caught, and debated going around, but even that posed challenges. There were several other pockets of steam all around her. She climbed on top of her staff, perching as she had seen Elaine doing, and quickly surveyed the area in front of her. She found a narrow pathway that she thought she could follow and hurriedly flipped forward, taking the path so that she could join Elaine before heat and fire engulfed her again.

"What have you asked Bastan?"

"I have asked him whether or not you were trustworthy. I have asked whether or not you were someone who could be worked with."

"I can only imagine the kinds of things Bastan would say to those questions."

"Bastan was quite complimentary of your skills as a thief." Elaine glanced over, and there was a hint of disdain on her face as she said it. "Had he not been, I don't know that we would have been quite as willing to work with you."

Sam frowned. She hadn't realized that Bastan was the one responsible for ensuring that she had a chance to train as a Kaver. "I suppose I should thank him, then."

"Well, you shouldn't dismiss him quite so freely," Elaine said.

"I don't think that I'm dismissing him freely at all. I'm just fully aware that Bastan is only concerned about Bastan." Even as she said it, Sam knew that wasn't entirely true. Bastan had already proven that he had a soft spot for her. She didn't need to hear it from those who worked with him, men like Kevin or another of Bastan's men like James.

"I'll be sure to share with him your assessment of his priorities."

Sam shook her head. "It's not my assessment of his priorities, it's me being realistic about the kinds of people that I have spent my days with. I know them. You might know *of* them, but I know them."

Elaine stared at her for a long moment before nodding once to herself and jumping forward again. She made a series of quick leaps and turned back, motioning Sam to follow. When she reached Elaine, she paused. They had only been at it for a short while, and already, she was tired.

Where would they even pause to rest for the night? There wasn't anywhere safe that Sam could see, and if they intended to pursue Marin across this steam field, Sam couldn't imagine how long they would have to go before finding her.

"Are you sure that Marin is out here?"

"What do you see?"

Sam frowned, looking around her. It was difficult to make out anything, especially as the steam continued to rise all around them, bursting free in certain places. "I don't see anything," she said.

"Because you're not looking, not really."

"I thought I was."

Elaine frowned, looking over. "You haven't had your Kaver abilities for very long, and yet already, you've become so dependent upon what you call augmentations."

"I know, I know. You want me to master my abilities so that I don't require augmentations to face my adversary."

"No. I want you to realize that there are other abilities that you have been born to."

"Such as what? I am unaware of any other abilities."

"How many others do you think can balance on the staff like you are?"

Sam glanced down at herself. She had been sitting on top of the staff, trying to peer out over the steam field much the way that Elaine now did. Sitting in this way, with her legs bowed out, she swayed with the soft breeze, keeping a balance as she did. Heat swirled all around her, though it wasn't intolerable. It wasn't a pleasant heat, either, but elevated above it, Sam was able to tolerate it much better than she would have were she on the ground.

"I learned to balance from you and Raylene."

"Did you? You have certainly improved since you first came to me, but you had a certain level of ability even before you came. That is something you're born to, not something you can be taught. It can be honed, much like anything can be honed, but imagine if your Scribe were to attempt to balance on your staff the same way. Would he have a similar ability?"

"Alec has trained for something else his entire life."

"No. Alec was born to something else."

"So, you're saying that I can only do this because I was born with the ability? I've seen other people who have good body control. Kyza knows that working with Bastan has brought me into contact with plenty of others who have similar abilities."

"Working with Bastan has brought you into contact with his type of people, but while they may be able to manage themselves in a fight, they do not share the same ability as you."

"Why does it even matter? What's the point of you telling me this?"

"The point," Elaine said, "is that there are things you need to learn about your natural Kaver ability that you cannot learn when you're depending on augmentations. When you faced Marin, do you think she was augmented?"

"Yes."

"And yet, how long did her augmentations last?"

Sam tried to think back to when she had last faced

Marin. It had been a while. Long enough that she wasn't sure that she remembered it quite clearly. "I don't know, they seemed to last the entire time we fought."

"And how about your augmentations?"

"Alec wasn't able to provide too many," Sam said.

"You wouldn't have been able to defeat Marin without some supplementation. You weren't trained well enough at that point."

"And now I am?"

"I doubt that you would be able to defeat Marin without augmentations yet. She is gifted. She has always known how to use the full potential of her Kaver abilities."

"And what are those abilities?"

"You think that you depend upon your Scribe for everything, but that simply is not the case. Your Scribe has been helpful, but you do not required his help to do many of the things you think provides through augmentation."

"So, what can I do without a Scribe to help?"

"The more you practice, the more you'll begin understand your abilities and realize that there are many things you can do without augmentations." Elaine scanned the horizon and fixed on a spot in the distance. "Think of how you believed that you needed augmentations simply to cross the swamp. Do you still believe that?"

"Maybe. It certainly would make it easier."

"Easier doesn't mean that it's necessary. You have now sat on your staff for long moments without so much as needing to move. That has not required any augmentation. I've seen the way that you are able to slip across the steam field, and I've seen you in the swamp. You do not need augmentations for that."

Sam glanced over at her. How much had Elaine been watching her? If she'd seen her in the swamp, then maybe she had followed her, which made Sam uncomfortable. She didn't like the idea of Elaine following her without knowing that she did.

"What other things can I do, then?"

"There are many things, and you will discover those in time. For now, you should continue to observe those who have mastered their abilities."

"Even if that means learning from Marin?"

"Why do you think we're chasing her?"

"I thought we were chasing her so that we could bring her back to the city to face punishment for what she did."

"There would be value in that, but even more important would be gathering Marin so that you can have someone else to guide your instruction."

"Why not you?"

"There are things that even I haven't mastered," Elaine said.

"Then where is she? How are we going to find her?"

Elaine nodded into the distance, and Sam followed the direction of her gaze, staring out. The steam made visibility difficult, but as she stared through it, watching in between the gusts of wind that sent the steam billowing northward, Sam saw the faint sign of movement in the distance. It was nearly to the mountain, far enough away that, if it was Marin, she wasn't sure they would be able to catch her. And if she wasn't alone, she likely had her Scribe with her. According to Elaine, she didn't need augmentation, but having her Scribe with her might mean that she was.

"Are you sure we should go after her without any enhancements?"

Elaine nodded. "I am certain that we should."

With that, Elaine flipped forward, and raced across the rocky ground. Sam had no choice but to follow.

13

FINDING A KAVER

They reached the base of the mountain late in the day. Sweat streamed down Sam's brow, and she no longer even bothered to wipe it away. She was tired, but not nearly as tired as she thought she would be. Elaine had traveled with a mixture of jumps and sprints across the ground. The combination had carried them quickly forward, and they reached the lower foothills of the mountain as the sun disappeared behind clouds high overhead.

"I don't see her anymore," Sam said.

"No, but we should overtake her soon."

"If we overtake her and we're exhausted, I'm not sure that it will be much of a fight."

"There are two of us and one of her."

"And yet she will be augmented," Sam said.

"You still put far more stock in that than you need to."

Sam wasn't sure that she did. She had seen the way Marin was able to handle her even when Sam had augmentations. Without them… she wasn't sure she would be able to defeat Marin even with Elaine's assistance.

They continued up the slope of the mountain, and as dusk began to fall, Sam noted shadows in the distance.

She said nothing, only nodding. Pockets of steam were rarer now, and as they climbed, she had only to worry about fatigue, not the danger of crossing the steam field. Then again, fatigue was enough of an enemy that she knew better than to dismiss it too easily. She was tired, exhausted from everything they had done, and now, she somehow had to face Marin and figure out a way to capture her—and her Scribe.

Even when they did, how were they going to get the two of them back out?

Sam tried not to think of that. It did no good other than to make her more anxious.

Elaine scurried forward, and as they neared the movement of shadows, she swung her staff, connecting with a loud crack.

Sam swore under her breath.

She joined Elaine in the fight, swinging her staff at the same time. "I guess we're not going to wait, are we?" Sam said.

Elaine grunted and jumped over a sweep of Marin's staff. "You could help," Elaine said.

Sam looked around. Where was Marin's Scribe?

Elaine might dismiss the benefit of augmentations, but Sam knew better than to dismiss it out of hand. There were far too many benefits to completely dismiss the possiblity. But where was he?

She glanced back to Elaine and Marin and saw that Elaine seemed to be managing well enough, so Sam raced forward, searching for Marin's Scribe.

Master Jessup. Bushy Brow. She remembered his voice and the scornful way that he had taunted her when he'd caught her, though she was pleased to have returned the favor.

She jumped with her staff, launching into the air. For a moment, she considered adding an augmentation. If she took only the briefest pause, she would be able to scratch a few things onto the easar paper she had in her pocket, which might help as she tried to find this man.

He wasn't the one she needed help with, though. He wouldn't be much of a threat, if any. He might have captured her, but he hadn't been the one to trap her. That had been Ralun.

She jumped on top of her staff, perching for a moment. There was value in holding this pose, and she wondered if maybe that was the entire reason Elaine had demonstrated it for her. She saw no sign of the Scribe.

He had to be here, somewhere.

"Samara!"

She glanced down and saw that Elaine was on the ground, trying to fend off Marin.

She jumped forward, flipping around as she did, and swung her staff toward Marin. The other woman spun around, catching Sam, deflecting her attack.

"Isn't this sweet," Marin said. "Mother and daughter, fighting together."

Marin twisted, moving faster than Sam could keep up

with. There was no question that she was augmented, though she would have limits to it, wouldn't she?

Then again, if her Scribe was still out there somewhere, the only limits would be the amount of blood they had. Maybe that was Elaine's plan. If she could delay things long enough, they would run out of their blood, and there would be no way for them to replenish it, at least not while Marin was fighting them.

Then again, if Marin defeated them because of the augmentations, it wouldn't matter. She needed to delay Marin.

"You don't seem all that concerned with seeing me here," Sam said.

"And why should I be? You pose no threat."

"No threat? I defeated you the last time we were together," Sam said.

"You didn't defeat me, your augmentations did. And without your Scribe, how do you intend to replicate that?"

Sam spun around, swinging her staff down toward Marin. The other woman blocked, her movement fast and the follow-up brutal. Sam staggered forward, barely able to keep on her feet.

Marin grinned. "See? You might have some training now, but you're still not fast enough."

"Face me without your augmentations."

Marin cocked her head, grinning widely. "What makes you think that I'm not?"

"Because you're moving too quickly."

"Only because you fail to understand the full potential of your abilities, Samara," Marin said.

Marin jumped, and while in the air, she spun around,

her staff twisting rapidly. She brought it down, and Sam rolled, missing one end, but she didn't miss the other. Marin's staff slammed into her stomach.

When had she separated the two ends?

Pain roared through her, but she tried to ignore it, focusing only on finding a way to stop Marin.

She needed to do more than simply stop her. If they managed to capture Marin before the blood ink ran out, it wouldn't matter. The Scribe would be able to counter anything they did, and he would be able to use whatever remaining ink he had to offer another augmentation to Marin.

Buy time.

That was all she had to do. Somehow, she had to find a way to bide her time.

And where was Elaine?

Sam pushed off to the side and tried to get to her feet, but she couldn't. Pain in her stomach made it difficult. Even if she survived, would she be able to make it back to the city?

Marin kicked at her, and Sam brought her arms up, blocking, and threw her back. She shoved with the force of her frustration and her anger, and Marin went flying.

Sam frowned to herself. How was that possible?

She didn't have an augmentation; all she had was her irritation.

She heard a grunt and staggered to her feet, readying for Marin's attack. The sound that she heard likely meant that Marin had knocked Elaine down, in which case, all that stood between Marin and escape—or her death —was Sam.

What had Elaine been thinking? There was no way the two of them would be able to defeat Marin without any augmentations.

A shape approached, and Sam brought her staff up.

It was Bushy Brow.

"You," she said.

"You shouldn't have come after us."

"You shouldn't have tried to attack me. Then, maybe I wouldn't have come after you."

He took another step, and she noticed he had a sword in hand.

Sam smiled to herself. What were the odds that he knew how to handle a sword? She figured they weren't very good. Most of the university master physickers were only able to handle a pen, and not much more than that. Alec couldn't do anything with a sword, so she doubted that this stupid man could.

She took a deep breath, steeling herself for a surge of pain, and flipped toward him, spinning her staff around in midair and cracking him in the back of the head. He staggered forward, dropping his sword when he did. Sam jabbed him on the back of the head once more for good measure, wanting to keep him immobile. It wouldn't do for him to come around and help Marin again.

"Good, you found her Scribe."

Sam jerked her head around, as Elaine appeared from behind a tower of rocks. She carried Marin as well as Marin's staff.

"You survived?"

"You didn't think that I would?"

"I didn't know. With what she did, I wasn't sure you would have been able to."

"I think your distraction was enough."

"Yeah, I'm... I'm sorry. I should have listened. I was trying to find her Scribe."

"And I told you that didn't matter."

"But he's here. She was augmented."

"She wasn't."

"The way she moved—"

"The way she moved is the way any Kaver can move, especially with the right training. In time, you can have that training, but if you go rushing off without waiting for it, and if you go off thinking that you know enough, you will suffer. Do you think Marin needed her augmentations to challenge the Thelns? Do you think she needed her Scribe in order to face the rest of us?"

"I... I guess I did."

"She didn't need augmentation. Even if they had easar paper, Samara."

"Her Scribe would have had access to easar paper."

"He wouldn't. He wasn't known as a Scribe. That's how he was able to remain hidden within the university."

Sam frowned, but realized Elaine was right. Marin hadn't revealed the presence of her Scribe, which meant that without others knowing, it was just as likely that he wouldn't have had access to easar paper. Without it, she couldn't have had any augmentations.

"Then she did all of this without them?"

"That's what I've been trying to tell you."

Sam stared at Marin. She breathed regularly, and a massive knot had formed on the side of her head. Elaine crouched down next to her and tore strips from Marin's cloak, and began wrapping her wrists with the fabric. When she was done, she moved on to her legs.

"That should hold her for the most part," Elaine said.

"If she doesn't need augmentations, then how do you expect that to hold her?"

"I didn't say that she didn't need augmentations at all. All I said was that she didn't have them when she faced you. In order for her to tear free from this, she will need more than what she can generate on her own."

"Will I?" Marin rolled her head to the side, looking up at Elaine. "That was a nice hit, Lainey."

Elaine sighed. "Marin, why did you make me do this?"

"Has it always been about you, Lainey?"

"You know that it's not."

"And yet you concealed from me the connection you had to Lyasanna. Me. I was your commander."

"And she was the crown."

"She is not the crown," Marin said, a sneer twisting her face. "She might have you convinced that she represents the crown, but she does not."

"And now look at you, little Samara, you stand here, thinking that Lainey has taught you everything that you need, but she hasn't. And she can't. As much as Lainey wants to, there are only so many things she can teach. Isn't that right, Lainey?"

Elaine sighed again and jerked Marin forward until she was seated in front of them. "I captured you, didn't I?"

"You captured me, but I'm curious whether you could do it alone or whether you always need someone else with you. First, it was Haffar, and now, you have Samara."

"Don't talk about him."

Marin glanced from Elaine to Sam. "No? And why shouldn't I speak of him. Have you chosen not to share with Samara the details of her father?"

"No more than you've chosen to conceal from her."

"Ah, but I did that to *you*, not to her."

Sam stepped forward. "You did that to *me*, not to my mother. You took *my* memories, you took who *I* am, not anything from my mother."

Marin looked over at her. There was a hint of the woman that Sam had known, but it was hidden behind a mask. "I'm sorry that you were caught in the middle, Samara, but everything that happened to you is your mother's fault and not mine."

Elaine shook her head. "Why do you continue to spread those lies?"

"Because they are not lies," Marin said. "No more than the lies that you have tried to spread about Tray."

"I know the truth," Sam said.

"Oh, I'm sure that you do, now. I'm sure that because Ralun bothered to come to the city again, they were forced to tell you. Someone had to know."

"Why? Why did you do this to us?"

"Why? After everything that you've been through with me, I can't believe you can ask that question."

"Everything I've been through? Marin, you are the reason I have no memory of my childhood!" Sam jabbed her in the chest, pushing far harder than she intended. Marin's jaw clenched, but she didn't wince or make any other expression. "You forced a connection between Tray and me, making both of us believe that we were brother and sister. Why?"

"Someone had to look out for him," Marin said softly.

"I thought you were supposed to look out for him!"

"And who told you that?"

"Lyasanna told me that. She said that you were assigned to bring him from the Theln lands. She said that—"

Marin started laughing, and Sam shook her head, not even certain what to do or say. How was she supposed to react to someone like Marin, someone who couldn't be reasoned with?

"Lyasanna told you that I was supposed to rescue Tray?"

Sam nodded. "She told me that Elaine and others rescued her from the Theln lands. She told me that several were sacrificed in order to do so."

"And did she tell you the full details of my assignment?"

"Marin—" Elaine cautioned.

"Lainey. I think it's time that your daughter understands the truth of the Anders. She needs to understand just what kind of people she's serving. She needs to realize that her master—your Scribe—ordered her newborn son to be murdered."

14

ANSWERS AND QUESTIONS

S am stood frozen. She couldn't even take a breath. Her body trembled, and she resisted the urge to look over at Elaine, not trusting herself. She knew better than to believe Marin, but there was a ring of truth in what she said. Regardless of everything that she'd been through, Marin had never wanted to harm Tray. She had used Sam as a way to protect him, forming a connection—a bond— between them.

It all made a sick sort of twisted sense.

"Is it true?"

Marin looked up at her, and Sam finally turned her attention to Elaine.

"Is it true?"

"Marin would have you believe that it's true, but why would Lyasanna have ordered her son to be murdered?"

Marin laughed darkly. "You didn't know. Oh, blessed Kyza, you didn't know." Marin shifted back and propped herself up on her arms. "All this time, I thought she had shared with you, her most trusted advisor, her Kaver, and now I can see it on your face. You had no idea."

"Lyasanna wouldn't have given such an order."

"And why not? She wanted to protect the family. She was the first Anders Scribe in generations. Her presence was a disruption, and of course the Thelns wanted to form a connection with her. She couldn't have the Anders know that she had succumbed to the temptation of the Thelns. No one could know. So, she sent me, the only person she thought she could trust to complete a task that she thought was necessary. She sent me in, telling me that the child needed to be lost. None could know that he existed, or he would be used against the Anders."

Sam dropped to the ground next to Marin. "Is that true?"

Elaine stared at Marin, and she barely breathed. "She wouldn't have sacrificed her child."

"Then you don't know her nearly as well as I did."

"Why? And why take Samara?"

"I believed you complicit in her instructions. Since you were willing to take a child, I decided that I would take a child."

"How did you do it?" Sam asked. She was barely able to speak, and her voice came out in a ragged whisper. "How is it that you took my memories from me? How is it that I didn't know my mother? That I can't remember anything from my childhood?"

"I didn't take all of your memories. I took away your recollection of your mother. And I ensured that you and Tray knew of the other, and that you would grow up believing that you were brother and sister. You would protect him, and he would protect you. Your presence ensured that the other was safe."

Sam had a sick feeling in her stomach and looked around the bleak mountain. Darkness had set in full, leaving only the faint light from the moon.

"She wouldn't have done this," Elaine said.

"You put far too much faith in your Scribe."

"I put faith in my friend," Elaine said.

"Then you have the wrong friends." Marin stared at her, and there was something angry on her face. "I thought we were friends, and yet…"

"I believed that you died. When you were said to have gone after him, you were dead. That was what we heard."

"That was what you needed to hear. If I hadn't died, if I hadn't been willing to sacrifice my connection to her, Tray would have died."

"Why not tell me before now?" Sam asked. She cleared her throat, finally finding a way to speak. " her voice. "WhyEspecially once you knew that I had begun to work with Elaine. You knew what they would do."

"You can't believe her, Samara," Elaine said.

Sam glanced over. "I don't know who to believe. I don't know what to believe. First, Tray was my brother. Then he wasn't. Then I believed that Tray was Marin's son. Now I find out he's Lyasanna's son. And now? Now I learn that Lyasanna wanted him dead simply because of what he was."

"We have to speak with her," Elaine said softly.

"Do you believe that she'll tell the truth?" Marin asked. "After all this time, why would she share? All that could happen would be that she would lose you, and she would lose you," she said, pointing to Sam. "You are able to help her hold her position. She won't sacrifice that willingly."

Sam stared at her hands. She didn't know what to say or even how to feel.

"He's… He's still my brother."

"You did this," Elaine said. "You forced that connection. You're the reason that Samara feels she needs to go after Tray and rescue him from Ralun. This is on you."

"No. Sam has a connection to Tray because of me, that much is true, but I will take no blame for the rest of it. That connection keeps him alive, at least it does until Lyasanna realizes that you know." She looked over at Sam, and her gaze softened. "He *is* your brother. Your family is who you decide it will be. You don't have to be blood relatives to share that bond. It's no different from the connection you have with your Scribe. You aren't related, yet there is a connection, a bond. One that I know you feel. I've seen the two of you together."

Sam didn't trust herself to speak. And it seemed Elaine didn't trust Marin to speak. She smacked her with her staff, knocking her unconscious once more.

"You can't trust her."

"How can I trust anything?" Sam asked.

"I haven't deceived you."

"But you have. You knew that Tray was Lyasanna's son, and you didn't tell me. How is that any different from Marin's deception? How is Lyasanna's deception any different? You're using us, and we deserve better."

"I haven't used you. I've tried to—"

"You've tried nothing." Sam turned away and rested her staff on her legs, staring out into the darkness for a long time. Eventually, Marin came back around with a soft moan, and Elaine spoke to her, though Sam made a point of not listening. Why should she when she had no idea who to trust? After everything she had been through, now she had to deal with the possibility that there was even more deception?

She rolled her staff on her legs. The wood felt solid and comforting as it rolled beneath her hands, and she was tempted to stand and make her way back to the city, but at night, she wasn't sure that she even could.

Elaine came to sit near her, saying nothing.

"What do you plan on doing with them?" Sam asked, nodding to Marin and her Scribe.

"They will be detained and brought back to the city."

"And just how do you intend to do that? It took everything we had to get here, so for us to make our way back, it will be even harder trying to carry them."

"I didn't say we were going to take the direct route back," Elaine said.

"What other way would there be?"

"You keep even that from her?" Marin asked.

"Quiet," Elaine said.

"Lainey, she has a right to know, just as he had a right to live."

"If you're going to keep at that farce, you're going to have to do a better job." Elaine said.

"There is no farce. I wish that there were. I wish that I could believe my princess. And I wish that I didn't have to feel betrayed. But how can I?"

"We'll see."

"You are in for a severe disappointment," Marin said.

Sam stood and stormed away. She wasn't going to stay and listen, not wanting to deal with whatever Elaine and Marin might go on about. She started forward and looked out at the darkness. Heat wafted up to her, coming off of the steam field, and in the distance—impossibly far away —she could just barely make out the glittering lights of the city. It had taken the better part of the day for them to reach the mountains, and returning would take just as long, if not longer, especially as they now would have to carry two prisoners with them.

"Where do you intend for us to rest?" she asked without turning back.

"It's safe here," Marin said.

"Nowhere is safe," Sam said.

She made her way down the hillside and took a seat on the rock. She rested the staff on her legs, and leaned forward, letting her eyes drift closed. After a while, she stirred, heat making her uncomfortable, and she had to move, changing to a different rock. That one was only somewhat better. Sam tried to sleep, but it came in fits. She had flashes of visions, things that had been her experiences as a child, images of Tray and Bastan and, unfortunately, Marin.

That was the family she knew.

As much as she tried to move past it, she could tell that Marin had helped her over the years. She might not have wanted to, and her reasons for helping might have been twisted, but Marin had never meant to harm her, not until the end.

Something had changed.

Even early on, Marin had been willing to save

Lyasanna, explaining about Sam's abilities and allowing her the opportunity to try and help her.

With her mind awash with everything she'd learned and unable to find sleep, Sam made her way up the hill. She found Marin resting and nudged her awake with her toe. Elaine watched silently. The Scribe—Bushy Brow—rested next to Marin. Something about that unsettled Sam. She doubted they would be able to do anything without easar paper, but maybe they could.

"What changed for you?"

"What?" Marin blinked sleep from her eyes and looked up.

"You prompted me to help the princess. Something changed for you."

"Nothing changed for me. I was trying to help get Tray out of prison."

"He wouldn't have been there if you hadn't sent me to steal the easar paper. You needed that for you and your Scribe."

"There are many uses for easar paper. It would've been valuable for bargaining, but Jessup would have been able to use it as well."

"Why did you want me to help Lyasanna?"

Marin took a deep breath before letting it out in a long sigh. "When Ralun returned to the city, I knew you would get pulled into it somehow. I tried to protect you—"

"You tried to protect me? You're the one who had me go after the paper in the first place!"

"Only because you are the only one who would be able to. I didn't know that Ralun was there at that time. Once I did, I tried to place myself between him and you. And then, when it became clear that I might not make it, I decided you deserved to know about yourself. You deserved to know what you were, even if it meant sending you back to them."

"I still don't understand."

"It's possible that you never will," Marin said. "I don't claim to have made the right decisions, not all the time. But with your brother—with Tray—I know that I did. Had I not, that young man—little boy at the time—would not have survived."

Elaine sat silently.

"Why did you attack? Who were you serving when you poisoned the canals?"

"I was serving me."

"Why?"

"I'm tired of the misdirection. The Anders would have you believe that they are so different from the Thelns, but they aren't. The only thing that's different is how the power is manifested."

"The Anders are similar to the Thelns?"

"Why else do you think both require the power of Scribes?"

Sam looked down to Bushy Brow. He was breathing steadily and had a few welts on him from where her staff had knocked him out. "I intend to go after Tray."

"I will go with you."

Sam laughed bitterly. "Even if I could trust you, why do you think he would want to see you?"

"I saved him."

"He doesn't know that. To Tray, you were someone

who deceived him, no differently than you did with me. How can either of us believe you anymore?"

"Perhaps you can't." Marin glanced back to Elaine. "You haven't told her."

"She needs to learn on her own."

"What lie have you kept from me now?"

Marin looked up at her. "It's not a lie. It's how you can use your ability."

"It's not something that can be explained," Elaine said.

"Maybe you can't explain it, but I seem to recall being the one who attempted to explain it to you."

"And I was never able to do it, not nearly as well as you made it seem like I should."

"And that is somehow my fault?" Marin asked.

"What is it?" Sam snapped.

"You believe that you need augmentations to use your ability, but you don't. Oh, augmentation certainly can help. There are times when you can add to what you would otherwise do, but the magic is within you, Samara."

"There's nothing within me other than the blood that's used for my augmentations."

"Close your eyes," Marin said.

Sam glared at her. "Why should I listen to you?"

"I'm trying to offer something to you."

"Why? Do you think that you offering this to me will somehow make me more likely to believe you in the future?"

"I'm offering something to you as a way to start," Marin said. "Whether or not you believe me in the future is a moot point."

Sam glanced from Elaine to Marin before closing her eyes. "Now what?"

"Now think about the feeling that you have when an augmentation is placed."

"That's it?"

"That's not it, but it's near enough that it can help. The augmentation is simply a way for you to have access to that same power, it's sort of a way of cheating your magic. You're using the power of your Scribe to trigger your magic."

"What about when we use our combined magics to heal people?"

"Then you're using the easar paper. That is something else entirely. That is what triggers your magic."

"It doesn't work when we write on regular paper," she said.

"Doesn't it? I would argue that there are ways in which you can use your abilities even without easar paper, and even without you triggering it yourself. If you're determined to need your Scribe to trigger your magic, there's no need for you to use easar paper."

Sam opened her eyes and glanced to Elaine. The other woman just stared at her.

"And that's it? I just need to close my eyes and imagine what it feels like when I have an augmentation placed?"

"There is a little more to it than that, but it's different for each Kaver. I can help you with the first part, but you need to find the rest on your own."

Sam closed her eyes, and she focused on what it felt like when Alec placed an augmentation. She chose to think about the ones that were most commonly placed—

strength and speed—and tried to envision the cold sense that washed over her as he wrote on the easar paper.

There was nothing.

She shook her head. "Whatever you think will happen isn't."

"I didn't say it was easy. But you should know that the more you work at it, the easier it becomes."

"Can you do it?" Sam asked Elaine.

"Not as well as Marin. She was always the greatest of us."

Sam took a deep breath and closed her eyes again. When she did, she thought again about the way she felt when the augmentation washed over her. Once again, there was nothing. She changed her focus, instead thinking about the words that Alec wrote. He had a pattern that he used, the same words that he chose to trigger her augmentation, rarely deviating, especially now that they both knew how it would work.

A soft thrill worked through her, and with it came a cold flush.

Sam's eyes opened in a snap.

"You felt it, didn't you?" Marin asked.

"I don't know what I felt."

"It sounds as if you do. Keep working with it. Keep attempting to reach for the connection that you already have, the power that you have felt, that you know, and it will get easier."

"And if I can't?"

"If you can't, then you will always be dependent on your Scribe. You will never know the full potential of your Kaver magic."

15

COMPLICATIONS

A lec tried to distract himself from what was happening with his father and with Kara, frustrated by how little he'd been able to uncover. There was nothing in any of the old records that would reveal what might've happened to either of them. Everything referenced that he had managed to come up with regarding somnolence and change in alertness had been practically useless. So far, he'd only managed to find a few records that were of any value to him.

"I might have something here," Stefan said.

Alec glanced over at his friend sitting next to him in the library. The room was mostly empty, leaving them thankfully isolated, better to avoid questions. He didn't mind having others in the library, but being allowed a chance to study without anyone else was beneficial. He hadn't seen any masters coming through here, either, which was more surprising than anything else. Typically, there were at least a few who would come to the library, whether to research or to simply socialize, Alec didn't know. Maybe he'd find out when he finally became a master physicker himself.

"What have you found?"

"It might be nothing," Stefan said, pushing a record over to him.

"Something is better than what I've uncovered."

"You're not even researching alertness anymore. You've been spending most of your time looking at changes in vision."

Alec looked down at the record he had set out in front of him. He had been splitting his time, working on trying to find answers for his father while also trying to uncover what might've happened to the girl. Her vision hadn't changed much over the last few days, though it did continue to decline. Would there come a point when she was completely blind? If that happened, there might be nothing that could be done for her.

Before that happened, he was determined to use the easar paper. Until then, he was willing to research and look for a more traditional approach.

"It's troubling."

"The girl?"

"Stacia, but yes. I don't know what happened to her, and I can't find anything that references someone of her age who had such a rapid decline in vision."

"You mentioned once that you were concerned about something she might have been exposed to. Why is that?"

"Because there are various compounds that can be caustic. I'm not as familiar with what seamstresses work with, but it seems to me that if she were exposed to something caustic, it would explain the rapid change in her vision. She's been working as an apprentice for just under a year."

"If it was something caustic and she's had prolonged exposure, there isn't anything to do unless you can counteract it—and remove her from future exposure," Stefan said. "And even then, it's probably too late. The change in vision could be permanent." When Alec frowned at him, Stefan only shrugged. "Vision is interesting to me."

"There aren't too many masters who study vision," Alec said.

"Mostly because they don't need to. The opticians manage most illnesses."

"They don't manage illnesses at all. They help with lenses, but nothing more than that."

"But most people don't think of coming to the university for eye-related issues. For the most part, they will go to an optician and will be satisfied with anything that can be done for them. I'm surprised that this girl—Stacia—didn't go to an optician."

"That's just it. She did. She made it sound like she went to more than one."

"She must have plenty of money."

"Why is that?"

"You know how expensive opticians are."

Alec did know, and he had considered that as a complication, but hadn't pieced anything more to it than that.

"You said she told you which section of the city she was in. Maybe we should go and speak to her employer."

It was something that Alec had considered, but there

never seemed to be enough time. Then again, if he could discover what she might have been exposed to, maybe he could find a way to help her. Once he knew what she was exposed to, treating her—even with easar paper—would be easier and likely more effective.

"In a little while," Alec said. "I still need to figure out what we can uncover about what happened with my father and the other woman."

He hadn't told Stefan her name, not wanting to reveal that he had gone to Bastan for help. Eventually, he hoped Bastan would be able to provide some useful information, but Alec hadn't heard anything from him.

"Then look at this," he said, holding out the record.

Alec glanced at the page and quickly read it. It was old —based on the styling of documentation, probably several decades old. The way that physickers documented records had evolved over time, gradually taking on a different approach. After looking through records as often as Alec had, he had begun to identify the age of a record simply by the documentation style. It was an interesting observation, but likely meaningless. Most of the information was still there, though it was often times in different sections of the record.

"It says this individual was unresponsive for months," Alec said, reading the page, "and never recovered."

"I didn't say that this was going to help you, only that it seems to have similarities to what we're dealing with now."

Alec flipped through the pages, searching for the presenting symptoms. With the age of this record, it was difficult to find because it wasn't in the expected location.

That meant it was even older than he had thought. Even records several decades old still had the presenting symptoms in the same place. He finally found it, though it was near the back of the record. The man referenced by the record was a butcher, which didn't provide him with much information. By the time he had been brought to the university, he had been unresponsive for several days. Many of the same treatments that Alec tried had been attempted on the butcher.

"We should set this one aside," Alec said.

They'd set aside each record that shared similarities hoping to later compare them for trends, even if there weren't any obvious ones at first. All he wanted was to find patterns that he could piece together. Would there be enough for him to find an answer?

The door opened more noisily than it typically did in the library, and Alec glanced over. Beckah rushed in, breathing rapidly. She leaned on the table and looked over at Alec. "I need you to come with me."

"Why?"

"Because your patient needs you."

Alec nodded to Stefan. "Keep searching."

Stefan waved him away, and Alec hurried after Beckah.

"Which patient?"

"Kara," she said, whispering the name.

"What happened with her?"

"I don't know. She started to shake. I was on rounds with Master Julia and saw it. The junior physickers are working on her, but…"

Alec was thankful that she had come for him. "Junior

physickers are working on her when there's a master there?"

"The master physickers don't see this as anything that is needing their attention."

"Only because they don't know how to help," he said, not bothering to hide his frustration. "If they cared, they would attach their name to this patient."

"Why would that matter?"

"It matters because they don't want to be associated with a treatment failure," Alec said. "Most of them prefer to be right."

"Are you sure?"

Alec nodded. "I've seen it often enough now that it is the only explanation I can come up with."

"That's awful."

"It is what it is. Which is why I need to get down there."

They raced through the halls and reached the ward. Alec ran toward Kara's cot and found two junior physickers working on her, one of them holding her down. She was convulsing.

"What happened?" Alec said.

Neither of them looked up. One of the physickers—a fat young man by the name of Scott—was attempting to shove a fistful of leaves into her mouth.

Alec grabbed his wrist and jerked him back.

Scott looked up and glared at him. "What are you doing? We need to stop the convulsing."

"And how do you think to do that with canor leaves?"

"Canor leaves have many properties that will help with

convulsions. You haven't been a full physicker long enough to—"

"I know that canor leaves, especially when crushed the way you're doing them, have both positive and negative effects. Are you intending to stop her heart?"

Scott frowned. "Stop her heart? Why would I—"

"Because canor can be especially potent, usually when as fresh as what you're using. Now, were these dried leaves, I doubt there would have been any danger to her, other than the fact that they likely wouldn't have worked."

The other junior physicker, an older woman named Heather who Alec hadn't had many positive experiences with, frowned. "What would you prefer?"

"Prefer or what do we have available?" Alec looked at the table next to the bed. There were a few vials, and there was only one he thought could actually help. He grabbed it and opened the tincture of orphum. It would do little more than delay the trembling, but it would quiet the tremors enough that other treatments could be tried.

He placed three drops inside her mouth. Within a few moments, the trembling began to slow before stopping altogether.

"Now. Why don't you go and find me decoar stone, sezer oil, and gabtan leaves?"

"*All* of that?" Heather asked.

"All of that, unless you want her to seize again," he said.

She hurried off, dragging Scott with her. Alec watched until they were out of earshot.

"Why do they have to be so incompetent?"

Beckah grinned at him. "Not everybody has the same

experience that you have working with medicines. Gods, you know as much as most of the master physickers. I doubt anyone of them would say that to you, but it's true. When it comes to treatment combinations, you might know more."

Alec looked down at the woman, trying to think of what he could do for her. At this point, there might not be anything. If she had begun to seize, whatever process was taking place might have advanced beyond his ability to make a difference.

"She shouldn't have seized like this," Alec said.

"We don't know what's happening within her," Beckah said.

"No, but something changed suddenly." Even the last record that he had read through hadn't described a seizure like this. Something had to have happened, but what? Why would she suddenly start trembling?

Alec repeated his exam. He had studied her often enough over the last week that he would have noticed if something was changing, but she had been remarkably stable, much like his father.

After sedating her, her heart had slowed, and her breathing was regular once more. He looked for changes to her skin, but there weren't any. When he opened her mouth, he saw remnants of the canor leaves that Scott had been trying to shove into her mouth, but nothing else.

"What do you think…"

Beckah trailed off when Scott and Heather returned, both of them with the jars that Alec had requested. "Here's what you requested, Physicker Stross."

Alec took them without saying anything more, and he

unstoppered the tops and put some of each ingredient into a jar, combining the leaves with the oil before crushing the stone and adding that, ultimately forming a paste. The combination would taste foul, but there was nothing to do about that. He left it in the jar and took a small spoonful and stuck it on the inside of her cheek.

"This must be done twice a day. Either I can do it, or one of you can. This combination has been proven to soothe seizures. It will give us time to learn what happened."

"That is an interesting combination," Scott said.

"Interesting in what way?" Alec said.

"Only that I haven't seen it used before."

"Have you cared for many people with tremors like this?"

"I studied under Master Carl."

Alec watched him, frowning. "I'm afraid I don't understand the connection."

"Only that Master Carl has experience with tremors like that. He is considered one of the foremost experts at the university."

Alec hadn't known that. It seemed there were many things about Master Carl that he didn't know.

"And what treatments would Master Carl have attempted?"

"I don't know," Scott said, "but I've never seen him use a decoar stone."

"It's an older treatment, and it's one that can be incredibly effective, especially when used in the right way," Alec said. "It has a calming effect, and when added to the oil in the leaves, it augments the effect of both.

Given that we are concerned with her arousal, we can't use anything that will sedate her too much."

"You added the stone because you didn't want to use quite as much of the other two." Heather glanced over to Scott and nodded.

"If we used too much of either of the other compounds, then we'd miss out on our opportunity to try to bring her around." He wasn't sure whether there was anything that could be done to bring her around, but sedating her more, leaving her less likely to wake up, wouldn't bring him the answers he needed. "Now you need to keep an eye on the other unresponsive patient in case there is a similar reaction."

Both Heather and Scott nodded, and Alec turned away, leaving them with Kara. There wasn't anything he could offer beyond what he already had. Beckah followed him, trailing after him into the hallway.

"You trust that they will do what you asked?"

"Not really. I'll probably have to go back to ensure that they do."

"Why do you think she had that seizure?"

"I don't know. I only hope Bastan brings me information that can give us answers about what happened to her."

"And if he doesn't?"

"Then I will have to use the easar paper."

They walked a while longer before Beckah glanced over at him, a deep frown twisting her face. "Have you talked to Sam about it yet?"

"I haven't. She has been sending me notes that she is still preoccupied, so I know she's still in the city." And he had been sending responses telling her how irritated he would be if she left without informing him. He hoped that she was able to keep that in mind as she made her plans, but if she were to leave now, Alec wasn't certain he would even be able to go. He needed to help his father before he could even leave the university. Hopefully, Sam understood.

"What has her preoccupied? I thought she wanted nothing more than to go after Tray?"

"She does, and she might."

"That doesn't bother you?"

"Would it matter if it did?"

Alec reached the entrance to the university and frowned. It was a bright and sunny day, with the warmth of the sun radiating through the doors. He could return to the library and continue his studies, but that didn't feel like it would get him any closer to answers.

He needed to take something off his plate. If that meant solving the riddle of what happened with Stacia, that would be what he did first.

"Where are you going?"

"I think it's time for me to make a visit to the Hosd section."

"Why there?"

"Because I need to understand what happened to Stacia."

"You could leave that to someone else."

"I've promised to help her, and if I don't, I worry about what someone else might require of her."

"The junior physickers would help her. She's a patient in the ward. They wouldn't leave her to be harmed."

"I still feel as if it's my responsibility." They reached the bridge leading from the university over into the neighboring sections. Alec glanced over at Beckah. "You don't have to come with me."

"I might as well. What else is there for me to do?"

"You have your studies."

"My studies? I think I learn almost as much by spending time with you, Physicker Stross."

"You're going to be the reason the master physickers regret my promotion."

"No. The master physickers will regret your promotion for many reasons, but I am not one of them." She grinned at him.

Alec had not been to the Hosd section before, but he knew generally where to find it. As they made their way through the city, he paused a few times to ask for directions, and by the time they reached it, he had begun to have a growing trepidation. The section reminded him of Caster. There was a certain feel to it, and he had that familiar sense of unease that he felt while in Caster.

"We don't have to keep going," Beckah said.

"If we want to help her, we do."

He didn't even know where to begin. There had to be a seamstress shop, but he hoped there wasn't more than one. If he failed to find the one where she apprenticed, he could go looking for Stacia's grandfather.

At least it was midday, and there wasn't the concern that they might be robbed. Alec had taken his jacket off, but that did nothing to conceal the fact that they didn't necessarily belong in this section. They looked like outsiders, and Alec felt like an outsider.

"We need to see if we can find a seamstress shop," he said.

"This section doesn't look like it would have a seamstress shop," Beckah said.

"I thought there were the same sorts of shops all over the city."

"There aren't. Alec, every part of the city has their own particular way of doing things. Not all sections carry the same goods. Why do you think there are sections that are so predominantly one merchant or another?"

"I haven't given it a lot of thought. In my section, we had pretty much everything we wanted."

"You had many things, but your section is more self-contained than most. Especially compared to some of these outer sections, it isn't typical for them to have all the merchants."

"I still need to find where she worked."

"What if she wasn't telling the truth?"

"Why wouldn't she tell me the truth? She wanted to be healed, and it makes no sense for her to not share everything about her, especially if it reduces the likelihood that I will be able to help."

"I think there are probably lots of reasons why somebody wouldn't be honest with a physicker, especially if they were doing something they weren't supposed to."

Could that be it? If Stacia was involved in something illegal, she might've concealed it from him. He knew that Sam would have done the same thing were she in that situation. Especially when she was working with Bastan, she most certainly would have concealed the nature of her job.

"I need to find her grandfather, then."

"Do you think that will make a difference?"

"If he were able to speak, maybe it would."

First, he had to find the man, and then he could see if there was something he could do about helping him speak. If he couldn't, then perhaps Alec would have to use the easar paper, so that he could discover what he needed to help Stacia.

"I don't even know where to start," he said.

"I imagine you go to where the people are. Where do you think the people in the section would be?"

Alec looked around, but most of the shops looked dilapidated, and few of them had signs hanging out front revealing what they sold. People made their way along the street, but they did so with a certain cautiousness to them.

Where would he go if he were in Caster? He would go to Bastan. And Bastan operated a tavern, for the same reasons. He could get information, and it wouldn't raise any suspicion.

"I think we need to visit a tavern."

"I'm not sure that now is the right time to sit down and have a drink," Beckah said, smiling at him.

"I thought you would be open for a drink at any time of day."

"What does that mean?"

"Only that my report of you is that you tend to be a little heavy with your ale consumption."

Beckah shot him an irritated expression. "Your report of me?"

"I thought I should have one ready in case you decided to report on me."

They reached a center street within the section, and Alec found what appeared to be a tavern, but he hesitated before entering. The building was just as rundown as many others in this section, though the door appeared stout and freshly painted. There were no windows, something that was uncommon in his section, and uncommon more centrally within the city.

"We can go in and hurry out," Beckah suggested.

"All we need is to find out what we can about Stacia. I need to understand what she might've been doing so I can help her."

"You know, you could always ask her. If she knew that you'd come to her section, how would she react?"

"I don't know. If she's trying to hide something from me, she might not react well."

Alec stepped into the tavern. It was dirty inside, and the floor was packed earth. A few tables were scattered about the room, most with people sitting around them. Some played games while others talked, all had a mug or two of ale sitting in front of them.

One group of men glanced over when they entered, and watched as Alec and Beckah made their way toward an open table. He knew from his time with Bastan that it was best simply to hurry into situations like this, and at least feign confidence, even if he didn't feel it.

They didn't have to wait long before a waitress came by, and she leaned forward, a lopsided smile on her face. Her clothing was dirty, and the dress was far too baggy, as if she had either lost a considerable amount of weight, or it had belonged to someone else before her. Alec didn't see any signs of skin folds that would indicate lost weight, and saw no signs of any glandular issues, so he suspected that this was nothing more than a hand-me-down.

"Not too often that we get highborns in here," she said.

"I'll take a mug of ale," Beckah said with a smile.

"And you?"

Alec nodded. "I'll take a mug, also."

The waitress left them, and Alec scanned the room. "Bastan's place is quite a bit nicer," he said.

"I get the sense that Bastan is a little bit more than what he appears."

"I don't know whether he is more than he appears, but I'm certain what we see is exactly what he wants us to think he is."

"You think that Bastan is a lowborn who wants people to think he's more mysterious?"

"I think Bastan is a skilled businessman in his chosen profession," Alec said.

Beckah grinned and accepted the mug from the waitress when she returned. He took his, and looked up at her, deciding that he could ask his question. "Do you know Rynance Vold?"

"Why?"

"I'm looking for him."

"Why are you looking for him?"

"It's... It's about his granddaughter."

The waitress looked around the tavern and finally turned her attention back to Alec. "Wait here."

She hurried off.

"That was strange," Beckah said.

"I think everything about this place is a little strange."

They didn't have to wait long. The waitress returned,

and she had a man with her. The man was in his thirties and had a thick beard and dark eyes that seemed to penetrate everything. There was something about the way he stared at Alec that made him uncomfortable.

"I understand you're looking for Ryn."

"I am. His granddaughter came to me for help. She said that she worked for a seamstress in this section."

"There ain't no seamstresses in this section."

"I'm getting that sense," Alec said.

"And it's not safe for someone like you to be over here and asking questions about Ryn."

"Why is that?"

"Let's just say that it's not."

Alec looked over to Beckah, wishing he had Sam with him. If anyone had a way of navigating places like this, she would have done well. "Can you at least send word to him that I have questions about his granddaughter?"

The man glared at him for a longer moment. "Send word where?"

"If you find him, he'll know where."

Alec stood, leaving his ale untouched. He fished a few coins out of his pocket and set them on the table. He motioned to Beckah, hoping she had the sense to follow him.

As he backed away from the table, he had an unsettled feeling in his chest. It didn't disappear when they stepped outside, and it stayed with him as they made their way along the streets, hurrying toward their section, and back toward the university. He couldn't shake the sense that someone followed them, though he doubted that they did. There would be no reason to follow them.

Beckah said nothing on the way back to the university. Only once they were back did he realize that something was wrong.

"Beckah?"

She didn't answer. Her eyes had a glazed appearance to them.

"Beckah?"

She slumped. He barely managed to catch her in time before she crashed to the floor.

Alex scooped her up and hurried through the university and into the hospital ward with her. As he did, his heart hammered, wondering what had happened to her. Hopefully, the fact that he was with her meant that he could reverse the effect of whatever had taken place.

But what was it?

16

A FRIEND IN NEED

"You were with her the entire time?" Master Helen said.

Alec looked down at Beckah. She hadn't moved since he'd brought her to the ward. She rested quietly on a cot, her hair brushed back so that it didn't obscure her features. Alec had examined her and found her heart and lungs regular, her stomach normal, and no findings on her skin. She was no different from Kara or his father. He knew nothing, other than the fact that Beckah shouldn't have ended up like this.

"I was with her the entire time. We had been here, working with the unresponsive woman, and then I decided to venture out into the city to see if I could discover more about one of my other patients."

"Physicker Stross, I don't need to remind you that that is highly unusual."

"Maybe it is, but I didn't know any other way to help

her. I thought if I could understand more about where she worked and lived and what she'd been through that I might be able to restore her eyesight."

"You took on a patient with changes in eyesight and thought that was appropriate for the university?"

"It's a young girl with a rapid change in eyesight. I thought that it was interesting enough I could learn from it," he said, telling her the same as what he had told Master Harrison.

"Show me to her."

Alec guided Master Helen over to Stacia. He had been so focused on trying to help Beckah that he hadn't even had a chance to confront her about the seamstress shop and everything else that she had told him.

"Physicker. Have you come up with anything?" Stacia asked.

"I went to the Hosd section, thinking that I could find some information about what happened with you."

Master Helen arched a brow at him. "You went to Hosd?" she asked softly.

Alec nodded, keeping his gaze focused on Stacia. "There isn't a seamstress shop there."

"There is. I promise that there is."

"And I went with my friend to a tavern, looking to find your grandfather, but we were threatened."

"Physicker Stross?" Master Helen asked.

"Who is he? Who is your grandfather, if that's even who he is? And why were you not honest with me?"

"I… I didn't know if I could be honest. I wanted to get help, and Ryn was convinced that he could get answers here."

"Ryn? As in Rynance Vold?" Master Helen asked.

Stacia looked down at her hands and nodded slowly.

"Who is he?"

"Only a very dangerous man."

"A dangerous man with no tongue?" Alec asked.

"Rynance Vold has no tongue?" Master Helen asked.

"The man who was with her had no tongue, I don't know if he's the same one," Alec said.

"Doubtful. Rynance Vold leads the northern crime syndicate."

"Crime syndicate?"

Would Bastan know him?

It was likely that he would, which meant that Alec would have to go find Bastan and see what else he could learn.

"He has been nothing more than a rumor for a long time, but from what I hear, he's been looking to gain territory."

A rumor and now Alec—and Beckah—had been caught up in it.

"What really happened with your eyesight?" Alec asked.

Stacia shifted on the cot, keeping her gaze down on her lap. "I… I came into contact with something that burned my eyes."

"Why wouldn't you have told me?"

"I thought that a physicker would have been able to figure that out."

"Not when there's nothing that appears wrong," Alec said.

"You said that you would look into it."

"I did look into it, but I can't help you if I don't know everything that happened. Where is this chemical that you came into contact with?"

"Ryn has it."

"He does? And he's in the Hosd section?"

"Most of the time. I've been working for them for a few years, mostly doing a few small jobs here and there, and I was hopeful that I could get away. There wasn't any other way to support my grandparents."

Alec shook his head. It sounded far too familiar. It was something similar to what Sam had gone through with Bastan, though would Ryn have the same affection for Stacia as Bastan had for Sam?

If he did, it would make sense for him to try to get help for her.

"That's where you got money for healing, isn't it?"

Stacia nodded. "Ryn wanted to help, but he couldn't be seen helping. Does that make sense?"

"It makes as much sense as anything else," Alec said.

"So, can you help me? Can you bring my vision back?"

"Without knowing the nature of the caustic compound, any attempted healing would be potentially dangerous," Master Helen said. She directed the words at Stacia, but Alec could tell they were meant for him. It was a warning, another admonition to keep him from using the easar paper.

"But if we know there is a caustic reaction, it seems it would be a simple matter to restore her eyesight," he said to Master Helen.

"Nothing is a simple matter, and if you don't know the

true nature of the injury, attempting to restore her eyesight could be dangerous. There could be a residual effect, and you would be continually attempting to make such repairs. At a certain point, the energy and effort involved might be more than what you can withstand."

He swallowed. "It seems I must return to the Hosd section and find Ryn." He looked over at Beckah lying unresponsive on a nearby cot. "But not until she's recovered."

"Yes," Master Helen said. "What did she come into contact with?"

"Nothing. We went from here where we were working on the other patient, and I was the only one mixing the restorative, and went to search for Ryn. We went to a tavern, and asked questions—"

"Which tavern?" Stacia asked.

"I don't know. All the taverns seemed alike."

"Not in Hosd. The taverns there are pretty different. Most of them side with Ryn, but some don't, and those are the ones you have to be most concerned about."

"Why is that?"

"Because if they think you're working with Ryn, they'll attack."

Alec looked over to where Beckah lay motionless. "But we weren't attacked. All we did was ask about Ryn and ask about you, but we were served our ale *before* we started asking questions."

Stacia's eyes widened. "They got you."

"What do you mean they got me?"

"At the taverns that support Ryn, if two highborns

walked in, they would immediately be suspicious. They would've put something in your drink. If they were able to determine that you weren't a threat, they would have added an antidote." She frowned at him. "How is it that you're not hurt?"

"Because I didn't have a drink."

But Beckah had.

"What do they use to poison people with?"

"I don't know. They used to use something that would only cause vomiting. It was their way of deterring anyone who might come after them, and it protected Ryn. Lately…"

Alec looked over to Master Helen. "Can you see what you can do for Beckah?"

"What is it that you intend to do, Physicker Stross?"

"I need to get more information."

"It seems the last time you went to that section, you were attacked."

"Which is why I don't intend to go alone."

"You will find that your… friend… is preoccupied at the moment."

"Where is she?"

"There is a certain assignment she has been given. If you intend to confront this Ryn, you will need to go a different way."

Alec breathed out heavily. There was only one other way he could attempt to find Ryn, and that involved Bastan.

But would he help?

Alec looked over at where Beckah lay motionless. Now, there were four of what appeared to be similar—

and possibly related—poisonings, and one of them had seizures. That didn't make a whole lot of sense, but he needed to find answers before their conditions worsened, and he needed to understand more before anyone else was harmed.

17

THREAT TO CASTER

"I don't understand," Alec said, looking over at Bastan. He had made it all the way to the Caster section again, dragging himself through the city, and once more wishing he had Sam with him, if for no other reason than her familiarity with these parts of the city. He didn't like coming here, though he felt infinitely more comfortable than Beckah when she had come.

"You think I am going to help you get information about this person?"

"But I understand they're moving in on your territory," Alec said. He hadn't even gotten the opportunity to tell Bastan about Ryn, but he seemed completely disinterested. That surprised Alec. He figured Bastan would be intrigued by any such rumors, regardless of the source. And this one came from Master Helen, so the source seemed as if it should be solid.

"There's no way anyone would make such a move," Bastan said.

Alec looked around the office. He marveled at the paintings along the wall. Though he'd been in Bastan's office before, he'd not really paid attention to the artwork. Sam had told him of Bastan's penchant for fine art. Some of these appeared to be by master painters, which he knew meant they were incredibly valuable. The most surprising was a painting of the canals that hung behind Bastan's desk. It was exquisitely made and depicted each of the sections of the city with the canals surrounding them. Something like that had value for many reasons, though Alec suspected that for Bastan it was merely a way for him to identify which parts of the city he needed to focus his attention on.

He turned his focus back to Bastan. "We were threatened in Hosd. And now Beckah—"

"Your friend?"

"The other physicker—student physicker—she was with me the last time we came here," he said.

"Why would you be threatened? Was she too vocal?"

Alec almost laughed. It was a reasonable assumption to make about Beckah. She could be too vocal at times, and she had been quite vocal when she had been here before.

"We went asking questions. There was a young girl who came to the university looking for healing."

"What did she come in with?"

"Does it matter?"

"Maybe."

"She came in with a progressive blurred vision. She's young—probably no older than fifteen—and said she was working for a seamstress and supporting her family." Alec still felt like a fool for believing her, though she had preyed on his inherent desire to help. She couldn't have known Alec would be the one assigned to see her—the physicker who worked with each person who came in was not guaranteed—but once she had him, she had said the right things and forced him to offer his help.

No. That wasn't quite right. Alec would have helped regardless.

"Blurred vision doesn't seem like a very typical problem for someone of that age," Bastan said.

"It's not. That's why I offered to do whatever I could. I thought I could help, but it was difficult finding anything that might explain why she had suffered the gradual loss of vision."

"You were doing this while trying to understand what happened with your father and Kara?"

"That has been just as difficult to understand," Alec said. "I'm doing what I can, but…" He shook his head. "I haven't been able to find any information that might lead me to a solution. To take my mind off it, I spent some time researching various treatments that might be effective for blurred vision."

"And you found nothing, so you went looking for more information about this girl."

"I did."

"What section is she from?"

"Hosd."

Bastan clenched his hands. "I see."

"You do?"

"Let me tell you what I know about that section. First, there are no seamstresses in Hosd, so whatever your young patient told you was a fabrication. Second, they are near enough to the swamp that they are somewhat different from other sections. There is crime, but not as much as in other places, especially not as much as in some of the outer sections."

"Like Caster?"

Bastan glared at him. "Caster doesn't have much crime, either. Not the way you would like to think. I ensure this section is safe."

The way he said it told Alec that Bastan had been angered by the mere suggestion that there was crime in his section, but Alec had seen it. He had lived it. There were thieves here—and Sam had been one of them.

"I needed more information, and believing the information she'd given me, I went in search of a seamstress shop and her supposed grandfather, whose name was Ryn—"

"You are a fool, aren't you?"

"What?"

"You have significant book smarts. You must, otherwise you wouldn't have been promoted to full physicker as quickly as you were, but you know nothing about the city."

"I'm a part of the city."

"Now that you're at the university, you're set apart from the city." When Alec frowned, Bastan merely shook his head. "Tell me, before you went to study at the university, what did you think of it?"

"I thought there were skilled physickers there, and—"

Bastan shook his head. "No. What did you *think* of it."

Alec frowned. "What are you trying to get at?"

"I'm trying to get what were your feelings about the university before you went there." He looked around the room before his gaze settled on the door that led out into the tavern. "I have plenty of people who work for me who have an opinion about those who are at the university. Most of them see it as a place where only highborns— those with money—can go for restoratives. The rest of us are stuck with people like your father, and often times with people who aren't nearly as good as your father." He turned his attention back to Alec. "So, what I'm trying to get a sense of is how *you* felt about the university."

"Before I went there, I… I thought it was impossible. I wanted to learn from the university, but only because of the knowledge that was available there."

"And now?"

"I still want to learn from the university, Bastan. That's why I'm there. That's why I stay there. My hope is to change things, and that in time, I will help to find a way to convince the physickers to work with those who don't have the necessary financial means to obtain healing."

"Just like your father?" Bastan asked, a hint of a smile on his face.

"My father didn't leave the university because of the difference in what they charge," Alec said.

Bastan arched a brow.

"It doesn't matter why he left, not really."

"It does matter. Everything matters when taking a measure of a man."

"He left because of what happened with my mother."

"Does he blame them?"

"No. He blames himself."

When Bastan frowned, Alec only shook his head. "Please, don't make me go through this with you. Just know that my father feels he was wrong."

"How often has your father been wrong?"

Alec stared at Bastan. "He's lying sick and possibly dying at the university and you're questioning my father's skills?"

"I'm trying to get a sense of him."

"I don't know. Before he shared with me the reason that he left the university, I would've said that he was rarely, if ever, wrong."

"And now?"

"He changed. Whatever happened then"—and Alec wasn't going to tell Bastan the details of how his father argued about his mother's treatment with the other master physickers—"changed him. He began to look at things differently. Now, he's willing to do whatever it takes to provide the necessary healing to anyone. And he's much more of a scholar." Alec shook his head, unable to get the image of his father lying motionless out of his mind. "Why does it matter?"

"It matters because your father is the reason that all of this is taking place."

"I thought you said you didn't know?"

"I wasn't sure, but after what happened with Kevin, I went in search of answers myself."

"You went yourself?"

"You don't think that I'm capable?"

"That's not it at all. It's only that Sam has told me that you don't like to put yourself out there and risk exposing yourself."

"For the right reason, I will."

"And having your colleague injured is the right reason?"

"Is there any better reason?"

Alec breathed out heavily. "What is it? Why do you think my father is tied to this?"

"I asked your father to obtain something of value for me. And he did."

"The eel venom. I was there when you used it."

"And your father did not speak of it to anyone?"

Alec shook his head. "I've already told you that he didn't," he said.

"Which is why it is surprising that someone else discovered the venom. They are using it in a different way, but it is no less effective."

Alec's eyes widened. "Eel venom is responsible for what's happening?"

"I don't know. From the information I've been able to collect, that is the only connection between those who have been taken ill."

"Wait. My father. Kara. Kevin. And Beckah?"

"Beckah?"

"When we were at the tavern. She was poisoned—or whatever it was. Stacia—the young girl with the vision problem—claims that we were likely poisoned out of mere suspicion, appearing highborn. Had we not asked about Ryn, we would have been treated with an antidote."

"An antidote. Your father made it sound as if there wasn't an antidote."

Alec shrugged. "I don't know anything about the venom."

"Then maybe it's time for you to begin searching for answers."

"I don't have any venom. I don't have any way of testing it."

Bastan gave him a strange smile. "That, I think, I can help you with."

18

INTO THE SWAMP

The barge moved through the canal, barely pausing as it drifted beyond the boundary of the city. Alec tried not to pay too much attention to the growing distance from the buildings as they moved out into the swamp. He had been out here one other time, and he had felt just as scared then as he did now. Only this time, he didn't have Sam with him for support.

A soft wind blew, sending in the stench from the deeper portions of the swamp, and Alec longed for some of the paste that he mixed to ignore some of the foul odors of the medicines he often had used when healing patients. It was silent other than the steady sound of the barge captain poling through the water, a rhythmic sort of splash as he pushed them forward. They moved slowly, and Alec tried not to think about the fact that they were heading toward a spawning ground for eels.

"How is it that you know of this?" he asked Bastan.

The older man stood next to him at the railing, staring

out over the swamp. He had been mostly silent since they'd started out. "Your father."

"My father wouldn't have shared, not if he knew."

"No. I don't think he intended to share, but—"

"You followed him."

"He was an unknown, much like you are. I wanted to ensure that the price I paid was worthwhile, and that he was completing the task that we set for him. Other than that, he has proven completely trustworthy. Had he not, I wouldn't be here with you now."

"Even if it meant helping the others?"

"The others mean nothing to me."

"None of them? Not even Kevin?"

Bastan breathed out heavily. It was the most frustration that Alec had seen from him. "Well. Perhaps for Kevin I would have brought you here. Not for any of the others."

"You would have just let them die?"

"We don't know that they would have died. All we know is that they're immobile."

"Immobile? We have a word for it at the university. Those who study such things call this comatose."

"And how many at the university study such things?"

"Not enough. Not nearly enough." Had there been others, Alec would have had someone he could have gone to, but there wasn't, and he didn't.

"I followed your father when he left the city. He took a small skiff, not a full barge like this. And he navigated himself."

"My father had access to a skiff?"

"I wasn't able to determine whose it was, only that

your father used it. He is… resourceful."

"There is much about my father that I haven't known."

"There is a thicket of reeds not too far from here," Bastan said. "That's where we're heading."

"And when we get there?"

"Then we go fishing."

Even when they caught the eels, Alec wasn't sure what they would be able to do with them. How was the venom extracted? His father must've had some technique, but Alec wasn't privy to it. Had he thought about it, he might have gone to the apothecary and searched through his father's notes.

"Did you see how he withdrew the venom?"

Bastan shook his head. "No. We've attempted to capture a few eels to see if we could do it ourselves, but we've never found a way. I was hopeful that with your knowledge…"

"So that's it. That's why you revealed this secret to me?"

"There is a price to knowledge," Bastan said. "Your price is that you need to share with me. Mine is that I had to reveal to you something I would otherwise choose not to. I consider it a fair bargain. If you feel otherwise, we can turn back, and I will deposit you back near the university where you can continue to watch your father fade."

"No. Let's keep moving."

Bastan nodded.

The barge traveled onward, turning away from the city as it went, heading deeper and deeper into the swamp. He thought about how Sam had used her canal staff to come out into the swamp. He couldn't imagine how she had done it. How was she able to come this way without a barge—or even a skiff as his father had traveled?

It was late when the captain brought the barge to a stop. Much as Bastan had claimed, there was a thicket of reeds, all growing densely together. Alec doubted he would have been able to find it on his own and was impressed that Bastan had managed, though he suspected it was more about the captain than about anything Bastan had done.

"Here?" he asked.

"Now we fish," Bastan said.

Fishing turned out to be nothing more than setting out nets and sweeping them through the water. It was nothing like fishing as he would have expected. Then again, Alec had never known anyone who actually tried to capture one of the eels. Why would they?

It took nearly thirty minutes before they caught anything.

"Pull it in," one of the men with them said urgently. He was a large man, but he spoke rapidly, and there was tension in his voice. It seemed as if he wanted nothing to do with the eel.

"It's moving too much," one of the others said.

"Doesn't matter. Pull it in."

As they started to pull, one of the men slipped.

"Kyza!" the smaller of the two said, reaching for the other. The man pin-wheeled as he started to fall off the edge of the barge.

With a loud splash that disrupted the quiet of the

night, he fell in.

"Grab him," Bastan roared.

The other men on the deck hurried over to him and yanked on his shirt, pulling him up.

"Hurry!" the man said. "I can feel something on me."

Alec started forward, wanting to do anything he could to help, but he stepped in a puddle of water and slipped, falling backward. He landed hard and winced.

By the time he managed to stand again, the other man had been pulled back onto the barge. Bastan glanced over at Alec before waving him over. "Is he injured?"

Alec tried to shake off the pain from his fall and scanned the man. He was lying on the deck, soaked and lying in a growing puddle of the pungent swamp water, but he saw no sign of injury.

"I'm fine," the man said. "I felt something near my leg…"

Alec turned his attention to the man's leg. There were parts of the fabric of his pants that were missing, almost as if chewed through, but the skin was unharmed.

"He's…"

Alec frowned. That wasn't entirely true. There were two puncture marks on the man's leg. With better lighting, he would not have missed them, but he almost had.

"What is it?" Bastan asked as he crouched next to Alec.

"Do you see those?" Alec pointed to the puncture marks.

"I see two small points of blood. Puncture wounds."

Alec ran his hand along the man's leg and felt a slight ridging, possible swelling.

It formed a half circle, and he could make out the

outline of the eel's teeth.

"Is that it? Did he get me?"

Bastan looked over at Alec, who nodded once. "You were bit," Bastan said. "But seeing as how you're still alive, I don't know how much to make of it."

"I got lucky," the man said, sitting up.

"Tanis, I don't know that anyone would ever call you lucky," the large man said.

Tanis grunted and pulled up his pant leg, looking at the injury. He stared at the chewed fabric for a moment before he examined the flesh of his leg, running his hand over it much the same way that Alec had. "That's it?"

"We must've pulled you free before the creature had a chance to fully clamp on," Bastan said.

"It felt like it was trying to tear my leg off," Tanis said.

Alec frowned. If they were after eel venom, where would the creature have it? Many animals had venom in their fangs. There were plenty of snakes that were milked for their venom, though that venom had beneficial characteristics. Especially the choran snake. They were found in the deeper areas of the canals, and they were rare, but when they were able to be caught, the venom was used to create a high-quality anesthetic.

If not the teeth, then what?

Unless the eel had to intentionally inject the venom.

"What is it?" Bastan asked.

"It's him. We have to assume a bite is how the eel injects its venom. We should have seen it working on him by now. There's no mistaking the fact that he was bitten."

"We don't know that it was an eel," Bastan said.

That was true. "I thought you said this was a breeding

ground."

"It is a breeding ground."

"Maybe that's it," Alec said.

"What?"

Alec shrugged. "There are some animals that don't have the same toxicity when immature. Maybe the youngest of the eels don't carry venom."

He looked over at Tanis. How large would that eel's mouth need to have been to have made a mark like that? It seemed as if it would have been a sizable creature, but Alec didn't know enough—or anything, really—about eels, so he had no way to determine if it was an immature eel.

That left the other possibility that there was something else in the swamp that had attacked him, and either wasn't poisonous, or it had chosen not to harm Tanis.

"Let's get back at it," Bastan said.

Tanis and the other man had gotten to their feet, and they grabbed the net, tossing it back into the water. "This time, you're going to be the one who goes in," Tanis said.

"Let's not have anyone go in," Bastan said.

Tanis looked back with a smile. "Well, if someone has to go in, at least let it be him. I already had my shot and gave them a little snack. We can let Orbal be the one to give them the next snack."

Orbal shook his head. "How about no one is a snack this time?"

They turned their attention back to holding on to the net, sweeping it through the water with steady slow strokes.

Alec started drifting off as he watched, waiting. His

mind wandered, thinking about what Sam might be doing and wondering what Master Helen had meant when she said Sam was preoccupied with some assignment.

He needed to get to her so he could tell her what had been happening, especially what had happened to his father and now Kevin and Beckah. She probably wouldn't have a whole lot of sympathy for Beckah, since Sam had a strange sort of jealousy regarding Beckah that Alec didn't fully understand.

He lost track of time. It could have been minutes or hours before the men began talking excitedly.

"We got one," Tanis said.

They both jerked, pulling on the net, but whatever was within it fought, threatening to pull them into the water. The barge moved with it, and the captain used the pole to resist, trying to hold them in place.

"This one is a fighter," Orbal said.

"Stay with it," Bastan said.

"Just make sure we don't go in," Tanis said.

"You won't go in if you keep pulling on it," Bastan said.

The two men heaved on the net and finally managed to drag it onto the barge. Alec stayed back, giving them space, not wanting to be too close to whatever they had caught.

When they tossed it onto the deck, foul-smelling water streamed away.

There was a thumping as the eel attempted to escape.

"Hold it down," Bastan said.

"With what?" Tanis asked.

"With your hands," Bastan said.

"Hands?" Alec asked. "If they get bit—"

"Then stay away from its mouth," Bastan said without looking over at Alec.

Tanis lunged forward, surprising considering he'd already been attacked, though he probably felt that he'd survived one attack so another wouldn't be nearly as bad. He threw himself on top of the eel, spreading his hands out so he could flatten it onto the deck. The creature continued to thrash.

"It's too slick!" Tanis said.

"You could try spearing it," Alec said, watching with a horrid sort of fascination. The eel continued to try to twist its mouth around and bite, forcing Tanis to release his grip and shift, using the netting to hold the eel down.

"I thought we didn't want to kill it." Bastan glanced over at him.

"If you spear it along the body, and you keep away from the vital organs, it's possible that you won't kill it, and might be able to hold it in place so that we can study it."

Bastan glanced over at the captain, and the man only shrugged. He turned and disappeared into the cabin of the barge before returning with a long, slender pole that reminded Alec of Sam's canal staff. The end of it was sharpened, and the captain handed it to Bastan who shook his head.

"Not me. Him."

He indicated Alec.

"Me? I don't think I'm the right person for this—"

"You're the one who had the idea."

Alec took the spear and held it. It was not as heavy as Sam's canal staff. At least if this failed and the eel died, there was the possibility that they could capture another one. It'd only taken thirty or so minutes to capture this one, but he would rather it not come to that.

He approached carefully. Tanis got to his knees and started to shift away.

"Get it before this one gets me too, Kyza claim you. I already have one bite on my leg, I don't need a matching one."

The eel snapped.

It happened quickly—far too quickly—and the creature sank its teeth into the man's arm, and surprisingly, swung its pointed tail at the same time, poking into Tanis's stomach.

He grunted and stopped moving.

Bastan grabbed him and tossed him back. "Spear the damned creature!"

Alec stabbed down with the spear, catching the eel in the middle of its body. He pinned it to the deck, and it thrashed against the spear, but held in that way, it couldn't go anywhere.

"Hold this," he said to Orbal.

When the man grabbed the spear, Alec hurried over to Tanis. He looked at the arm wound. It was a bite, not much different from the one on his leg. Skin was torn, but the wound was deeper than the one that had punctured his leg, and though blood poured from it, there was nothing remarkable about it.

Alec turned to the place in the man's stomach where he'd been punctured by the tail. The flesh around it was already starting to blacken.

That was the poison.

What was the purpose of the bite?

Alec looked down at the eel. It was long and slender, with a massive head and an enormous jaw filled with double rows of super-sharp teeth. The creature had eyes that were black as night, and it watched him, almost as if trying to gauge how it would snap free from the spear through his body. The creature's lower half was long and slender, and ended in a barbed tail.

How had he never known that before?

There was probably quite a bit that no one knew about canal eels.

Sam had shared with him how they had bitten her staff when she attempted to come through the swamp. It was possible the bite was little more than a diversion, a way of holding its prey as it punctured it with the tail.

"That's it," he said in a whisper.

"What's it?" Bastan asked, looking up from where he still knelt beside Tanis. He held the man's hand and squeezed as he lay there unmoving.

Alec returned to examine Tanis. He checked his pulse, and it was already starting to slow. Now, it was slow enough that he wouldn't be surprised if his heart stopped. Without any supplies, Alec didn't think there was anything he could do, and even if he had supplies, there might not have been anything for him to do. The blackening around the man's stomach had continued and had now worked up into his chest.

There was nothing they would be able to do to save him.

"Alec?" When he didn't answer, Bastan grabbed him by the arm. "Physicker Stross."

Alec shook himself. "The tail. That's where the poison is."

"The tail?" Bastan asked, looking over at the eel.

Alec nodded. "The bite isn't contaminated. Look at it. The skin is macerated, but it would be painful, nothing else. Certainly not enough to kill him." And not an arm wound, not like that. There were plenty of animals whose bite wounds could kill someone, but one like this would only maim a person. "But look at where the tail punctured him."

Bastan turned his attention to the belly wound, and his eyes widened as he stared at the blackening around the wound that continued to spread. "That?"

"Look at the tail, Bastan," Alec said.

"It's spiked."

"Barbed. I know of other animals with barbed tails, some poisonous, some not. The first bite clearly had no effect, and there is no sign of poison at the site. The second time, the eel nearly chewed through his arm, but no blackening, like where the tail impaled his abdomen. It's whatever the eel has in its tail. That's the key."

"You don't have to seem so excited about it," Orbal said, leaning over Tanis.

Alec shook his head. "I'm not excited. Please don't think that I am. If there were anything we could do to help him—"

"Then you need to do it," Bastan said.

"Bastan, there's nothing I can do—"

"Nothing? I seem to recall a specific technique you and Samara have. We are here for all of us. Now, do you have that capacity to help him or not?"

198 | D.K. HOLMBERG

Alec breathed out. He shouldn't resist, especially since Bastan was right, and they were here for both him and for Bastan. He could help, couldn't he?

"I need to have some privacy," he whispered.

"Where? We're in the middle of a swamp."

His gaze drifted to the captain and then to Orbal.

Bastan chuckled. "They won't say anything. They work for me."

"Are you sure that's enough?"

"Are you sure I won't push you into the swamp?"

"You won't do that."

"If you don't even try to help this man, I certainly will."

The threat in his tone was crystal clear.

Alec patted his pocket, feeling for the easar paper. He had only a scrap with him, not much, but enough that he thought he could provide some help. Hopefully, the vial of both his and Sam's blood was fresh enough and hadn't fully dried up.

There were steps he took to ensure it didn't, but they only lasted so long. He pulled it out of his pocket and looked for something he could use to write, but there was nothing. He couldn't ask Bastan or the captain for fear of bringing attention to what he was doing.

That left only his finger.

It took more of the paper when he used his finger as he couldn't write nearly as tightly as he would otherwise, but Bastan was right. He needed to do something to help Tanis.

And in this instance, he knew exactly what had happened, which meant he should be able to counter the effect.

Puncture wound to the abdomen. Poisoned with eel venom. Rapid onset of necrosis. Concentrated bardl leaves, hyph oil, and verr would help counteract the necrosis.

Alec frowned. That would only counteract the necrosis, but what could he do to counteract the venom?

Antivenom needed to counteract the effect of the eel toxicity. Maceration to the arm should be sutured.

He added the last quickly, knowing that it mattered not nearly as much, but he felt better doing so. Alec waited, and when a slow wash of cold went over him, he was hopeful that he had been successful.

He capped the vial of blood and put it, along with the easar paper, back into his pocket. Then he approached Tanis, looking to see if anything had changed for him.

"If it's going to work, we should see an effect soon."

Bastan nodded at him and continued to hold Tanis's hand.

As Alec stared at the man's stomach, the black lines of necrosis began to fade. At least that much had been effective. That was more straightforward, using a combination of medicines that he knew could work on necrosis. The other part was less certain. He didn't know whether there was an eel antivenom or not. He assumed there was—at least, he assumed there must be, considering what Ryn used—but he hoped the magic of the easar paper didn't rely upon that.

Long moments passed before Tanis took a gasping breath.

"What happened?" Tanis asked, turning to look at Bastan.

Bastan grunted and released his hand. "Nothing more

than you got bit again."

"Again? I always knew I was tasty, but this is a little ridiculous. Where?"

Bastan nodded toward Tanis's arm. "Your arm," Bastan said.

Tanis held his arm up, but the wound had healed, leaving nothing more than a long scar. Tanis frowned at it. "How…"

Bastan looked up at Alec, and Alec realized he had made a mistake. He shouldn't have attempted to restore Tanis's arm along with everything else. The injury was deep, but it would have healed over time. It would have invited fewer questions had he simply left it.

"Maybe you weren't bit nearly as bad as I thought," Bastan said.

Tanis grunted, and he shivered. "I feel… I feel like I just got in a fight."

"Be thankful that's all you feel," Bastan said.

"What are we going to do with this?" Orbal asked.

Alec shook himself, remembering the eel remained pinned to the deck. It continued to thrash against the spear, its tail flailing as it tried to strike anything.

"We need the tail," Alec said.

"How much of the tale?" Bastan asked.

"I don't know. Maybe all of it."

Bastan stood and unsheathed his sword, and in one fluid movement, he sliced the head of the eel clean off.

The thrashing continued for a moment more before all movement stopped.

"Now, Physicker Stross, let's see how much your father has taught you."

19

DISSECTION

It was strange sitting in the apothecary without his father. Even stranger still was the knowledge that his father wouldn't be able to return unless Alec was successful with finding a cure. Usually, his father was the one who would be responsible for finding the cure. Now, it was all up to Alec.

A single lantern glowed on the table, giving a flickering light. He sat alone in the shop, the stench from the eel cloying in his nostrils. He picked at the flayed-open body, searching for a gland that might contain the venom. He worked carefully, the surgical skills that he had acquired with Master Eckerd coming into play. What would Master Eckerd have thought had he known that Alec would use these skills in this way?

He probably wouldn't have said anything. It had been weeks since he'd had any sort of conversation with Master Eckerd, even longer since he'd had a chance to spend time with him in the surgical suite. Now that he was a full physicker, would he even have those chances again?

Did he even want to?

Alec had some skill in surgery, but it wasn't his passion. He much preferred thinking through and making the diagnosis and coming up with a treatment plan rather than cutting through flesh.

The eel anatomy was interesting. A long, bony spine ran the entire length of its back, ending in the barb at the tail. That seemed to grow out of the spine, a part of it. Alec had carefully cut the barb free and found that it was hollow. He traced back from it, looking for where the venom would pulse out from.

For a long time, he found nothing. Alec had to remove the entrails, discarding the intestine into a bucket that would need to be burned later. He wanted no evidence of the fact that he had dissected a canal eel within his father's shop. He carefully extracted the spine also, wanting to have full access to the inside of the eel. He identified the heart and the stomach, and was not surprised to find a few small fish partially digested within it.

Where would the venom sack be?

There was only one spongy section of tissue that Alec hadn't identified. It was near the rear of the eel, but it wasn't as spongy as what he would've expected for a fluid-filled sac.

Working carefully, he cut into the spongy tissue.

Yellowish fluid seeped out.

Alec froze. That was it.

How would he collect it?

He cut the spongy tissue free and placed it in a shallow

metal bowl. Somehow, he needed to extract all of the venom, at least as much as he could. He had been expecting a fluid-filled sac, but this was something else entirely.

Alec worked carefully, squeezing out as much of the yellowish fluid as he could. He collected it in the bowl and then poured it into a metal canister. He chose not to use a glass canister, not wanting to risk the possibility that it might break.

With that canister full and secure, he moved on to the next eel.

They had captured five. After the fifth, Alec had told them he thought that would be enough. He wanted to allow for some margin of error, especially since he hadn't been able to find the venom sac during his initial inspection on the barge, but that didn't seem to be the issue any longer. It was a slow and tedious process, despite the fact that he now knew where to find the sac. Now all that was left was for him to test it.

But what would he test it on?

Alec didn't have the experience his father had with experimentation, but he'd watched him a number of times over the years. He needed a test subject that he could try the venom on to ensure that it worked. When he did, then he could start looking for an anti-venom to counter it. He wasn't sure what that would be, but the fact that he had been able to document it on the easar paper told him that an anti-venom existed.

Alec stared at the pile of eel tails, or what was left of them after his dissection. But he hadn't looked at the heads yet. Bastan had been nearly surgical with how he removed the heads, slicing them cleanly free, killing the eel quickly.

He had only bothered to bring back a few of those. The rest had gone back into the water.

Alec set one of the eel heads on a tray. Even in death, the black, beady eyes seemed to stare at him. There was something almost unnatural about these creatures. It had a terrifying-looking mouth. Using the knife, he pried it open as wide as he could. It had rows of razor-sharp teeth with two incisors that were long and pointed at the sides of the mouth.

A drop of milky water dripped from one of the incisors.

That was strange. The heads had dried out since retrieving them, so it couldn't be from the canals.

Unless… It wasn't water.

Could he have missed something? Alec had assumed that the yellowish substance he'd extracted from the spongy sac was the venom, and that still seemed likely, but maybe there was something else.

He carved along the creature's skull, carefully peeling back the flesh. On either side of the long fangs, he found two small sacs.

Alec's breath caught.

Could he extract these?

Doing so would be difficult, especially since he didn't have the appropriate instruments. His father didn't keep surgical instruments at the apothecary, since he wasn't a surgeon. He slowly cut the flesh away, leaving only the sac attached to the fang. Once it was done, he tipped the head upside down over another shallow bowl and made a small puncture in it, just enough to let the fluid leak out into the bowl.

It was milky, the same as what he had seen drip from the incisor.

This was not likely to be the venom. Alec remained convinced that the venom was the yellowish fluid that he'd take from the other sac . That meant this was something else.

But what could it be? What would its purpose be?

He made delicate work of doing the same thing with the remaining eel heads that he had.

When he was done, he sat back, staring at the bowl. He needed some way of experimenting with it, but on what?

Maybe Bastan would have the answer.

Alec grabbed the canister of the yellowish extract and stuffed it into his pocket. He then took bowl that held the small amount of milky fluid he'd collected from the tooth sacs and poured it into a smaller canister, covering it to ensure that the work he had done would not go to waste. He left the apothecary and made his way toward Caster. It was late, and Alec knew he should wait until morning to go for Bastan, but he needed answers now. He wanted to understand the purpose of these fluids. One was the venom—he was certain of that—but what was the other?

Maybe it was nothing significant. Or maybe it was the key to understanding what had happened to his father and others. If he could understand the way the fluids from the eels were used, maybe he could finally figure out how to help these people recover.

When he crossed over the canal leading to Caster, he got that feeling again that someone was watching him.

Alec hurried forward. He didn't like the sense of someone following him, certainly not here in a section of the city that he knew to be dangerous. He hurried forward and occasionally cast a look over his shoulder, but saw nothing.

Alec hurried onward, keeping his hand over the jars in his pocket as he ran, racing toward Bastan's tavern.

When he turned a corner, there was an enormous man standing in front of him.

For a moment, he thought it was someone who worked for Bastan, but it wasn't anyone that Alec had seen before. Over the last few weeks, he'd been to Bastan's tavern often enough that he recognized many of the people who worked for the man, and this wasn't one of them.

"Physicker," the man said.

"I think you have the wrong person," Alec said.

"Oh, I don't think that I do."

"Can I help you?"

The man grunted, and he lunged for Alec.

He kicked, trying to get free, but the man was quick. He wasn't a Theln, but he was similar in his massive size and speed, but there was something else—the strange, awful odor that Alec attributed to the Thelns.

He hurriedly looked around him.

There was no one else here. Had he made a mistake coming at so late at night? He knew he should he have waited.

But then, he had been too eager. He wanted to share

with Bastan—and have the opportunity to test—but now he would be captured.

The man grabbed his cloak, and Alec tried to pull free, but he held on to it tightly.

Alec spun, pulling his arms out of the cloak, keeping the jars in his hand as he did. With his arms freed, he raced forward.

Two other individuals appeared at the other end of the street.

Alec skidded to a stop.

He couldn't be captured, and even more important, he couldn't be captured with the venoms. There may not be a way for him to get free, but there might be a way for him to ensure that he didn't sacrifice everything they had worked for.

It was possible for him to find more of the eels, but he feared he was running out of time.

Alec lunged for the nearest alley.

The figures chased him. The alley was long and dark, and there was no end to it. He would be trapped here.

He hurried to the end of the alley and carefully set down the two jars. Then, he spun to face his attackers.

The largest of them approached first. Alec should have taken more time to train with Sam. If he had, maybe he would been better able to evade them, and lose them in the streets, or maybe even if they did catch him, he would have been less injured.

"What do you want?"

"We are in need of a physicker," the nearest man said.

"There are plenty of physickers at the university."

"Ah, but we are not near the university. Besides, you are the physicker we need."

As the man approached, Alec understood. He had been targeted.

But why?

The man grabbed him, wrapping him up. Alec didn't even fight. There was no point in it. He cast one last look toward the wall where he'd set down the jars and hoped the natural darkness of the alley would conceal them. Somehow, he would have to get free and return to fetch them.

As he was dragged away, his only thought was that he hoped Bastan had been keeping an eye on this part of the city as he claimed he did. He hoped Bastan had been watching over him as he watched over so many others. If he didn't know and as a result sent no help, Alec wasn't sure he would be able to escape.

20

BACK TO CASTER

S am was exhausted when they returned to the city.
There had been another way back, a looping path
that led over higher ground, leaving the steam fields in
the distance. Every so often, there would be a burst of
steam nearby, and Sam jumped. She wasn't the only one
to do so. Marin's Scribe had jumped just as often as she
had, though the longer they went, the less he jumped. By
the time they returned to the city, everyone had gone
quiet, and Sam had abandoned attempts at using her
magic the way Marin described. She wasn't sure whether
it would even work and had not been able to replicate the
strange chill that had washed through her the one time
she had managed. That seemed more a fluke than
anything else.

"Where are you going?" Elaine asked Sam. They
entered the city through one of the southern sections, and
it wasn't one that Sam was all that familiar with, but from

here, she knew she could make her way to more familiar parts of the city.

"I think I've had just about enough of being around all of you," Sam said.

"We still need to return them to the palace."

"You mean *you* need to return them to the palace," Sam said. "Or, more likely, you intend to take them to the prison."

Elaine held her gaze. "Now isn't the time for this, Samara."

"You're probably right, but considering that Marin isn't able to escape, and that her Scribe doesn't seem able to do anything more than walk, I think you're okay."

"And where will you go?"

Sam looked around. "I don't know."

Elaine nodded to her. "We will confront her together."

"And what will that change? If it's true, then what if everything Marin has told me is also true?"

"I have the same questions."

"No, you have different questions than I do."

Elaine watched her for a while before nodding and turning away. Sam was thankful that she didn't continue to argue. She had half expected Elaine to force her back to the palace, and if she did, Sam wasn't sure she could refuse.

She needed to go to the university and see Alec, especially after what she'd learned. It felt like it had been ages since she'd seen him, rather than only a few weeks.

Sam wandered through darkened streets. She ignored the shadows of buildings on either side of her, not mindful of the people that were here. These were sections of the city that she didn't know nearly as well, but armed with her canal staff, she didn't fear someone catching her by surprise and jumping her. Maybe she should.

She wandered steadily toward the west, and it was late by the time she reached Caster.

Sam crossed the canal, barely thinking about it as she flipped over and landed on the other side. A group of men who had been loitering near the canal turned toward her, and she tapped her staff on the ground.

One of the men sneered at her. "Interesting trick you have there, girly," he said.

"Listen. I don't know who you are, but I'm not in the mood," Sam said.

"You don't come to Caster unless you're in the mood," the man said.

Sam breathed out in annoyance. She spun her staff and smacked him in the cheek, sending him flying back to his friends. The others turned toward her, and Sam flipped up, landing in the middle, wielding her staff around in a sweeping arc, taking out legs. She was rewarded with sharp snaps as bones broke, and she felt little remorse—and little satisfaction.

Everything fell silent. The battle was over, and she had knocked down five men with barely more than a second thought. She had no augmentations, nothing other than her canal staff.

"Leave girlies alone," she said to the man. When he tried to sit up, she thunked him in the head with the staff once more for good measure.

She made her way through the streets, and her steps brought her to Marin's house. There was no one there, not anymore. The building was nice—at least nice for Caster, and it had been a place where Sam had discovered more about herself. She stared at it, wishing answers could come more easily to her.

After a while, she turned away and headed along the street, keeping toward the edge of the buildings and generally off to the side, not wanting to draw too much attention. She didn't need to get into another fight, though if there was another group like the last, she wasn't opposed to teaching them manners.

When she reached Bastan's tavern, she hesitated only a moment before heading in. Once inside, she separated the two ends of her canal staff and tucked them beneath her cloak. She took a seat toward the back of the tavern and scanned the inside.

There was activity, and much more than was usual for Bastan. It was too early for him to have this many people here.

The door to the kitchen opened and a familiar face poked out, carrying a tray. When he saw her, James angled her way and took a seat across from her. Where was Kevin? James was fine, but she was much more comfortable with Kevin. "I haven't seen you here in… Well, in a long time."

"Yeah, I've been busy."

"That's what Bastan says." James watched her for a moment. "What happened? You seem as if you lost someone."

Sam shook her head. "I don't know that I lost someone so much as I lost faith in someone. My mother," she said.

James grunted. "You know, sometimes, parents do

things that we don't understand until later. They think it's in our best interest, but little do they know that sometimes, our best interest is keeping an eye on us and saying nothing."

"No, I don't think this was her acting in my best interest."

"No? Well, I'll get Bastan." He stood and made his way toward the back of the tavern.

"James?" James paused and turned. Normally, she wouldn't hesitate, but then normally, it was Kevin here. "Would you... Would you have any food?"

A slow smile spread across his face. "For you? Of course, I would."

He disappeared into Bastan's private office before reappearing and heading to the kitchen. Sam didn't have to wait long before he brought out a tray of food and set in front of her. It was roast with vegetables and what appeared to be fresh bread. Everything smelled delicious, and Sam barely paused before digging in. "I have coins," she said between bites.

"I'm pretty sure Bastan would throw me out if I tried to charge you."

"Bastan only wants his money."

"Not from you."

James tapped the table and turned away, leaving Sam to her food. She ate in silence. Her mind raced as she tried to think through everything that she had seen and experienced, but she had a hard time processing it. Her mind felt a blur, and everything seemed to buzz within it.

"I'm glad to see you. There's something I might need

your help with…" Bastan stood in front of her before taking a seat across from her. "Something happened?"

"I found Marin."

"I get the sense that you finding Marin wasn't so good for you." Bastan leaned forward. "Did she hurt you?"

"Not the way that I thought she would."

"And what way was it?" Bastan asked.

"She… She explained why she did the things she did."

"The way you say that tells me there's something to it that bothers you."

"Of course there is. I thought when I found my mother, everything would be better for me."

"And it's not?" Bastan rested his arms on the table and watched her. There was concern in his eyes, the kind of concern that Sam had grown accustomed to seeing from him, though she didn't know what to make of it. Bastan cared for her, and he might be the only one who had been straight with her for as long as she'd known him. He'd wanted her to do jobs, but that was it. He had never asked her to do anything else, and he had never treated her as anything other than a thief, the type of thief that he had trained her to become.

"It's not. My mother—Elaine—hasn't provided me with the answers I was hoping she would. And everything that I've learned has only led me to more questions."

"What kind of questions?"

"The kind that has me wondering if I've been doing the right thing."

Bastan sighed. "I'm not sure any of us can say we're doing the right thing."

"You sure can't," she said with a laugh.

"I do what I can to run my business. I take care of those who work for me, and I look out for them. Sometimes, I'm the only one who does. I do my best to ensure that this section stays as safe as I can make it. Now, Caster is never going to be like one of the inner sections, and we're never going to have highborns coming in here and throwing around money, but Caster is much safer than it could be if I wasn't here."

"I know, Bastan. I didn't mean to imply that—"

He raised his hands, holding them out from him. "I'm not worried about what you imply, Samara. I just want you to know that some people work because they are after a certain thing. I've known plenty of people in my day who wanted only power. When I was younger, that was all I cared about. I thought if I could gain enough power, I would be able to make good money, so I could make a move on one of the highborn sections. After a while, I came to realize that it wasn't money and power that I cared about but the ability to protect those who were important to me." He leaned forward. "Have you ever wondered why I've never made a move beyond Caster?"

"You have contacts all over the city, Bastan."

"Contacts doesn't mean that I'm attempting to move beyond my section. And I have no problem having influence outside of our section. That influence is what keeps everyone else safe. Kyza knows that the damn royals aren't about to keep us safe."

"Probably because they don't have the necessary resources," Sam said in between bites.

Bastan watched her, a smile coming to his face.

"Resources. Oh, I'm sure that's the reason they don't venture this far out. It's not that we create something of a buffer."

"What kind of buffer?"

"The kind that doesn't matter, Samara. These sections are expendable, at least in the minds of highborns. None of them would care if we fell apart. If the city were to fall, it would do so section by section, giving the highborns a chance to escape."

"They can't escape, they're in the center of the city."

"They only want you to think they're in the center of the city. Think about the palace. It's situated near enough to the river for easy access out of the city. All it would take would be a skilled captain to guide them to freedom."

Sam frowned. It wasn't the palace that was at the center or nearest the river, it was the university.

She kept hearing that the Scribes had power similar to that which the Thelns possessed, but Sam had never given it much thought beyond that. What did it mean that they shared similar power?

"I'm sorry that you had a bad experience with your mother."

"The worst part of it is that I've been blaming Marin, and I'm not sure I should have been."

"I thought Marin was responsible for what happened to you when you were young."

Sam hadn't told him all that much about it other than to let him know that Marin was responsible for her lack of memories, but Bastan must have looked into it on his own. That didn't surprise her. "As far as I know, she was. But she did it because of an assignment she'd been given."

"What assignment would make her think that it was okay to steal a child's memories?"

"The same assignment that was given to her where she was told to kill a child."

His eyes widened. "You?"

Sam shook her head.

"Tray," he quickly guessed. "Then why were you involved?"

"Because she blames my mother. She presumed Elaine knew about the assignment and thought that Elaine should have known better, or maybe she was acting out of malice." Sam shrugged. "I don't really know. And at this point, I don't know that it even matters. All I do know is that Marin is the reason Tray is still alive, at least if I believe her."

"With the way you're moping here, it seems as if you do."

"I have no reason not to. That's just the problem."

"And the person who gave the order?"

"Someone who should have known better."

Bastan stared at her. He didn't press her for more information, and he didn't try to get her to open up about anything else. He simply stared, compassion in his eyes. "What do you intend to do?"

"That's the question, isn't it? If I continue to serve the way that I have, I am somehow complicit."

"I doubt that."

"Even if I know and still choose to serve?"

"People aren't all good or all bad," Bastan said. "Everyone has shades of gray." He leaned back and smiled. "I mean, look at me. I'm sure plenty of people think that

I'm no good, but it's not as if I don't care about those working for me."

"Bastan, I don't think you conceal that nearly as well as you think you do."

He chuckled. "No, I suppose that's probably true. And I'm not sure that I want to conceal it. I want to the people who work for me to know that I've got them. That I will do everything I can to protect them."

Sam still couldn't believe that she had once thought that Bastan only wanted to use her. Either he had hid it well from her or she had simply been oblivious to the fact that he cared more for her than he had ever let on.

"I don't know what to do," she said.

"I've had that same experience many times in my life," Bastan said. He looked around the tavern, and his gaze drifted over all the people that worked with him. Sam couldn't recognize all of them, but she detected enough that she knew there were plenty of people here who served Bastan. Most did so because of the safety he offered. More than a few wanted the financial benefit— Bastan made it very clear that he paid well and had decades of having done just that to back up his claim—but some, like Kevin, wanted nothing more than to be a part of something. It was the same thing Sam felt, and it was what she had thought she was getting through her training as a Kaver. "What you need to do is take a step back and look at who you are and what's important to you."

"That's just it. What's important to me is—or has been —Tray. And now I don't even know what to make of it. If he's not my brother, I don't know that I have the same purpose."

"Why do you let them tell you who is or isn't your brother?"

"Bastan, I was coerced into believing that Tray was my brother. I know that we aren't the same."

Bastan stared at her for a long moment. "Have I ever told you about my brother?"

"You keep your personal information pretty close to the vest," she said.

"Mostly because there are others who would think to use it against me."

Sam chuckled. She had a similar experience.

"Well, my brother and I were raised in the Haver section, and we—"

"Haver? That section is highborn, Bastan."

"Is it? It's more centrally located than Caster, but I'm not sure I would consider Haver highborn. Anyway, we couldn't be any more different if we tried. My brother and I have never gotten along. When I started having success with my business dealings, I tried to bring him in, but he wanted nothing to do with it. At one point, I suspected him of reporting me, and it took more than a little influence for me to avoid that reporting."

Sam smiled widely. "Influence?"

"I deal in influence. It's not as if you don't know that."

"And by influence, I presume you are talking about how much you had to bribe someone."

"There's only one type of influence that matters in the city, Samara. All most people care about is how much money they have."

220 | D.K. HOLMBERG

"You're not that different," she said.

"I'm different in that my influence is all about getting enough money so that I can keep my business dealings safe."

"Bastan, it's not all about money with you. I've seen you willing to use violence to get the outcome you want."

"What can I say? I have to protect my people and my business dealings."

"So, what happened?" Sam asked.

Bastan frowned. "What do you mean, what happened?"

"What happened with your brother?"

"Ah. Well, with him, I had to cut off communication. I haven't seen or spoken to him in the last ten years. I don't even know what's happened to him."

Sam laughed, shaking her head. "I don't even understand the point of the story, Bastan."

"The point is that even your blood relatives may disappoint you. You're born into a family, but that doesn't mean that it has to be the family you choose. Think about it and decide who will be in your family. Who has your back when things get dicey? That's the family that matters."

He fell silent, and Sam looked up at him. "There was something you were going to tell me about when I first got here. What was it?"

Bastan shook his head. "I'm not sure it matters."

"Bastan…"

"Go find that friend of yours. Sounds like you haven't seen him in a while."

"What's that supposed to mean?"

"Just do it, Samara, all right?"

Bastan tapped the table and stood, scanning the tavern again.

"I want you to know that I got a place for you," Bastan said. "With me, I'll always have a place for you."

He turned away, leaving her with her tray of food and sitting silently.

What would she do?

The answer was there, but it was one that left her feeling uncomfortable. And it was one that she wasn't sure she could do on her own. Could she confront the princess without augmentations? Did she dare even attempt it?

If she didn't confront her at all, did it mean the princess would get away with everything that she'd done?

Sam hated that idea almost as much as anything else. More than anything, she wanted to know whether the princess was responsible for what Marin had claimed. She needed to confront her, if only to have those answers.

When she did, she had to be prepared for the possibility that Elaine would challenge her. Sam didn't know if she was ready to face her mother. But, if what Marin said was true, did she have any choice but to do that?

SEARCH FOR ALEC

The atmosphere inside the palace was somber. Sam thought maybe it was only imagined, and that maybe she was perceiving something that wasn't there, but maybe not. There were no guards. More surprisingly, there were no Kavers.

Had something happened?

Then again, it was early morning. She had spent most of the night outside of the palace and had remained in Caster far longer than she normally would have. Bastan had not returned, though Sam would have liked it if he had. As frustrating as he could be, there was just something about Bastan that made her feel comforted. Maybe that was his point. He was the family that she had. Despite everything else, and despite all of the tasks that he had assigned her, Bastan was one person who had always been there for her. He was her family.

Sam hesitated as she made her way toward Elaine's quarters. There wasn't anything there that would be helpful, not without her understanding exactly what Lyasanna had done. And wasn't that the reason she had returned to the palace? She had come for answers, which meant that she had to reach Lyasanna and confront her.

Sam change direction and headed toward the Anders section of the palace. Sam climbed the stairs, keeping her hand resting on the separated end of her staff. When she reached the level, she turned the corner, storming along the hallway, and came face-to-face with Master Helen. "Samara. It was my understanding that you were out with Elaine on an assignment."

"I was. We're back."

"Back? Did Elaine happen to complete her objective?"

"Objective?"

Master Helen shrugged slightly. "From what I understand, you left the city with a particular objective?"

"I would say that we left with that objective," she said.

Master Helen watched her for a long moment. Sam was left with a slightly unsettled feeling. She'd never felt that way with Master Helen before, especially as the woman had been assigned to help her work through her amnesia, but the woman watched her now with a strange sort of inquisitive gaze.

"Where is Elaine?"

"I don't know. I left her when we returned to the city."

"You left?"

"I did. Why does it matter? I wasn't raised in the palace, and there are other parts of the city that are just as much home to me."

Master Helen studied her for another moment before grabbing her arm and pulling her away, guiding her down the hall and away from the Anders section. When they were down the stairs, Sam tried pulling free, but Master Helen had a strong grip—much stronger than she would have expected.

"What are you doing? Why are you taking me away from here?"

Master Helen shook her head. "Not now. Not here."

She guided her free of the palace and over to the bridge. Sam didn't feel threatened—not really. She felt confident she could escape at any point if she needed to, and curiosity kept her from attempting to pry herself free.

"Why are you taking me to the university?" Sam asked.

"How long has it been since you saw your Scribe?"

"A few weeks. Why?"

"You need to speak with him. There has been a development."

"A development? First you asked me about an objective, and then you talk to me about a development? Why speak in such coded terms?"

Master Helen paused at the door leading into the university. "There are some things that those within the palace aren't aware of," Master Helen said.

Sam frowned. "Such as… Wait. Lyasanna didn't know where Elaine went?"

"Lyasanna sent others on a specific task to destroy a particular objective. Elaine had a different approach in mind."

That told Sam that Lyasanna assigned others with the task of killing Marin. Likely to silence her. It also meant that Elaine had defied Lyasanna's orders and gone after Marin herself.

Sam considered Master Helen for a long moment. "Do you know?"

Master Helen frowned. "Know?"

Maybe that was too much to hope for. She needed an ally, and she wasn't sure if Master Helen was going to be that ally. But maybe Master Helen would be the one to help her get back to Alec. Maybe she would help her have a chance to be better connected to him.

Once inside the university, Sam looked around, feeling the strangely unsettled feeling that she had each time she came here. How was it that Alec felt so comfortable here? This wasn't a place that she could ever stay, not for long.

"Why are you bringing me here?"

"Because your Scribe needs you," she said.

"Why does Alec need me?"

Sam followed Master Helen as they made their way through the university. She was curious now, though she wanted mostly to get back to the palace to find out what Elaine had done with Marin. Her mother clearly still believed Lyasanna, so she would have likely taken Marin right to her, or at least told the princess of her capture. But then what? Would the princess have her death sentence for Marin carried out in order to keep hidden the fact that she had ordered Tray's death all those years ago?

"Master Helen, I know that Alec might need me, but there are other things that need my attention."

"Such as you going after your brother?"

"I haven't gone after him, not yet. But I intend to." More than ever, she felt she needed to go after Tray.

"That can wait, this… This is a more pressing matter."

As they continued down the hall, Sam realized where they were. When they reached a set of doors, Master Helen pushed them open and they entered the hospital ward. Sam had been here once before, when Beckah had brought her here to try to identify Marin's Scribe by his voice.

The medicinal odor assaulted her nose. She remembered it from before, but it seemed somehow worse the time.

"Did something happen to Alec?"

"No. Alec is fine. It's—"

Sam's breath caught. "His father," she said, hurrying over to the cot occupied by Alec's father.

He looked almost as if he were asleep, but he didn't move. Sam touched his shoulder, and tried to shake him, but there was no reaction.

"He won't wake up," Master Helen said. "Whatever has been done to him prevents him from awakening."

"And what is it? What happened to him?"

"We aren't sure."

"Alec knows his father's here?" Sam asked, looking up at Master Helen.

"He knows, and he has been part of the search for answers, but there are no answers, not yet."

"How long has he been like this?" Could Alec have needed her, and she hadn't been there? Everything she had been through made her wonder whether she should have come to find Alec first, long before going with Elaine in search of Marin. If Alec had needed her, and she hadn't been there, was she now responsible for the fact that his father was like this?

"He's been like this for a little while. He is not the only one."

"How many others?"

"There are now three."

"Three?" She looked around the room, but she didn't have the same appraising eye that Alec had for determining whether people were injured. He was able to take a single look at someone and make a diagnosis, which was something that Sam often wished she shared with him. Instead, what was she good at? She could fight, and she had proven that she had the ability to do some other things, but there were times when she thought what Alec was able to do—his knowledge and skill set—were more impressive than what she was able to do with her Kaver abilities.

"Come with me," Master Helen said.

She guided Sam to another cot, and she looked down, realizing that she recognized the person lying there.

"Beckah?"

"She was with Alec when this happened."

"Was he… Was he harmed?"

"I told you, Alec is unharmed."

"Where is he?"

Master Helen frowned. "He has been here fairly diligently the last few days, especially since his father came. And then when Beckah was afflicted, he remained here, unwilling to leave. I'm surprised that he is not here now."

"All of this is strange," Sam said.

"There is something else," Master Helen said.

"What is it?"

"I think that it is somehow tied to a man you know quite well."

"What man?" Sam asked.

"Bastan."

Sam stared at Master Helen. Of course it would be Bastan. "Has Alec gone to see him?"

"I don't follow the comings and goings of physickers, Samara."

"Yet you follow them enough to tell me that he has been involved with Bastan." She looked around the room. "Is he in his room now?"

"Perhaps, but his room will be in a different location than what you probably knew."

Sam followed Master Helen along the hallway until she climbed a set of stairs that led to a section of the university where she had only been a few times. Down one way, she saw the student section, where Alec once had his quarters. Master Helen continued, guiding her away from there, not bothering to stop.

The hallway widened, and there were more paintings hanging on the walls, along with a few sculptures, and sconces glowed with bright lantern light. Everything about this section was much nicer than where the students spent most of their time. She remembered the room Alec had been given when he first came to the university, the way that it seemed cramped. There was something cozy about it, and she knew Alec had never minded the size. He was never one to need much excess, though it seemed silly to her that given the enormity of the university, the students were given such small rooms. Then again, there really wasn't a need for anything larger. With the library and other places like that for them to go, the students were rarely confined to the rooms; they had many other places that they could spend their time.

"Promotion brings privilege," Sam said.

"Why should it not?" Master Helen asked.

"Do the physickers really need much larger rooms?"

"It's not a matter of need so much as it is a matter of demonstrating value."

"Value?"

"There is value in having full physickers. Just as there is value in promoting some of those physickers to the rank of master physicker. In time, I suspect your friend will be able to reach such a promotion, though it will take work on his part."

"You don't think Alec is able or willing to do the work?"

"It's not his ability or willingness to work, but more his interest in remaining at the university."

"I think all Alec wants is to stay here and study."

"Does he?" Master Helen glanced over at her as they strolled through the hallway. All of the doors along the hall were closed, and they seemed to be the only ones moving about this early, though Sam was sure others were up and about. It was possible she simply hadn't seen anyone yet. "He continues to disappear from the university from time to time, putting himself in danger."

"Danger? You know exactly what he's doing and why he's doing it."

"Just because I know what he's doing doesn't mean that he should be doing it."

"Even though he's a"—Sam leaned toward Master Helen and lowered her voice—"Scribe?"

Master Helen glanced at her. "Just because he has the ability to document in such a way does not mean that he has committed himself to the university. There are many who have gained that ability and have abandoned it."

"Why would they abandon it? Alec sees the university as his way of understanding everything that he needs to know about what he can do."

"Because the university is not designed to teach everything that he needs to understand that particular ability. He can learn what it means for him to treat and heal the human body, and he can learn to have an inquisitive mind —though I suspect he already has that—but he will not be able to learn what it means to be a Scribe. That is something that must come from himself, and he must determine what he wants to do with his ability."

Sam frowned. "Why won't you teach him? I've been learning from Elaine and other Kavers so that I understand what I can do."

"Your ability is more of a physical one. You must have it demonstrated to fully grasp the extent of your talents. What your friend is capable of doing is quite a bit different, and that is why certain things cannot be completely taught. Some grow frustrated by this and leave."

"Where do they go?"

Master Helen continued down the hallway, saying nothing.

"Where do they go?" Sam asked again.

Master Helen paused and looked back. "They leave for

a place where they feel they might get answers. They leave our city and abandon us, placing us in greater danger."

Sam stared at her. Could Master Helen be saying what Sam thought she was?

"The Thelns. That's what you're saying, isn't it? I already know that they want Scribes, but I didn't realize that the Scribes willingly left here and went to serve them."

"There are many things that we do not like to speak about. That is one of the most difficult."

"Why?"

"Because, Samara, if your friend leaves here, he will find the answers he seeks."

Master Helen turned away from her and hurried down the hallway, leaving Sam staring after her, wondering why that sounded ominous when it was exactly what Alec would want.

22

CAPTIVE

The building was run down. One of the walls seemed to be practically caving in, letting in some of the smells from the night. Alec noted the stench from the swamp most prominently, though there were other smells—those of rot and filth that he tried to ignore.

They had brought him here, depositing him in a chair and not bothering to tie him up or bind him in any way. Did that mean they didn't view him as a threat?

Then again, he wasn't a threat, not really.

The large man stood at the doorway, blocking his only way out, unless he attempted to push through the wall. Considering the way it sagged, it was possible he might actually be successful if he attempted it, but that wasn't something he thought he could do.

In the faint light given off by the two lanterns hanging on either side of the door, the man didn't appear nearly as large as he had in the darkness. Maybe that was the effect of the shadows. He had a plain face, other than a rather sharp-looking jaw. His eyes were flat, but they seemed to take in everything, sweeping around the room as if to catch someone trying to break in—or break him out.

Alec had long ago given up on attempting to engage him in conversation.

He had spent the time returning to this section attempting to talk to two men, but they had said nothing other than they had need of a physicker.

He wasn't entirely certain which section they had brought him to, but he had a sinking suspicion that it was Hosd, if only because of the proximity to the swamp. Wherever it was, the buildings of this section were quite run down, even more so than in Caster.

How long would they hold him here without telling him what they wanted?

He had tried to come up with what he would say, but even that probably didn't matter. Until he knew what they wanted, there was no way for him to prepare how he would respond.

After a while, the door opened, and a solid-looking man entered. He had gray hair that reminded him of Bastan's and deep blue eyes that quickly scanned the room before settling on Alec. He was dressed in a jacket and pants that appeared far nicer than anything one would wear in such a run-down section. He seemed to be unarmed, though Alec had learned from Bastan that those perceptions could be easily mistaken.

"You are the physicker," he said in a deep baritone voice.

"Why do you have me here? There are plenty of other physickers, and you could simply go to the university—"

The man smiled at him. "Go to the university? I think not. Even if we could gain access, there are places that even I don't dare go."

"Who are you?"

"I'm the man you came looking for."

Alec's eyes widened. "Ryn?"

"Why were you looking for me?" He stayed near the door, near enough to the large man that he seemed prepared for Alec to attack. Even if Alec knew enough to fight, he was not only outnumbered, both Ryn and the other man were quite a bit larger than he was.

"I was taking care of someone at the university, and she mentioned your name."

"She did, did she? That is a shame. She should know better than to invoke my name, especially outside of this section."

"Her vision is fading, and she wanted to get help. I don't think she intended to tell me. It was her—"

"Her grandfather. Yes. I am quite familiar with him."

"Then he can tell you that I have offered to help her. I came to this section trying to find more information about her and what happened to her."

"Is that right? You came here looking for information, but why did you go to Caster?"

Alec tried to steady his breathing. Anything he said now would potentially cause trouble. How would he explain his connection to Caster?

"I helped someone else from there. I went to check on them."

"Really? Is that standard practice for physickers now? I

didn't realize they cared so much that they'd leave the university to look in on those they have healed."

"I haven't been at the university very long," Alec said. "And—"

"You haven't, yet you are a full physicker?" From the way he asked it, it seemed as if he understood what that meant. Which meant that Alec had to be even more careful. If Ryn understood the distinctions between the physickers, he needed to ensure he didn't say anything that might run counter to what he knew.

A different thought troubled him. Might Ryn be the one responsible for what was happening to his father and the others? He still didn't know how the four poisoned were connected. How would they have interacted with each other? Or with Ryn, for that matter.

"I'm a full physicker," Alec said. "And I care about those that I help. That's the reason I offered to help Stacia, even though she didn't have money to pay for her healing."

"Unusual. Most of the time, the physickers are most concerned about getting their money first. Why are you different?"

"Not all healers feel that way," Alec said. "There is a growing movement for us to take care of those without the means to pay."

"Indeed?"

Alec nodded. "That's what I've been trying to tell you."

"What you have been trying to tell me is that you went to Caster to check on one of your patients. What is their name?"

"I'm not able to discuss that."

"No?" Ryn asked, a smile coming to his mouth. "What do you think will happen if you do?"

"We take an oath not to share such information with people outside the university. If we did, it could cause problems, raising concern unnecessarily. Some people don't want others to know when they've been ill, certainly not if they've been ill enough to need the help of the university."

"And what do you think will happen if you don't?"

Alec swallowed. "It's... It's a man by the name of Kevin."

Would Ryn make the connection between Kevin and Bastan? It was possible that he would, especially given that Kevin had served Bastan for a long time. He didn't know anything other than the fact that Ryn was trying to gain territory on Bastan, though they were separated by a significant distance in the city, so it didn't really make sense for them to be competing for territory.

"And what happened to Kevin?"

"He suffered from a severe infection. It started with a cough, and he had fevers and chills, and eventually wasn't able to walk. I used a combination of—"

Ryn held his hand up, silencing Alec. "You sound like a physicker, but you don't have the same attitude as many of the physickers. And I must admit that I am disturbed by the fact that you came to my section."

"I was only trying to help Stacia."

"Stacia is sick because of her own mistakes," Ryn said.

"You don't want to help her? All I need to know is what she was exposed to, and then I can work with her to see if I can counteract the effects."

"No."

"I didn't come here to disrupt anything for you. I didn't even know anything about you. She said she worked for a seamstress."

Ryn smiled slowly. "A seamstress? Is that right?"

Alec nodded quickly. "That's what she said."

Ryn turned to the man at the door and nodded. "Bring the *seamstress* to me."

The man looked at him for a long moment before nodding. He left them alone, but Alec didn't think there was anything he could do to get free. He didn't dare attack Ryn, especially as he had the sense there were others on the other side of the door that would be able to stop him if he did.

Ryn reached into his pocket and pulled out a scrap of paper. "What is this?"

Alec looked down at the paper, trying to keep his expression neutral. Even without looking, he knew what it would be.

Easar paper. The scrap of paper had been in his pocket when the man had grabbed him and torn his cloak free. Alec had managed to get the venom out of his pocket and thought that he had it hidden, but everything else in the pocket would still have been there, including the easar paper… and their blood.

"I take notes on what I see. It's part of my training at the university."

"Notes? These are quite interesting. It seems as if someone was attacked based on the way you described this. And I must say that the ink used is most interesting."

Alec struggled to keep his expression calm. "My pen was—"

"Why are you really here," Ryn asked.

"I don't know what you mean."

"I think you do."

Alec took a deep breath. He wasn't sure that telling the truth would make a difference with this man, but there didn't seem to be any way for him to get free, so lying wasn't going to get him answers, either.

Maybe he could engage him in conversation and convince Ryn to get talking, which might get him to share more than what he intended.

"There are several people who have come to the university comatose."

"Comatose?"

"Sleeping, or at least seeming to. They won't wake up. Something happened to them that causes them to become unresponsive."

Alec watched Ryn as he said it. Would he reveal his role in it?

"When we came here to learn of Stacia, one of the other physickers with me was poisoned," Alec said. "I suspect it was in her ale, as it was the only thing she consumed."

"Is that right?"

"From what I understand, she was poisoned because we started asking of you, and had we remained, you might have offered an antidote."

"Is that right?"

"Isn't it?"

Ryn stared at him and seemed to be amused more than

anything else. He tapped one foot slowly, a rhythm that reminded Alec of the steady poling of the captain as they headed into the swamp. Had they come past this section as they took the barge out into the swamp?

Maybe Bastan wasn't the only one who had been watching his father.

"What are you using?" Alec asked.

"I have no idea what you mean."

"I think you do. It has something to do with eel venom, doesn't it?"

The corners of Ryn's eyes twitched, and Alec knew he was right.

"No one is foolish enough to try and capture one of the canal eels," Ryn said. "Anyone who has tried has been pulled into the water, and few come out safely."

Alec hadn't heard that. Maybe that was nothing more than a way of scaring him, or maybe it was true, at least in this section. Here, with their proximity to the swamp, they might have a different experience with the eels.

"And to be honest, the eels are clever. Those who have tried to fish for them and catch them have failed. It's almost as if they know."

"Unless you know where to go to find them."

Ryn stared at him. "You're more than a physicker, aren't you?"

"What did you do to them?"

Ryn snorted, and the door opened before he had a chance to answer.

Alec looked over and saw an older woman enter. She had silver hair that she tied back behind her head with a strip of leather. The corners of her eyes were deeply wrinkled, and her brow had a deep crease. Her mouth was pinched in a frown, and she glared at Ryn as she came into the room.

The glare didn't soften when she realized Alec was there.

"You called me here?"

"Only because someone came to my section looking for the seamstress."

"I really wish you would stop calling me that."

"I call you what you are to me." Ryn turned to her, and for a moment, rage flashed on his face. "You didn't tell me that she went to the university."

"Because I didn't know that she went."

"No? And how would she get the necessary funds to head to the university? That would be beyond her means."

"I don't know," the woman said. "Perhaps she stole them."

"She didn't need nearly as much as you think," Alec said quickly. He gambled, hoping he could convince the seamstress to share more with him if the chance arose. "I already told you that I haven't been charging for my healing services," Alec said to Ryn.

"And I have told you that the university would not allow such a thing."

"Full physickers are allowed to set their own prices."

Ryn frowned. "Not even a junior physicker?" He glanced over at the seamstress. "She's going to be the reason this fails."

"If he's the only one who came here—"

"He wasn't the only one. There was another, and now

she's lying in the university with the rest of them. We do not need them to turn their attention to us."

"There's no reason for them to."

"Who? The university? All the physickers want is a way to heal them. If you tell me what you did to them, and if there's some way I can restore them, we won't bother you at all."

Ryn turned back to Alec, and he chuckled darkly. "Why would I care about the university? There's no one there who could cause difficulty for me. We're too far removed from the center of the city for them to care. No. It's your other connection that I care about. It's the reason you were in Caster—the *real* reason you were there."

"Bastan?" he whispered.

Ryn took a step toward him, his entire body tensed. "Do not say that name around me."

"Why? Why are you trying to hurt Bastan?"

Ryn stared at him, studying him for a long moment. "You don't know?"

"I don't know anything. I'm simply trying to help those who have come to the university for my services."

"Well, I think I'll leave it to the seamstress to help me determine whether or not that is true." Ryn turned to her. "Get answers from him."

With that, Ryn strode from the room, leaving Alec staring at the thin older woman. For some reason, terror began to work through him.

23

INTO DANGER WITHOUT
AUGMENTATIONS

Sam and Master Helen finally reached Alec's rooms, and Sam still hadn't said anything. She wasn't sure how to address the issue with Master Helen, not knowing whether there was anything she could say that would bring her better answers. Maybe the answer was simply that there was more to being a Kaver and a Scribe than Sam understood. There were limits to what Elaine was willing to share, though was that for Sam's benefit or for the city's?

Master Helen knocked and waited a few moments before knocking again. When there still was no answer, she pushed the door open and looked inside.

The room was empty. Sam poked her head in and looked around, searching for signs of Alec. This was his room. It held the scent of him. There was the musty odor of books, and she noted a stack of them in one corner. She saw papers on his desk, where she imagined he made notes about the various treatments he tried. A narrow bed was shoved against the wall, giving more room for the large desk. A single chair was angled toward a hearth.

It wasn't much larger than the student rooms, but it did appear much cozier. It suited Alec.

Everything about the university suited Alec.

She couldn't imagine him leaving here and heading to the Thelns lands, even if they might find answers by doing so. Why would anyone venture there willingly, unless in search of answers?

Then again, Tray had gone there. He had willingly left, thinking he couldn't find the answers he sought by staying in the city. But Tray was not only part Theln; he was part Kaver, which meant some of his answers *would* be found within the city, but perhaps not the ones he wanted. He wanted to understand what it meant for him to be part Theln, and he probably didn't worry about what it meant for him to be a Kaver, especially not if Marin had shared anything with him.

That was something Sam needed to find out too. What had Marin shared with Tray? Could she have told him what it meant for him to be part Kaver? Or maybe she hadn't known, not before Beckah had used her connection to the easar paper to augment him.

"He's not here," Sam said.

"I am able to see that as well," Master Helen said.

"It's late. Where would he have gone?"

A troubled expression crossed Master Helen's face. "If he wasn't at the ward, and he's not here, the only other place would be the library. He spends many hours there."

Master Helen swept out of the room and down the hallway. Sam followed, trying to keep pace, but Master

Helen walked quickly. Sam scurried along the hall, feeling her canal staff bang against her shins as she did. She suppressed the urge to swear. Though it might help her feel better, it would do no good.

They entered a wide hallway on a lower level of the university. Master Helen reached a pair of double doors and pushed one open, hurrying inside.

Why was she moving so quickly? Did everything she did happen quickly?

Sam stepped inside after her. The room was impressive. There were rows and rows of shelves all laden with books. The enormity of it was overwhelming. At the far end of the room, she noted a table, and a young man sat at it. He had a long face, and he was leaning over a several open books, staring at them. A lantern glowed on the table.

Sam turned her attention to the rest of the library. The room was enormous, and likely ran the entire length of the university. How many books were here? Why would the university need so many? How many possible ways could there be to heal someone?

"Stefan?" Master Helen said, stepping forward.

The young man at the table looked up. He stood, clasping his hands in front of him. "Grandmother."

Sam glanced over to Master Helen. "Grandmother?"

Master Helen shot her an admonishing look. "What are you doing here at this hour?"

"I'm… I'm trying to help Alec. He was researching patients who were comatose. We weren't able to find anything. There haven't been many records, but I did come across—"

"Do you know where he has gone?" Master Helen asked.

Stefan blinked. "He's not with me. He has been spending quite a bit of time in the wards, so he might be there."

"He's not there."

"Then his room?"

Master Helen shook her head again.

Stefan shrugged. "I don't know, then. Now that he's been promoted to full physicker, it's hard to keep up with him."

Sam recognized the irritation in his voice. This was someone who had known Alec before his promotion. Why had Alec not spoken of him? The only person she knew from the university was Beckah, and her mere presence and the time she spent with Alec frustrated her, even though Sam knew that it shouldn't. Now that Beckah was injured, she felt some sympathy, though it was hard to muster much. She couldn't get past the idea that Beckah had some other interest in Alec, even though he claimed that she did not.

"Come with me," Master Helen said, turning away and sweeping back out of the room.

"Grandmother?"

Helen stopped. "What is it?"

"When you see him, let them know that I have a few records that might be beneficial. I can't say with certainty whether these are what he's been looking for, but I think..."

"You think what?"

"I think they might help. They are old, probably from

before some parts of the city existed, but they reference a specific type of poisoning that is very similar to what we're seeing."

Master Helen's jaw clenched, as if she was debating something. Finally, she nodded. "I will share with your friend what you have discovered."

She started away from the library, grabbing Sam's arm and leading her out.

"Where are we going?"

"Your friend has been foolish to continue to leave the university, as I have said. I fear he has ventured away again, and more likely than not, he's gotten himself into some sort of trouble."

"If I know Alec, he hasn't gotten himself into any trouble. He's probably just off somewhere studying."

"If that were the case, he would not have disappeared and gone to the Hosd section. That place is dangerous, even for you."

"I'm a Kaver. There aren't many places that are dangerous to me anymore."

"You might be surprised. I think arrogance with your abilities can be a downfall. I would've thought Elaine would have cautioned you about that."

They left the university, and Helen guided her toward the bridge in the distance. If she was going to have Sam walk through the city, it would take much longer than if Sam were to jump the canals. Winding through streets and looking for crossings would be a much more time-consuming way than what Sam was accustomed to.

"Where do you think he's gone?"

"There are two possibilities. Either he has ventured back to your section and tried to reach Bastan or…"

"Or what?"

"Or he has made the mistake of trying to travel back to Hosd. I wouldn't put it past him to think that he needed to find answers about what happened to his friend and his father."

Sam knew that Master Helen was right. If there was anything Alec could do that would help them understand what had happened to them, she knew he would pursue it. Alec wasn't scared, even though there were times when he should be. He often let his dedication and purpose take him places he shouldn't go. It was much like when he had gone with her chasing after the Thelns. He had been fearless, unmindful of the fact that he was powerless against them. Without him, she wasn't sure she would have been able to escape the Thelns. She had needed his augmentations.

"Where should we go first?"

"I think the safest answer is to go to the section you're most familiar with," Master Helen said.

"I can move more quickly on my own," she said.

"Fine. Go see if you can find your friend, but I will be coming behind you."

Sam smiled to herself, thinking what Bastan would say if he met someone like Master Helen. There had been a time when Sam thought her nothing but a kindly old woman, but she had since learned that the master was quite a bit more. Alec respected her and feared her a little bit.

Sam nodded and grabbed her staff from beneath her

cloak, and began screwing the ends together even as she approached the edge of the canal. She launched herself across, bouncing a few times before landing on the other side. She took off in a sprint, hurrying as she went.

Why would Alec have been spending time with Bastan?

And why hadn't Bastan shared that with her?

Sam didn't even spend time with Bastan, not anymore. She probably should, especially now with the revelation about Marin, and Sam's uncertainty about her role as a Kaver. What would Alec have been doing with Bastan?

Maybe it had to do with whatever had been happening to the people he cared about in the city. Could Bastan have been helping him find out what had taken place?

As she neared the Caster section, Sam slowed.

Three men made their way across a distant bridge.

It was late enough that Sam took note of them. Almost as notable was the fact that those men were enormous, almost as large as Thelns, though not quite as big. Experience from living on the streets of Caster for as long as she had—and her gut instinct—told her to follow them.

Bastan had been attacked. Were they part of that?

Maybe all of this was part of that.

She used her staff and jumped to the rooftop, streaking across the slate tiles, careful with her footing so that she didn't slip. When she reached the edge of one roof, she jumped to the next, moving quickly from one to another, flashing across the top of the streets.

The men turned a corner and Sam hesitated.

It was more than just the three men.

Two of the men carried someone.

Sam scurried ahead, trying to get to a point where she could look down and see who they carried. Could it be Bastan? If it was, she had to help him, and practically bubbled with excitement at the idea. She could only imagine how much he would owe her if she had to rescue him from some attacker. And here he had claimed that he was safe in his section.

But as she neared, she knew that it wasn't Bastan.

A flop of curly hair fell into the person's face.

Sam's breath caught.

Alec?

She jumped down, back onto the street, prepared to attack, when two men converged from either side.

"You don't want to do this," she said.

"I think we do. You shouldn't be following."

"You shouldn't be hurting my friend."

Sam swung with her staff, and one of the men grabbed at it, practically pulling it from her. Sam swore under her breath. What was she thinking fighting without any augmentations?

But she was skilled. It wasn't as if she didn't have any way of defending herself and attacking. With the training that she'd received from Elaine and the other Kavers, she was able to fight back.

Sam dropped low, swinging the staff along the surface of the ground, spinning it toward the man's leg. He jumped over, but his colleague did not, and she swept his feet out from underneath him. Sam flipped up, bouncing on the end of her staff as she spun in the air, swinging the staff down.

The man ducked, rolling out of the way.

A pair of swords appeared in his hands.

Where had he hidden those?

"I'm not helpless," she said.

"And we're not the only two that you face."

Sam spun, realizing almost too late that two more men had converged on their position.

What was this about? This was more than a simple abduction of Alec. She had thought he had just been a victim of random street violence. And with Alec dressed in his typical well-made clothes, he was a likely target. Occasionally, street thugs would try to ransom the person they attacked, thinking they could get even more money by selling them back to loved ones. That only worked if they knew who they had abducted and knew some way of sending word to the people who would be interested in buying them back. With Alec in Caster, the attackers would've had no way of knowing that.

And if they weren't about his coins, then they were after Alec.

Why?

She pushed those thoughts out of her head and focused on the fight at hand. Sam had to either send them all off or somehow escape and catch up to Alec to see where they were taking him.

She jumped up on the end of her staff, perching for a moment as she surveyed the street. As she feared, there were four of them. She had knocked down one, leaving him slightly injured, but not badly enough that he couldn't fight her. She wished she could have gotten one good blow with her staff. One clean attack would have made things a little bit easier for her. Now, without that, she had to figure out some way of taking down four men —for large men—without any augmentations.

Could she reach the rooftop?

If she could, she could run along the buildings and maybe get away from here, perhaps quickly enough that she could catch up with Alec and his abductors.

Someone kicked at her staff, and rather than falling, Sam pushed off, swinging in around as she did.

She tried to put some space between her and her attackers, but the street wasn't very wide here. It was wide enough for her to swing her staff in a circle, which forced them back, but they surrounded her in a way that put several of them behind her.

Sam didn't like that, and continued to dance around, fearing that she was leaving too much of her exposed.

Someone moved behind her, and she spun, kicking the end of her staff back, hoping to catch that person.

She flipped forward, swinging around again, and managed to catch one of the attackers on his side. Knocking him forward.

Something struck her from the side, and Sam staggered.

She had enough sense to swing her staff as she fell, and that at least fended off the attacker from catching her again.

She continued to swing around, but the men were less fearful of her than they should have been.

If only she had some way of augmenting herself.

What was it Marin had said? She had told her that it was a matter of focusing on the way it felt, that the power came from within her?

Sam wasn't sure she believed that the easar paper was a cheat to power that occurred naturally within Sam, but then again, she had faced Marin, and she had seen the way the woman had fought without augmentations. If Sam could capture even a part of that, she might be able to, if not defeat, at least escape from these men.

As she continued to spin around in a circle, trying to fend them off, she focused on what it felt like when Alec performed his augmentation, when the power swept through her. She tried to think of the words he would write, imagining them in her mind. That brief distraction gave her attackers a chance to converge.

As they did, that familiar feeling washed over Sam.

It came as a cold wave that worked through her, starting from her toes and working up to her neck. She breathed it in, hoping her visualization of an augmentation would give her the strength she needed.

When she spun the staff around again this time, it came with more speed.

Sam laughed to herself.

She flipped into the air, and when she came down, she swung.

The staff moved quickly, striking one of the men in the back of the head, and he staggered forward, falling in front of her.

She flipped the staff around again, smacking him on the side of his head. He grunted and stopped moving.

How many were left? Were there two or three?

Sam tried to focus on the battle, but the augmentation made everything faster. It made her faster. It made her strength even more impressive.

She swung around again and cracked one of the men in the skull. He staggered forward, and she danced out of the way, moving too quickly for him to keep up.

She jumped. There was strength in her legs that wasn't normally there, and it carried her up and into the air, where she was able to spin around. She swung the staff, bringing it down in an arc as it cracked into the nearest man's skull.

He fell.

And then there was silence.

She looked around. There were three men, not four. One of them had gotten away.

And so had the two men who were carrying Alec.

Sam raced through the streets, moving away from Caster. She had a good idea where they were heading, especially given what Master Helen had said about what Alec had been up to.

But if that was the case, why? What was so valuable about Alec that would make someone in Hosd come after him? Could they have learned that he was a Scribe? Would they think to try to use him for their own purposes? Or was there something else? Could it simply be because he had gone into that section seeking answers?

Sam would find him. And she would free him.

She raced along the streets, searching for movement, chasing after Alec in the darkness. Her heart hammered, and she prayed she wasn't too late for her friend.

TORTURE AND RESCUE

"You shouldn't have come here," the woman said.

"I came to help Stacia. She came to the university looking for answers. Her vision had been blurring, and she wasn't able to see, and she was afraid she couldn't care for her family."

The seamstress took a step toward him. Alec realized that she had a pair of knives, one in each hand.

What was this?

Ryn's words rang in his head.

Get answers from him.

Alec suddenly remembered that he wasn't confined to the chair. He had stayed there because there was something about Ryn that had terrified him, but he wasn't trapped, not in such a way that he had to remain seated while the seamstress approached. He could get away.

"What does he think I will tell you?" Alec asked, backing to the far wall. If nothing else, he would attempt to break free.

The seamstress didn't say anything, and she continued to come toward him.

"What happened to Stacia? What was she exposed to that started to impair her vision?"

The woman hesitated. "She was not supposed to be looking into the jar," the seamstress said.

"What jar?"

"When it splashed in her face, I tried to rinse it out, but there was only so much that could be done. I told her we would watch for any signs of impairment. At first, there was nothing. We thought she was unharmed."

"What jar?"

"Eventually, the toxin began to take effect."

"What jar?"

"And the only man who we thought might be able to provide answers was already impacted."

Alec blinked. "You're the reason my father is comatose."

The seamstress looked up at him. "Your father?"

"The apothecary. You're the one who stole from him. How did you know?"

"I don't know what you're talking about."

Alec ignored her knives and took a step forward. "What happened to them? There are now four people who suffer from whatever it is that's happening. And Stacia. If it's all about the eel venom, I need to find a way to counter it."

"I'm afraid there is no counter to it."

"None?" That wasn't necessarily true. Alec had discovered that when he used the easar paper to help save Tanis. There had to be some antivenom, and some way for him to help the others. If he could get access to the easar paper, he might be able to, but he had to get out of here first.

"You see, Ryn followed Bastan several nights ago when he went out into the swamp. He thought he was after his territory. He saw the way he was able to take down that large man with a single arrow."

"So, he wanted to know how Bastan managed it," Alec said, realization sweeping through him.

"When Bastan went back out into the swamp, he followed. And then he followed him to the apothecary."

Alec swore under his breath. All of this was because of Bastan? All of this was because of eel venom used to stop the Thelns?

And now, his father lay unmoving. Beckah was poisoned. Kevin and Kara.

The seamstress raised the knives.

Alec glared at her. "What answers do you think I have that you need knives to get from me? I'm more than happy to share everything I know if it will help those that I care about."

"I'm sorry," she said, coming toward him.

Alec backed up against the wall. He tried kicking at it, but it didn't budge. Despite its dilapidated appearance, it somehow held, stronger than he would have thought.

He heard a shout out in the hallway, and the seamstress hesitated, looking over her shoulder.

Alec used that brief moment to kick, using the technique Sam had taught him, and knocked one of the knives free from her hand. He grabbed it as it clattered to the ground and held it out from him.

"Do you even know how to use a knife in violence?" the seamstress asked.

"Do you?"

"Why do you think he calls me the seamstress?" She made a slashing motion toward him, and it was almost too fast for him to see. He jumped back a step, barely missing the blade as it swept toward him. "It's because I'm the one who gets answers."

She slid toward him, and Alec tried to spin, but the knife pierced his stomach. He looked down, his eyes wide as pain started to surge through his belly. His hand went to the injury instinctively, dropping the other knife where it clattered to the ground. The woman twisted, and Alec bit back a scream.

"Now, tell me about Bastan."

"I don't know anything about Bastan."

She twisted the knife again. "You know more than you let on. Why were you with him? And what does he want with Ryn?"

His vision began to blur. How much blood had he lost?

"Please," he begged. "You don't have to do this. I can help. I know that you care about Stacia. I could see it when we were talking."

"Stacia made a mistake. That sort of mistake is not permitted around Ryn."

The woman brought her knife back, and Alec couldn't even put his hands up to defend himself.

The door smacked open. He looked over, expecting to see either Ryn or the other large man, and was shocked when he saw Sam come spinning into the room, her staff a blur.

She threw it, and it collided with the woman's head, sending her flopping forward.

The seamstress managed to get up more quickly than he would have expected, and she flourished her knives, spinning them in such a way that Alec feared for Sam. Without augmentations, what could she do? She could fight with her staff, but if the seamstress tossed a knife at her, would she be quick enough to avoid it? He didn't want Sam attacked—and hurt—just because she came to try to help him.

"No, Sam—" he started, barely able to get the words out. His voice was weak. Even if he survived this, and even if Sam somehow managed to rescue him, he didn't have enough strength to withstand healing.

Sam jumped forward, moving more quickly than he remembered her being able to, and swept her staff down and then back up in a sharp movement, knocking the seamstress to the ground. She brought the staff back around, and it collided with the woman's head, knocking her out.

And then Sam was in front of him. She looked down, concern filling her lovely face. "Alec, stay with me."

"Sam? How did you find me?"

"You're not exactly difficult to find," she said.

"Then why didn't you find me sooner?" Alec clasped a hand over his belly, wincing as he did. "I've... I've lost quite a bit of blood."

"We're both here," Sam said.

"We might be, but I don't have any paper."

"I thought you always kept some with you?"

"I did, but it was taken from me when I went to find Bastan."

"Why have you been spending so much time with Bastan?"

"With you gone, I figured I might as well get to know him a little better. I thought he might be lonely," Alec started, his attempt at levity falling flat. His pain was almost unbearable. He tried to ignore it, but it throbbed inside his belly. Every breath he took seemed to make it worse. He tried not to think about what internal injuries he'd sustained, but it was difficult. His mind continued to race through the diagnoses, and he knew just how badly he was hurt.

"Stay here, I'm going to see if I can get some easar paper and—"

"You don't need to worry, Samara."

Alec's head rolled over, and he saw someone he wasn't expecting.

"Master Helen?"

She strode into the room and pulled a slip of paper from her pocket. Sam quickly grabbed the fallen knife and made a sharp slash across her palm. She then dipped her finger into Alec's belly and mixed the blood.

Master Helen leaned forward and began to write. Alec didn't have the energy to look at what she was writing, but the pain began to ease, starting with a slow sort of cold sense that washed through him, and building to a hot intensity. With each moment, he felt the agony recede.

And then it was gone.

He looked down at his belly, and the wound was completely healed.

Alec took a sharp breath and sat up. "What are you doing here?" He looked at both of the women as he said it. How were they able to find him? And now that they had, what were they about to do?

"We're here because of you," Sam said. "I went looking for you at the university and ran into Master Helen. When we discovered you were gone, she told me that you had come to this section before, searching for answers about some person you are healing."

"How did you know to come to this place?"

"Because I saw you getting dragged through the city," Sam said. "I would've gotten to you sooner, but I needed to make sure I knew everything I might come into contact with."

Alec breathed out. "We need to find Ryn. I don't know what he's up to, but he's doing something with the eel venom."

"Venom?" Master Helen asked.

"My father had acquired eel venom for Bastan. That was what he used when the Thelns attacked the last time."

"Eel venom would be incredibly dangerous. Why would Aelus have risked it?"

"Because there are other uses for eel venom," a voice said.

Alec looked over and saw Ryn standing near the door. There were two men standing next to him, and they reminded him of the men who had been a part of his abduction. Both of them carried something that looked like darts, and they flicked them faster than either Sam or Master Helen could react, and they fell.

"Interesting. You should not still be here," Ryn said to

Alec. "And they should not have managed to get past my defenses. I am quite curious about all of this. It seems you have many more questions to answer for the seamstress when she awakens."

Alec glanced down to Sam. He needed her to recover, but in this state, he wasn't sure that was even safe to attempt. At least he thought he understood what had happened. He was convinced that Ryn was using eel venom.

And Master Helen had the only solution he knew of to help Sam—easar paper.

Alec scrambled forward, rolling off to the side to put Master Helen's body between his and Ryn's men. He reached for the easar paper that lay on the ground and quickly dabbed his finger in the pool of blood ink and scrawled a few quick lines.

Venom toxicity. Antivenom applied. Slow reflexes, attempting to try—

He didn't have a chance to finish.

One of Ryn's men charged at him, and Alec rolled over, trying to grab for Sam's staff. When the man reached him, he spun the staff around, connecting with the man's leg.

"Come on, Sam," he said. "I need you to get up."

A cold washed over him. As it did, strength seemed to seep away from him.

Had he made a mistake? He had already used the connection between him and Sam, and that might have drained more strength than he realized.

No. There had to be enough left.

Alec tried pushing back, but he could barely move. His entire body felt as if he had just run a great distance.

Was this all from his attempt to use an augmentation? Or was this because he had already been healed using the easar paper and now his attempt to heal Sam was too much?

"I think you will need to explain why that paper is so important to you," Ryn said. He had stormed closer to Alec, close enough that he could smell the man. He had the stench of the swamp on him.

"No," Alec said. "And whatever you do, Bastan will find you."

"Will he? I don't think Bastan cares enough to find me. If he hasn't searched for his brother after all this time, what makes you think that now will be something different?"

Alec froze. Brother?

Had Bastan said anything about a brother?

"Sam!"

Suddenly, she moved.

It wasn't just that she moved, but she flipped into the air, pushing off with the end of her staff, and came spinning around, striking the nearest man with the free end. She continued in a fluid movement and caught the second man. With both of them down, she turned toward Ryn.

But he was gone.

Alec breathed out heavily. "Sam. We need to—"

"I know. We need to get out of here. Can you help me with Master Helen?"

"I hope so."

"Let's get her back to the university. I think I can get us

there quickly," Sam said, walking to the wall and kicking it. It caved in, and as it did, Alec realized that he hadn't placed an augmentation. He'd healed her but hadn't augmented her strength or speed. How was it that she was able to do that without him placing an augmentation?

"Not the university," Alec said.

"Why not? Helen needs help."

"And we'll get it for her, but first, we need to go to Caster and talk to Bastan."

"Why?"

"Because Ryn is his brother."

25

A DIFFERENT SORT OF CALLING

Sam continued to look over at Alec as they approached Caster. She couldn't believe he been captured and couldn't believe he was the reason that she had been forced to fight. Typically, it was because of something she had done, and she was the reason they had to find a way to fight free, so for it to be Alec this time, she found that... almost amusing.

"Who is this Ryn, beyond being Bastan's brother, that is?" Sam asked, still unable to believe it and wanting answers from Bastan.

"Well, apparently Bastan's talents run in the family. Ryn apparently runs the Hosd section as Bastan runs Caster."

"How did you end up getting involved with him?" Sam asked. They walked through the streets, and she kept her staff out, using it as a way to deter people who might think to attack them. She wasn't about to get into another fight, though she wasn't afraid to do it if it came down to that. Now, though, she had two people to protect. Master Helen followed, though she did so behind her, moving slowly. Sam had to adjust her pace to keep from getting away from her.

"He's the one who's apparently responsible for what happened to a young girl I was healing."

"And this has to do with eel venom?" Sam had a hard time believing that the eels were responsible for anything. They had attacked her staff a few times, but nothing more than that. Thankfully, she hadn't fallen into the canals—or the swamp—where she had to worry about the eels devouring her.

"Trust me, it has everything to do with eel venom."

When they reached Caster, Alec started to veer away, heading to one of the side streets.

"It's this way to Bastan's tavern."

"We can't go there, not yet."

"Why not?" she asked.

"Because there's something here that I lost."

He stopped in front of a darkened alley and started down it. Sam hurried forward, casting a glance over her shoulder at Master Helen, who waited patiently, her hands clasped in front of her. She hadn't said much in the time since they had left Ryn's hideout, but Sam thought the woman should at least say something that might keep Alec from doing something foolish.

"Where are you going?"

"I had ducked down into this alley when they came after me," he said.

"A dark alley? Didn't I teach you better than that? Caster can be dangerous, and—"

Alec leaned down and he picked something up off the ground. Sam frowned when he turned back to her, holding some kind of jar out toward her.

"This. This is what I was hiding. I didn't want them to get it, especially since I didn't know who they were or how hard it would be for me to get this back."

"What is it?"

"You have extracted eel venom," Master Helen said. Her eyes widened. "That… That should not be possible."

"Why?" Sam said, turning back to her.

"We have tried. Even when we can capture an eel, we have not been able to find their venom."

"There are two different types," Alec said, leaning back and grabbing another jar from the ground. When he straightened, he turned and faced Sam, a smile on his face. She had seen that smile before. It was his excitement at something he'd uncovered.

"Let's get out of the alley," Sam said, guiding both Alec and Master Helen. Master Helen's gaze continued to drift down to the jars in Alec's hands, and Sam placed herself in between the two of them not wanting Master Helen to think to grab them from Alec. Sam didn't know how hard it had been for him to extract the eel venom, but she saw the way he protected it, so he must think it valuable for him to have risked himself coming down the alley so he could hide it from his attackers.

Once out of the alley, she turned to Alec. "And now what?"

"Now, we can go to Bastan," he said.

She glanced at Master Helen, who nodded in agreement. "I think I would be beneficial."

Sam guided them through the streets. She stuck to the wider streets, still feeling a bit of concern that one of Ryn's men might try to jump them again, and had no interest in dealing with that, especially since she didn't know how powerful his men might be. They managed to sedate her, knock her out. Had Alec not risked himself, Ryn and his men would have captured her.

They reached Bastan's tavern shortly afterward. They had no further issues, and when they entered the tavern, she looked around, expecting to see Kevin come out of the kitchen as he often did, but he wasn't there. There were a few familiar faces, though not Kevin and some of the others who typically ran the kitchen.

"Kevin was attacked," Alec said, looking over at her, seeming to notice what she was focusing on.

"What do you mean he was attacked?"

"He was searching for information about what happened to my father. I had come to Bastan after my father was brought to the university. My first thought had been to search the shop to see what he'd been working on that he might have accidentally ingested. When I realized someone had taken the eel venom from his cabinet, I knew I had to go to Bastan. I hadn't even realized he's asked Kevin to go in search of information. When they found Kevin in a similar state as my father, Bastan came for me at the university. We have no idea who attacked him or the woman at the hospital, but we now have a total of four who have fallen."

"And Beckah, too, right? I saw her in the ward when I went looking for you. I'm sorry, Alec." She was surprised to realize she actually meant it. She was sorry. "Who else?"

"The young woman I spoke of. Her name is Kara. I don't know much more about her than that other than that Bastan knows her. He recognized her when I brought him to the ward." Alec made a point of keeping his gaze fixed on Sam as he said it, and she saw Master Helen staring at him. Was Alec not supposed to have brought anyone to the ward? Would he be punished for doing so?

"We have to help them," Sam said.

"I'm trying," Alec said.

"That was why you were coming here?"

Alec nodded. "I needed something to test the venom on so I can get a sense of what it might do. I needed to know what potency it had so that I could figure out how I could counter it. I wasn't sure there was a way to counter it, but there must be." He leaned in and lowered his voice. "I had to help one of Bastan's men, a man by the name of Tanis, when he was injured while we were fishing for eels. I used a scrap of easar paper, and I wrote that there was an antivenom."

"So?" Sam said.

"So, most of the time when I do something like that, I use a known antidote, or some known treatment, and this time, I wasn't sure whether there was any treatment. Because of that, I wrote that there was an antivenom, not knowing whether or not that was true."

"And you think that because it worked, there must be an antivenom?"

"There has to be something," he said.

Sam guided them across the tavern and stopped in front of Bastan's door. She ignored the looks of the men around the tavern and knocked twice.

"Interesting that he would use a place like this as his hideout," Master Helen said.

"I don't think Bastan is hiding anything," Sam said. "In Caster, he's pretty open about his role in this section."

Master Helen frowned, and Sam waited for the door to open. When it did, Bastan looked out, his face haggard, and his eyes drawn. "Samara. Is this really the best time—"

"Alec was attacked," she said, stepping inside and pushing Bastan out of the way. She nodded to Alec and Master Helen to follow her in. When they did, she closed the door, giving them some privacy. "He was coming to meet with you, and he was attacked."

"When was this?"

"I don't know, maybe a few hours ago," Sam said.

"And you think it's remarkable that Alec was attacked at that hour?" Bastan turned his gaze to Alec and shrugged. "He's not from this section, Samara. Even if he were, that wouldn't protect him, not late at night."

"It's not that. It's that the man who caught him was after him because of you."

"What man?"

Alec glanced from Sam to Bastan. A slight flush worked up in his cheeks, and Sam shook her head. "It's fine. You need to tell him."

"His name is Rynance Vold. He is in—" Bastan cut Alec off.

"I know who he is and where he is," Bastan said. "What I don't know is why you would have any contact with him. That section of the city is dangerous."

"I always thought you believed that Caster was

dangerous," Sam said, resisting the urge to ask more about his brother.

"Caster is dangerous, but I keep it as safe as I can. The Hosd section is far more dangerous, and it's far more likely that outsiders would have difficulty with people there."

"Well, Alec was attacked because he went there looking for information about a girl he was trying to help."

"What does this have to do with me?"

"It's all tied to eel venom," Alec said.

"Are you certain?" Bastan asked.

"Ryn said as much when we were talking. Presuming he was going to kill me, he admitted that he had been the one who poisoned my father and took his supply of venom. They... They followed you when you went after him in the swamp."

Master Helen stepped forward and grabbed Alec by the sleeve. "Aelus knew the secret to eel venom?"

"My father was the one who managed to acquire a supply of it so that when Bastan attacked the Thelns, we were prepared," Alec said.

"And he didn't share this with anyone?"

"He didn't. I don't think my father wanted anyone to know."

"And I told him not to," Bastan said. He rested his hands on his desk, leaning toward them. As he did, he loomed, his presence seeming to get larger. It was a trick, but Bastan was so accustomed to commanding rooms that he managed to do so even with a master physicker. "I expected a certain level of confidence from him when I employed him," Bastan said.

"You can't keep secrets like that, Bastan," Master Helen said.

He watched her. "Do I know you?"

She shook her head. "No. But I know of you."

"Good. Then you understand the kind of man that I am."

"Stop," Sam said, stepping between them. "You're not convincing anyone, Bastan. You don't need to be so intimidating, or pretend to be."

"Who's pretending?"

"You are. You have no intention of doing anything to Master Helen. I know you better than that."

"Do you?"

Sam eyed him. What was Bastan's reason for acting like this? She looked from Master Helen to Alec and wondered if it had anything to do with Bastan's perception of family and connections that he thought he needed to protect. He didn't need to do anything to protect Sam. She was able to protect herself, especially when it came to Alec and Master Helen.

"Tell us what you know about the eel venom," Sam said.

"I know nothing more than his father acquired it for me. He said he had a specific toxin that might be effective against the Thelns. He never told me what it was."

"But you followed him," Alec said.

"I followed him. I needed to know what it was so I didn't have to—"

Bastan smiled. He spread his hands out and stepped back, looking at each of them.

"So, you didn't have to pay him for additional supplies?" Alec asked.

"I'm a businessman," Bastan said. "If there's a way of reducing my costs, then... Well, then I take it. Your father—"

"My father doesn't charge much for his services."

"If you think that, then you are mistaken," Bastan said. "When it comes to *this* particular kind of service, he does charge, and his fees are enough that I would love to reduce them if I could."

"How much did my father charge for the eel venom?"

"Fifty gold coins," Bastan said.

Sam coughed. "*Fifty*? Where would you have gotten the kind of..."

She turned her attention to Alec. He had gone pale. She could only imagine what he was thinking. Alec revered his father and revered the knowledge he had passed on to him, and if his father was responsible for somehow using that knowledge to cause harm to others, that would be difficult for him.

"Alec, you don't know—"

Alec shook his head. "I do know." He turned to Master Helen. "You knew this, didn't you?"

"I knew that your father had taken on a different sort of calling."

"Calling?"

"He wanted to continue to serve the city."

"How is this his way of serving the city?"

"You would be surprised. If your father found some

way of countering the Thelns, it would be incredibly valuable."

"But my father isn't a Scribe!"

Master Helen shrugged. "There are many of us who question. Your father left the university after being promoted to master physicker, but I'm not sure if he was ever tested to determine whether he could be a Scribe. If we can't restore him, we may never know."

"Are we going to have this ongoing debate?" Bastan asked.

"Maybe we wouldn't have to if you weren't hiding things from us," Sam said.

"I'm not hiding anything from you. I think your anger is misplaced."

Sam let out a frustrated sigh.

"Were you able to extract the venom?" Bastan asked Alec.

Alec nodded, barely able to meet Bastan's eyes.

"And?"

"And I don't have any way of testing a cure."

"What?"

"I don't have any way of testing an antivenom. And—"

Bastan pushed past him and reached the door. "Wait here," he said.

When he was gone, Sam walked over to Alec and put her arms around him, pulling him into a tight embrace. He looked as if he needed it, though he shouldn't feel bad about having been deceived as he was by his father. Her mother had deceived her. Marin had deceived her. Sam's entire life was about deception.

"Where do you think he's going?" Master Helen asked.

"Maybe to find a test subject," Sam said.

"It would kill them," Alec said. "Without easar paper…"

"I have easar paper," Master Helen said. She patted her pocket. Sam eyed the pocket, wishing she had the same supply. All they had were scraps, and even that supply was almost gone. Then again, now that she had discovered the secret that allowed her to perform augmentations without writing on the easar paper, would they have the same need?

"Even with easar paper, I wouldn't subject anyone to that," Alec said. "I don't know what the effects are, not entirely, but I do know that no one deserves to suffer from the eel venom. I saw it up close once, and that was enough."

He shivered, and Sam squeezed his arm, trying to reassure him. She wasn't sure she did anything to fully reassure him, but it was all she could offer.

Bastan returned, and he carried a wooden box with him. "Here," he said, thrusting the box toward Alec.

Alec took it carefully and lifted the lid before slamming it shut once more.

"What is it?" Sam asked.

"Rats," Alec said.

Sam stared at the box. "You just happen to have rats?"

"I run a kitchen, Samara. Every kitchen has rats."

"Remind me not to eat near your kitchen ever again."

"Remind me not to offer you free food. Perhaps the next time you're hungry and come to me, I can let you starve."

She glared at him, and Bastan only shrugged.

"I need a place to work. I can go back to the apothecary—"

Bastan shook his head. "No. I want to know if this works. We are going to help Kevin."

"Just Kevin?" Alec asked, looking up at him.

"If you find the key to helping Kevin, you will find the key to helping your father. You can use my office."

"And if it's not effective?"

"Then we will keep looking."

"What about Ryn?" Sam asked.

"Ryn is of no concern. He has long wanted to move in on my territory, but there is a reason I have managed to hold on to it as long as I have."

"That's not quite what I'm getting at," Sam said.

"Then what are you getting at?"

She looked at him, thinking back to the story he had told her about his brother. Could this Ryn person actually be his brother? If he was, why would Ryn suddenly attack now? What reason was there for him to come after Bastan?

"Ryn told Alec something when he was holding him."

"Knowing what kind of man Ryn is, I suspect he told Alec many things while holding him captive."

"Only one of those is something that I think you should be aware of."

"And what is that?" Bastan asked.

Sam glanced over to Alec, who was staring at the jars, his gaze every so often flickering over to the box. He was engrossed in the project, completely prepared to begin his experimentation. Master Helen shared the same interest, and yet with her, there was something in the way she looked at the jars that made Sam uncomfortable.

"Samara?"

She tore her attention away and looked over at Bastan again. "He claimed you were his brother."

Bastan glowered at her. "I think we have already had this conversation, Samara. I have no brother." With that, he turned and left the room, and Sam stared at the door, wondering what really had happened between Ryn and Bastan.

26

TEST SUBJECTS

Alec looked at the box. The rats inside would make perfect subjects on which to experiment with the eel venom, but how would he start? He opened the jars and set them on either side of the box. One of the jars had the yellowish fluid—that which he had extracted from the rear of the eel—while the other had milkier fluid, which he had taken from the fangs.

"Why are they different colors?" Master Helen asked.

"There were two sources of venom, three sacs," Alec said. "I don't know what the difference is. The yellowish venom came from a spongy sac in the lower half of the body and was excreted through the eel's tail barbs, and two secondary sacs in the upper jaw, excreted the milkier venom through hollowed incisors."

"Two?"

Alec nodded and glanced up. "Why?"

"We have studied the eels for a long time," she said.

"I understand. The master physickers must know

something about the eels, especially since they chose to use them to protect the city."

"It's more than that. The eels have particular properties that are strange."

"Such as their fangs?"

"Have you considered the reason that the master physickers—and the Scribes—have used the eels to protect us from Thelns?"

"No one has been willing to share with me. Anything that I might have considered doesn't matter."

"Use your mind, Physicker Stross. You are much smarter than that. You don't need someone to tell you something that you can observe for yourself."

"What is it? Does it have to do with the Kavers and Scribes?"

"In some way, the powers are connected. There is a balance. We have never really understood why the combination of Kaver and Scribe has made a difference, only that it does. There is something about the combination that is more effective than when it's done by itself. In that way, we have searched for information about the eels. They have the power to kill but they also have the power to heal."

"Heal?" Alec looked at the two jars and thought back to what he had seen of the eels. "When the eel attacked one of Bastan's men, there was no healing to it."

"And yet you managed to find some sort of antivenom, didn't you?"

"I don't know that there is a true antivenom. All I know is that when I wrote on the easar paper, I commented on the possibility of an antivenom."

"What have you been able to determine of eel flesh?"

"The flesh?"

She nodded. "Did you run any tests on it?"

Alec thought of the eels he had dissected. He had discarded most of what remained after he'd removed the sacs, tossing them in a metal bucket that he had ignited. At the time, he thought he was doing it to protect his father's reputation. "No. There wasn't anything to the flesh. I couldn't imagine eating them."

"And why not?"

"I... I guess I don't know."

"The master physickers have long understood that eel meat has curative properties. It's not something that we make well-known, especially since, if we were to do so, we would run the risk of people wanting to harvest the eels themselves and use their meat for healing. The eels provide a certain protection for the city, so in turn, we must offer them protection, so that we can keep them safe."

"But if eel meat could counteract the poison, why wouldn't you have told me that when my father and the others came into the university?"

"I did not believe this was an eel poisoning. Anytime I've seen anyone poisoned by an eel, there was a puncture wound and—"

"And necrosis around the wound."

Master Helen nodded. "You have seen it."

"It's from the barbed tail."

"The tail? Not the jaws?"

Alec shook his head. He lifted up the milky fluid and shook it. "I don't know how toxic this is. That was the reason I wanted to test it. When one of Bastan's men was bitten by the eel, nothing happened. It was the tail—and the puncture wound—that was what would have been fatal."

"And that is what your father must've harvested for Bastan?"

"It has the same coloration," he said, pointing to the yellowish liquid. "But I don't recall him collecting any milky fluid."

"Maybe he didn't know to look for it," Master Helen said. "After all, who would think to look for a secondary site for the venom?"

There was logic to that thought, but Alec wasn't sure. Why wouldn't his father have first searched the mouth and jaw for the venom source. Since snakes excrete their toxins through their bites, wouldn't that have been the first place he father would have looked?

With no evidence that his father had any knowledge of the milky venom, that was what he had to test first.

He thought he had enough information on what would happen with the tail venom, and the way that it would cause immediate necrosis and ultimately death. But he had no idea what would happen with the milky fluid.

He looked around Bastan's office for something with which to administer the venom, and his eyes settled on a pen on the table. He stepped over to retrieve it and dipped it into the milky fluid. With a small amount of the venom now in the pen, he approached the box and one of the rat's crawled up the side, sniffing toward the pen's tip. Alex held it closer, and the curious rat actually opened its mouth. He let a few drops go into its mouth before withdrawing it.

"What are you trying to do with this?" Master Helen asked.

"I'm trying to see if there is any effect. There has to be some purpose to it."

"What if it's nothing more than digestive juices? What if it's only saliva? Think of what you know of the human body, Physicker Stross. Make an analogy."

"No humans have hollowed-out incisors that would allow them to inject saliva or digestive juices directly into anything they chewed." This was different, but he wasn't sure why it was different.

Nothing happened.

Maybe that wasn't the key. Maybe there was no purpose to it other than as Master Helen said. Or maybe there was something else that they were missing.

He went to Bastan's desk and grabbed another pen and dipped it in the yellowish venom. He took it, moving carefully, and hovered over one of the other rats. The rat crawled up to the pen and started licking it. There was a part of Alec that felt terrible about what he was doing. If this worked, he would kill the rat.

But if he didn't try, he wouldn't know exactly what purpose the venom had.

After a few moments, the rat started squealing.

The sound was awful, a piercing, horrid type of sound.

"I think you found the poison," Master Helen said.

"I hadn't questioned which one was the poison," Alec said.

"And now what?"

"I still need to know if the other is the antivenom."

"Try the milky fluid on the one you just poisoned."

Alec glanced over to it. He took the first pen he'd used and dipped it once again in the milky venom before bringing it over to the squealing rat. This time, the rat ignored it, not coming up to drink as it had before. Alec tried reaching his hand into the box, but the other rats raced at him, almost as if they intended to attack him.

Alec jerked his hand back.

"I'm curious whether the milky fluid does anything different to the creature once it's been poisoned."

Alec looked over at the first rat, the one that had received the milky fluid. That one had not done anything. He seemed well, despite the fact that Alec had fed him with eel fluid. What would happen if he attempted to give the rat the yellowish fluid on top of that?

Alec took the other pen and droppered it into the rat's mouth.

He expected the rat to begin squealing, the same way the other one had, but there was nothing.

"Maybe the milky fluid prevents the eel from poisoning itself," Master Helen said.

"Or maybe it *is* the antivenom," Alec said.

Could that be it? Could the eel have the key within it? That seemed almost too easy, especially considering how close he had been to losing Tanis.

The door flung open and he looked up. Sam glanced down, her gaze taking in the screaming rat in the box, before she looked up at him, meeting his gaze.

27

LOSING A FRIEND

Sam caught Bastan just outside his tavern. He was staring into the cloudless night, his face locked in a frown, and his eyes seeming to look off into nothing. A cool wind gusted, carrying the stink of the canals.

"What is it, Bastan?"

"You should go back inside, Samara. You have your friend there waiting for you—"

Sam joined him, leaning against the wall.

"He's interested in those rats more than he is in me right now."

"If that's the case, then I think you have some trouble."

"Oh, he won't always be more interested in those rats."

Bastan glanced over, and a hint of a smile played on his mouth. "It's not like you to be so salacious."

"What's salacious about that?"

"You need to talk with him about your feelings," Bastan said.

"We're fine," she said.

"Fine doesn't mean that you are where you want to be."

"And where do I want to be?"

"I can see the way you look at him. You would do anything to protect him. It's much the same way I look at you."

"Bastan?"

He looked over at her. "It's nothing quite like that, Samara. I've known you since you were this high," he said, waving his hand around waist level. "But I think you've forgotten the fact that I care about you."

"You made that clear repeatedly, especially lately."

"I've tried to make it clear because you have gone off and are exploring something I don't understand. You have an ability I don't understand, and as much as I would like to and would like to help you, it's something that leaves me feeling…"

"Powerless?"

"I suppose that it does. I've been the one who has protected you all these years, and now, I don't think I can anymore. Now that you leave Caster as often as you do, my reach is limited."

"Are you trying to expand your reach because of me?"

Bastan looked at her. "I protect those who I consider my own."

"Why am I your own? Is it because I've been your thief?"

"My thief? You've been more than that, Samara."

"What does that mean?"

"It means that I see you as family. I don't have much family of my own, and I've tried telling you just how important it is to choose your own family. I have chosen you." He met her eyes and held her gaze. It wasn't often that Sam saw Bastan so uncertain, but there was uncertainty in the way that he looked at her now.

"You don't have to protect me."

"You're mistaken."

"I don't think I am," she said. "I've learned enough that I can protect myself. I'm happy to continue taking jobs for you, and—"

Bastan shook his head, and a smile crossed his face. "You misunderstand me. I don't feel that I *have* to protect you. I *want* to protect you. To me, those are very different things. I do it because you are important to me. I see something of myself in you. You're... You're like a daughter to me, especially as I have no children of my own." Bastan looked at her for a long moment before pulling his gaze away.

He stepped away and headed down the street, and Sam debated whether to follow, though not sure what she would even say. How could she react to Bastan when he said something like that? She wasn't accustomed to Bastan being so emotional around her.

And yet, hadn't she longed to have a father? Hadn't she longed to know what that would have been like?

But when she thought about it now, she realized maybe she'd had one all along. Bastan had always been there, always with her, and always making sure that she didn't step too far out of line. He really was the father she never had. Oh, he had required that she take jobs, but never had they been jobs that were too dangerous. He had been the reason she learned to sneak around the city, and the reason she had gained some of the skills that she had. Marin had taught her some of the other parts of her skills, something that Sam realized she needed to think more deeply on.

After discovering her mother and the connection she had as a Kaver, Sam had thought she'd found her family, but now it came clear to her—she'd always had it.

"Bastan…" she said, calling after him.

He didn't answer and continued down the street.

Sam swore under her breath and hurried after him. She didn't even have her staff, which she should have known better than to leave the tavern without. Then again, she was close enough to the tavern that once she caught Bastan, she could return, and she could be back into a place of relative safety within Caster.

Bastan turned a corner, and when she turned to follow, he wasn't there.

Where had he gone?

The street was empty.

She heard a grunt down one of the nearby alleys.

Sam frowned. She raced forward, looking for signs of Bastan. Could some fool have thought to attack him? Why would anyone dare, especially in Caster?

She thought back to the recent incident when those sword-wielding men had attacked him. She had managed to be there that time, but now…

She rounded another corner and saw five men dragging Bastan off.

Something struck her in the back.

Sam swung around, wishing that she had her staff, but without it, she had to fight empty-handed.

Two men waited. Both were nearly as large as the other men that she'd fought.

"You're making a mistake."

One man grunted. "There's two of us. There's one of you."

Sam focused on what it felt like when she had an augmentation and tried to give herself speed and strength, thinking about the way it washed over her when it came on. Could she force herself to have another augmentation?

There came no following sense.

She backed up, but the two men had her wedged in. They blocked her from moving away from them, clearly experienced working together.

She looked at the nearby building. There was a window, but it would be locked and likely boarded over. Most people in Caster weren't foolish enough to leave their windows accessible at night.

Even without augmentations, she wasn't without skill. She needed to use that now.

Sam focused on what she had learned of hand-to-hand combat. It wasn't nearly as much as what she had learned about fighting with the staff, especially as her staff was her primary weapon, but she could be fast. She had quick reflexes.

She needed to use those skills against men that were larger than she was.

Stay low and keep out of their reach.

If she couldn't rely on augmentations, she had to get free. When she did, she could send word for others who could help her claim Bastan, though who would she go to? Who would believe that Bastan had been captured?

Worse, Bastan had headed off before she had a chance to tell him that he was something of a father to her. He had been captured not knowing that he was as important to her as she was to him.

More than anything, that sent a surge of anger through her. She would get to Bastan. She would tell him how important he was. She would tell him how much she appreciated all that he had done for her over the years.

She dropped and rolled, getting out from beneath one of the men trying to grab for her. Sam flipped her leg around, kicking, and struck him on the shin.

Pain jolted through her leg, but she was determined not to let it get to her.

Sam rolled again, and this time, she collided into one of the men. He wrapped her up, grabbing her around the shoulders, and she swung her fist down connecting with his groin. He released her, and she spun, bringing her knee up.

It was a double connection to his groin. At least he wouldn't be chasing her anytime soon.

When the other man lunged for her, she slipped beneath his grasp and rolled forward, quickly getting to her feet and racing back down the street.

By the time she reached the tavern, she glanced back, looking to see if anyone followed.

Inside the tavern, she looked around. She hurried back to the kitchen where there were a few familiar faces, and she found Tanis, the man Alec had healed. She didn't know him nearly as well as she knew some of the others.

"We need help. Bastan was taken."

Tanis looked at her. "What?"

"We were out on the street. He wandered off, and five men grabbed him. I tried to go after them, but…"

Tanis nodded and raced off, hurrying to one of the back storerooms. When he returned, he had several swords gripped in his hands, and he started handing them out to men in the kitchen.

"Whoa. What are you doing with those."

"You said he was captured. We're going after him."

"We don't even know where he's gone."

"It doesn't matter. We're going to find out what happened to him, and we are going to get Bastan free."

Tanis left the kitchen, and within moments, most of the people within the tavern were on their feet, half of them already armed with swords of their own.

Were *all* of these people with Bastan?

She knew that Bastan kept most of the people in the tavern on his payroll in some way, just as she knew he was always protected while here. She was surprised by just how many people were with him.

"You need to wait a minute," she said to Tanis.

"Wait for what?"

"Wait for me."

"And what do you think you can do that the rest of us can't?"

She stepped forward, reached up, and grabbed him by the collar, yanking him down. It surprised her, because she had much more strength than she was expecting. Tanis seemed surprised, too, and his eyes widened as her face loomed only an inch or so from his.

"You will wait for me. I care about Bastan as much as the rest of you."

When she released him, Tanis stared at her for a long moment before finally nodding.

Sam hurried back to Bastan's private office and saw Alec and Master Helen working with the box. The lid was off, and Alec was reaching inside, attempting something with one of the rats. She heard a soft squealing, and she shivered. No animal should make a squealing sound like that, certainly not one caged.

"What are you doing?" she asked, grabbing her staff.

Alec looked over at her. "Sam?"

"Bastan was taken. I'm going after him."

Alec looked down at the rats for a moment before standing and wiping his hands on his pants. "Then I'm coming with you."

"You don't need to. I can do this myself."

"No, I think that whatever you're doing, you need some help." He leaned down and grabbed the two jars on the table, quickly screwing lids back on them and stuffing them into his pocket.

Master Helen watched, and after a moment, she looked over to Sam. "What you are proposing to do will be dangerous."

"What I'm proposing to do is go after someone who has taken somebody I care about. I would do the same for anyone important to me."

"You haven't gone after your brother," Master Helen said.

Sam shot her a hard look. "Not yet. That's coming next."

She looked over at Alec. "Are you coming?"

"Just a minute. I need one more thing."

He turned to Master Helen. "You have easar paper?"

"Alec—"

"We need to help Bastan. I don't know why you have such reluctance about him, but he deserves our help."

"It's not that I'm reluctant to help Bastan, it's just that…"

"It's just that what?" Alec asked.

"It's just that I'm not sure we should be the ones offering that help to him," she said.

"Because he's a thief?"

"Because he's a djohn."

28

COMING UP WITH A PLAN

"Adjohn?" Sam asked, staring at Master Helen. She nodded. "Bastan is a djohn. I'm certain of it."

"What is a djohn?" Alec asked.

Sam couldn't take her eyes off Helen. "They are from beyond our city. They have some innate magical resistance, though I don't understand it very well. They're the men Bastan brought with him to fight the Thelns." If he is djohn, it would explain why he knew to hire them.

How was that even possible? How was it possible that Bastan had hidden something like that from her?

"Could you quiet that creature down?" She nodded to the squealing rat. It didn't matter. After another moment or two, the rat fell silent. She made her way over to the box and saw it lying motionless inside. The fur had blackened, and the skin beneath it had discolored. "What did you do?"

"I tested the venom," Alec said. "I used milky one on

the first rat and got no reaction. Then I used the yellowish one on a second rat, and it poisoned the rat. Hence the squealing. When I just tried to follow up the yellow venom with the milky venom, the other rats all but attacked me, so it died before I could give it the milky one. I decided to give the first rat the yellow venom, and it had no reaction. It's almost as if the two, regardless of which is given first, counter each other."

"You don't have to be quite so excited about that," Sam said.

"But… Don't you see what this means? Maybe I can find some way of helping my father and the others."

"You already had some way of helping your father and the others. You had the easar paper. Once you knew what it was, all you had to do was document the antivenom, the same way you did with Tanis."

Alec paled. "You're right. I don't know why I delayed. I should have gone straight back to the university after we returned to the city and tried to help my father and Beckah and…" He shook his head. "I was so excited about trying to figure out what it meant that we had these eels and to see if I could discover an antivenom, that I didn't."

"And now, there's not time," Sam said. "Now, I need you to come with me, so that we can go after Bastan."

"Where do you think they took him?" Master Helen asked.

"If the size of the men had anything to do with it, I suspect Ryn came after him."

"Why would his brother be so determined to come after him?"

"I think… I think that's my fault," Sam said, flushing.

"Bastan was trying to expand his territory and expand his reach."

"From what I understand of him, he has not done so before now. He has been content with his grasp on Caster," Master Helen said.

"He had been. But ever since I went to the palace to begin training, Bastan decided he needed to extend that reach."

"Because of what he'd discovered?"

Alec looked at her. "It's because of you, isn't it?"

Sam nodded. "He didn't tell me that, but I suspect that's what it is."

"He has been talking about protecting those he cares about," Alec said. "When I came to visit, he kept referring to family and talking about protecting those who worked with him."

"Yes, well I don't work for him, not anymore, but it seems as if Bastan sees me as family. And…" She flushed again. "Well, given everything I've gone through, Bastan is pretty much the only family I have. I need to go after him and I need to get him back before Ryn does something to him."

"I will help you," Alec said.

Master Helen glanced from Sam to Alec. "If you do this, you risk exposing the presence of the Kavers and Scribes in the city."

"I think our presence has already been exposed. The fact that we were able to fend off the attack is enough to have exposed us. We can mitigate some of that exposure if we go after Ryn, but I don't know how much we'll be able to limit."

Master Helen let out a deep sigh. "All the years I've been in the city, I have done everything I could to prevent the spread of knowledge about our existence."

"Why?" Sam asked. "Don't you think awareness of our existence would help keep people in line?"

"It's never been about keeping people in line. It's been more about preventing others from coming and attacking."

"You mean coming for the Scribes."

"What?" Alec asked.

Sam glanced from him to Master Helen. "That's what they don't want you to know. If you go to the Thelns lands, there might be a way for you to expedite your understanding of what it means for you to be a Scribe. They don't want that."

"Because none have ever returned. There is temptation —" Master Helen started, but Alec cut her off.

"I don't know why you would be so worried about the Scribes—others like us—going to Theln lands and understanding who we are and what we can do, but it's more than what you've shared."

"It's because the Scribes create the easar paper," Sam realized.

Alec looked down to the two jars in his hands. "And the paper is connected to the eels, somehow, isn't it?"

Sam looked at Master Helen, and her skin tingled as she suddenly understood the excitement that Master Helen had shown when she realized that Alec had found the eel venom. It was about more than his discovery of the toxin. It was about something it meant for her. "Is that it?"

"Those who are Scribes in Theln lands have long

known some secret to creating easar paper. We have snuck it from them, which is how we have the supply that we do, but we have never been able to learn how it's created."

"Did you think it had to do with the eels?"

"We have speculated on that," Master Helen said. "Given the fact that the eels have some role in protecting the city, especially with the numbers of eels we have counted in the canals, we have managed to prevent the Thelns from coming. Even the mechanism of how that works is not well understood."

"Then why would Marin have tried to poison the eels?"

"Because she was working for the Thelns," Master Helen said.

Sam shook her head. "I'm not sure that is what it was. If it was all about her working for the Thelns, she could have left the city long ago. Besides, she was only here to protect Tray."

Master Helen frowned. "What is this?"

"Marin. The reason she was in the city was to protect Tray. She needed to keep him away from his father, and though I don't know that it made sense for her to keep him so close to his mother, I think this was where she felt he was safest."

"What are you talking about, Sam?" Alec asked.

"Tray. Lyasanna told me that Tray was her son. And Marin confirmed it when we captured her." Master Helen gasped. "Marin was given the assignment to kill him, and she refused, and so because of that, she disappeared."

"Where did you hear this?" Master Helen said.

"As I said, from Lyasanna herself, and then from Marin."

"You found her," Helen said.

Sam nodded. "I thought you knew. I thought you knew that Elaine and I returned with her."

"Elaine never returned."

If she hadn't returned, where did she go?

Could Marin have escaped again? Sam had to believe it was possible, especially with the abilities that Marin had shown, but she didn't think Elaine would make that mistake.

Unless… Unless Elaine had chosen to murder Marin, to find a way to silence her so that Lyasanna's secret couldn't come out.

As Sam raised that question, she realized that at some point, she had started to believe Marin. When had that happened? When had she started to trust what Marin had told her over the words of her mother?

"And Marin involved you because of your mother?" Alec said.

Sam nodded. "Apparently, Marin believed that my mother was complicit, or at least did nothing to countermand Lyasanna's orders."

"We need to find them," Alec said. "We need to ask the princess about this."

"I was about to, but Master Helen grabbed me."

"And it's a good thing that I did," Master Helen said, nodding to Alec. "Had I not, what would have happened to your Scribe?"

Sam took a deep breath and tapped her canal staff on the ground. "I need to go after Bastan. Alec—You can choose to come with me or not, but I think your augmentations may benefit me."

"Maybe I don't have to go with you to place the augmentations."

"Why is that?" Sam asked.

"Well, you'll only worry about me if I'm with you, won't you?"

Sam nodded. "I can't have you getting harmed while we're trying to rescue Bastan."

"What if there was a way for me to remain hidden where I would be safe and where I can still place augmentations? It wouldn't be a guessing game, like it was when Jessup held you."

"But you won't know which augmentations I need."

"Which augmentations do we typically use? Think about it, Sam. We use strength, speed, sometimes we heal. If I am there and able to give you what you need to stay out of harm's way, we might not even need healing augmentations."

He was right, and that annoyed her. But why was that? Was it because he was suggesting that she go off on her own, or was there something else to her annoyance? Was it that she would once more be fighting by herself?

For Bastan, that felt right.

"Stay here. Give me a few minutes, and then begin adding augmentations. I want skin that can't be punctured. I want bones that can't break. And I want resistance to various toxins. Every so often, I want you to cycle them, so we're ready as the augmentations may wear off."

Alec nodded. "I think that's all a great idea."

She went to Bastan's desk and pulled out a bowl from

one of his drawers. She opened her palm above the bowl and made a quick slash with one of her knives. Blood pooled in her palm and then dripped into the bowl. She winced, ignoring the pain in her hand, knowing that it needed to happen so that Alec would have access to enough blood.

Alec glanced at the jars before he thrust one of them at her. "Take this. This is the eel venom."

"Alec—"

Alec shook his head. "No. I don't know if there's any purpose to it, but if nothing else, you can use this to end your fights."

"I don't have any way of administering the venom," Sam said.

Alec held out a pen to her. Sam chuckled.

"A pen? You know, I *do* have a knife."

"Fine. Dip either of them in the venom. You can use it to jab into somebody. It doesn't take long before it takes effect."

Sam thought about the rat and the way that it had squealed. She wasn't sure she wanted to hear a man squealing the same way, but Alec was right that she needed to have some other defense if she was attacked. She pocketed the venom and took the pen, slipping that into her pocket alongside it. She would have to be careful so that she didn't jab herself with the venom.

"Maybe you start with making my skin impervious," she said.

Alec frowned for a moment before his eyes widened. "Oh. Good idea." He took a seat at the desk and glanced up at Master Helen. "The easar paper?"

She considered him for a moment before pulling a few sheets of paper out of her pocket and setting them on the table. "You understand how valuable these are?"

"Maybe they won't be quite as valuable if we can figure out how to make it ourselves," Alec said.

Master Helen nodded. "I am going to return to the university. If these others were injured by eel venom, I will see if I can't help them with the antivenom."

Sam grabbed her arm, taking the jar of the milky liquid. "Not yet." Her abrupt move may have been a bit too forward with Master Helen, but she didn't care. "Depending on what happens, we might need it."

"Those at the university need it now," she said.

"Then use the easar paper to buy them time." Now that they knew what to try, the easar paper shouldn't carry the same risk, should it?

"That's a dangerous strategy."

"It will work," Alec said. "I've seen it work with one of Bastan's men."

Master Helen looked from Alec to Sam, frowning deeply. "Are you sure about what Marin said?"

Sam nodded slowly. "I don't know if it's true."

"But you believe it is true."

"I believe that Marin didn't have as much reason to lie to me when she said it. Maybe it wasn't entirely true, but…"

"Thank you," Master Helen said.

"For what?"

She breathed out heavily, her frown easing. "For giving me something to consider. For possibilities I had not thought existed." She headed toward the door and closed it behind her. Sam stared at it, feeling a strange unsettled feeling.

"That was…"

"Strange," Alec finished for her. "Master Helen can often be strange."

"Do you think you can do this?" she asked.

"You need to go get Bastan. You're right. He is your family."

"He said I was like a daughter to him," she said with a whisper.

"I'm not surprised. When I came here to talk with him, he… Well, let's just say that he made it very clear how much you mean to him."

Sam took a deep breath. "Are you ready?"

"Are you?"

She licked her lips, tapped the canal staff on the ground once more, feeling as if doing so gave her a measure of good luck, and grabbed her cloak, slipping it over her shoulders. She was tired, exhausted from everything she had been through, but this was something that needed to happen. Regardless of anything else, she had to go after Bastan and had to bring him back.

"I'm ready."

29

AFTER BASTAN

The Hosd section was too close to the swamp for her comfort, but now, with her ability to maneuver through it, she was able to approach the section along the swamp side, something that not many others could do. Sam hopped along on her staff, remaining perched as she went, occasionally flipping. Augmentations left her flush with strength and speed, allowing her to jump much farther each time she flipped out of the water, coming back to balance on her staff. She was careful not to flip too far or too fast, needing to maintain control of each rotation, and not wanting to come down too hard on the staff. If she did, she might splinter it before she even got a chance to go after Ryn and get Bastan.

Every so often, she felt pressure on the staff. She had grown accustomed to that while navigating the swamp and figured it was one of the eels. Maybe they knew she carried a jar full of their venom. Maybe that angered them.

At least with her augmentations, she didn't have to fear them tearing through her flesh.

Perched as she was on the staff, she was able to survey the section. There was movement that probably shouldn't be there at this time of night. A dozen or more men moved in the darkness, little more than shadows, but they went in and out of a building that butted up against the swamp.

Likely, they thought themselves safe.

The building she had rescued Alec from had not been along the swamp, though it had been near enough to it. And Alec had told her he had gone to a tavern to find information, but that wouldn't make sense for Ryn to hide out in a tavern. Then again, maybe he wanted to be more like his brother. Maybe Ryn thought he could create the same sort of tavern compound as Bastan.

Sam didn't linger. Doing so put Bastan at danger. She didn't know what Ryn wanted of him, but it probably wasn't anything good.

She flipped.

With the augmentations surging through her, it took a single flip from her point in the swamp to reach the shore. When she landed, she jumped again, rolling on top of a nearby rooftop before coming to her feet.

Sam crouched quickly and crept forward. She should have requested enhanced eyesight. It was something that she kept forgetting to talk to Alec about, but something that was almost as valuable as any of the other enhancements. With enhanced eyesight, she thought she could see what these men were up to, and where they were going.

There was no option but to go down.

She jumped.

She appeared in the midst of them, not bothering to conceal her sudden appearance. She reacted quickly, swinging her staff around, and she smacked into three of the men in one arc before they had a chance to realize she was there. All three fell, and none of them got back up. By her count, that left at least nine more remaining, though there could be many more than that. How many might she have to face?

Others converged on her.

She recognized one of the men from the attack in the street. He smiled at her.

"You shouldn't have come here for him," the man said.

"You shouldn't have let me escape," she said. She took the end of her staff and jabbed him with it. With her enhanced strength, the staff plunged through the skin of his stomach, and he screamed. It had turned into something like a spear, and blood spilled onto the ground.

That wasn't quite what she wanted.

At least he wasn't going to come after her.

She jumped. She lifted into the air, spinning around, swinging the staff in a rapid spiral. This time, she managed to connect with four people at the same time. All of them dropped as her staff struck the side of their heads.

The augmentations began to fade.

It happened slowly, with a washing sort of sensation, the same kind of sense she had as when the augmentations took hold.

How much time did she have before Alec realized they were fading?

Sam spun the staff around again. She was still augmented, and her strength was still greater than it normally was, but it wasn't quite as impressive. She cracked her staff along the sides of several men, knocking them down. She had to hurry before the augmentations failed entirely.

There were only two men still standing. She twisted her staff quickly, thankful that her speed remained intact. With a whip-cracking motion, she managed to strike one on the chest and the other on his forehead, and they both went sprawling down. She smacked them again, wanting to ensure that they stayed down.

Sam hurried back along the street, disappearing into the shadows. She panted, trying to catch her breath. While she did, she realized the augmentations had faded completely.

Kyza!

Come on, Alec.

He needed to repeat the augmentations. And she hoped he remembered the one for her skins. The last time she had faced Ryn, he had somehow managed to poison her, and without Alec here to heal her, she couldn't afford to make the same mistake again.

How long could she wait for another augmentation?

Sam didn't think she could wait very long. Others would surely come, and she would be facing a dozen or more once again. Even with augmentations, that wouldn't necessarily be easy. She didn't want to fight her way through Hosd, especially since she wasn't entirely sure how much protection Bastan would have around him.

She couldn't wait any longer. She crept forward, hoping

Alec hadn't gotten sidetracked by maybe the rats or something else, but as she did, she opened the jar in her pocket, and dipped the pen inside, hopefully loading it with poison. If it came to it, she wanted to be ready for an attack. But, without her skin augmentation, she had to be very careful.

The men had seemed to be moving in and out of one particular building. Sam focused on that and headed toward it. When she reached that building, she pulled the door open, and stepped inside.

It was an incredibly well-appointed home. A thick carpet as beautiful as any she'd seen in the palace covered the floor. Lanterns were stationed along the walls, creating a soft glow, almost a welcoming sense. A massive stone hearth occupied almost one entire wall. There were plush chairs scattered throughout the room. On one side, there was a long counter, and behind it a doorway.

This was a tavern.

Only... it was nothing like any tavern she had ever been in. This was nothing like Bastan's tavern. This was much nicer.

Bastan would hate that. From the smell of the food, she suspected the food was even better than what Bastan served.

Ryn trying to out-do Bastan didn't make any sense. Why would he copy Bastan's business model?

And where was Bastan?

The tavern was empty, unlike Bastan's on any given night, except for tonight. The men who worked for him, people that he depended on, people who were devoted to him, were making their way toward this section at this very moment. Sam was hopeful she could take care of this before they reached here. She didn't want any of Bastan's people—her people, she supposed—to get harmed trying to rescue him.

Sam went for the door on the other side of the room. That had to be where she needed to go, didn't it?

She pushed the door open and stepped inside. It was a kitchen, though this kitchen was not at all like Bastan's. Once again, it was much nicer. Bastan's kitchen was serviceable, more functional than anything else, and the people who worked in it, men like Kevin and now Tanis, were good cooks, but they had limitations. Part of it was related to the limitations from the food that Bastan was able to acquire, but part of it was related to the skill of the cook.

Broth boiled within some of the pots on the stove, and Sam couldn't help it—her mouth started to water.

She would *not* tell Bastan about this, especially if he didn't already know.

The kitchen was empty.

Why would the kitchen be empty? Why would the tavern be empty?

Unless they knew she was coming.

Kyza. This had to have been a trap.

Sam raced back into the tavern and skidded to a stop. There were a dozen people here. Maybe more.

And she had no augmentations.

"Just you?" Ryn asked, stepping out from a chair near the hearth.

"Do you think more are needed?" Sam asked.

"I would have thought he had more men than just you."

"I'm not a man."

"Clearly. I thought Bastan would have had more people under his employ than just a single young lady."

"He does. I'm his favorite."

"Is that right? So, when I capture you and torture you in front of him, you will be the reason he breaks?"

Several of the men started toward her, and Sam tapped her staff on the ground. "I wouldn't do that. Did you see what I did outside on the street?"

The men hesitated.

"Yes. That was me. And before you ask, I'm not going to tell you how I did it. Just know that the dozen of you don't scare me at all."

She swallowed. She hoped she sounded more convincing than she felt. Her heart hammered, and she desperately needed Alec to augment her again. What had happened to him?

"Ah, you would have me believe that we should be intimidated by just you?" Ryn asked.

"I wouldn't have you believe anything. I'm just telling you the truth."

"You weren't nearly so disruptive when you were here before. I think… I think that you have help." He motioned, and one of the men nearest the door scurried away.

Even with one man fewer to face, Sam wasn't sure the odds were any better.

Two men started toward her, and she grabbed the pen out of her pocket and slipped forward, jabbing one of the men in the leg, and spinning, stabbing the other in his arm.

She jumped back, swinging her staff around as quickly as she could.

"That's it?" Ryn asked.

Sam waited. "What more were you hoping for?"

Suddenly, the two men started to scream.

Their screams were pained, agonizing, and black lines began to work along their skin, up from their necks and onto their faces. Both men dropped and began convulsing.

Sam wanted to look away, but she wasn't able to.

This? This was the eel venom?

Kyza, but this was awful. Alec should've warned her, though then again, she *had* heard the rat screaming. What else had she expected?

"Come closer, and I'll see how many more of you want to suffer the same fate."

If nothing else, the sudden screaming had disrupted and shaken the confidence of the men arranged in front of her. They hesitated when they had not before. Each of them glanced at the others, and finally, they looked back at Ryn, as if needing assurance.

"Where is Bastan?" Sam asked.

"You won't live to get to him," Ryn said.

"No? I'm thinking that you might not live to keep me from him. Tell me where to find him, and I will leave you —and your men—alive. If you attempt to keep me from him, then I will do everything in my considerable power to destroy you. Don't think for a moment that I'm afraid of these men." She tapped her staff again, and all of the men jumped back a step.

"What is Bastan to you? Why do you care so much about him?"

"What does it matter why I care about Bastan? All that matters is that I do. And I'm not the only one. If you don't release him, there will be an army of his people converging on you. You will be destroyed."

Ryn snorted. "Destroyed? You speak in such absolutes." He waved his hand. With that, the other men suddenly found their resolve, and they hurried forward.

Sam focused.

She knew she could summon the connection to her Kaver abilities. She had done it before. All she had to do was think about the way the augmentation washed over her and focus on what Alec might have written.

Whatever had happened to Alec, she had to do this on her own.

For Bastan, she had to do this.

A wave of cold washed over her.

Sam took a deep breath. Speed and strength flowed through her, augmentations that she gave herself. She added to that impervious ability, not wanting to be poisoned.

Then she darted forward.

Her staff spun, moving faster than any of the men could react. She knocked down three before stepping back, moving off to the side, and swinging out with the pen gripped in her fist, stabbing another man in his chest. Continuing the motion, she flipped her staff around, and jabbed the end of it into one of the men's forehead. He crumpled.

Sam stalked forward, making her way straight toward Ryn. His eyes began to widen as he realized that the men he threw at her weren't enough. Several others came in, and Sam made short work of them, attacking them with her staff and driving them back. No longer was she afraid that she wasn't going to be strong enough or quick enough. The augmentations had taken hold, and she was able to use her staff to knock them back.

"Where is Bastan?"

Ryn managed to calm himself, and he even smiled. When he did, she saw something of Bastan in it, though Bastan didn't have nearly the predatory grin as what Ryn showed.

"You really are impressive," he said.

"I don't care if I impress you," she said.

"I can see why he favors you. And I can see why she was concerned about you."

She? What *she* would Ryn be referring to that might be concerned about her?

As she hesitated, she felt movement behind her.

She paused and swung around, bringing her staff in a rapid arc. The three men who had been stupid enough to approach were knocked back.

When she turned back to Ryn, he was gone.

Kyza!

Where had he gone? And… what had he meant when he'd said Bastan was concerned about her?

30

A KAVER COMES

Alec sat at Bastan's desk. The man had a comfortable place to work, and Alec understood why he chose this desk, and particularly this chair. There was something about the way it cupped him as he sat here, welcoming him. He made a few notes on the easar paper, scrawling words across the page, and working on his augmentations for Sam.

It was better that he remained behind. He was safer here.

And if he was careful with his augmentations, she would be safe where she went.

Working together, he could ensure that she remained unharmed. He was her Scribe, after all.

Alec chose the words carefully as he scrawled them along the page. From what he could tell, the words were just as important as the way he wrote them.

With each line, he felt a cold wash through him. It was how he knew the augmentation took hold. All he had to do was keep this up until Sam returned. With the sheets of paper that Master Helen had left, there was plenty. He didn't have to worry about running out before she returned. It was a luxury they'd never had.

Every so often, he glanced over to the box of rats. He still couldn't believe that the eel venom was countered by something within the eel itself. He also couldn't believe that the eel venom might be the key to creating easar paper. That surprised him as much as anything.

He stared at the page, counting moments before choosing to write something else. He didn't want to go too quickly. If he did, if he documented faster than what Sam needed, there was the very real risk that he would somehow overdo it.

After another brief pause, he started to document again, wanting to ensure that Sam was never without augmentation.

The door opened, and he glanced up.

"Apothecary. It is good that you're here."

Marin stepped forward, and Alec quickly grabbed for his pages of easar paper, trying to think of some augmentation that he might add to himself, but he wasn't quick enough. Marin managed to grab them and pulled them free of his hand, leaning forward.

"I think it's time that you're done with this."

"You don't understand."

"I think I do."

"Sam needs me—"

"She needs you because she's making a foolish attack on Ryn. I'm fully aware of that."

Alec looked past her. Normally, there would be one of

dozens of Bastan's men in the tavern, but Sam had wrangled them all, taking them out to pursue Ryn.

"Yes. There isn't anyone here to help you." She stuffed the easar paper in her pocket and looked at the box. She pulled the top off and reached inside, plucking the dead rat out of the box and dangling it by its tail. "Perfect. I was hoping you had figured out how to harvest the eels."

"I haven't figured out how to harvest anything."

"No? If I'm not mistaken, this is from eel venom."

"What are you doing? What are you after?"

"It's time that this be over," she said.

"What do you mean? What do you want to be over?"

Marin grabbed the jar of milky white eel venom and stuffed in her pocket. "I imagine this is what you have harvested?" Alec let his gaze drift to her pocket. If all she was after was the eel venom, he would let her take it. She didn't have the toxic one, not the one that Sam had with her, and there was only so much damage she could do with it. In truth, he had yet to discover what the milky venom did, short of hoping it was the antivenom.

"This is all I harvested."

"No. I can see from the way you answered that there is more. Why don't you go ahead and tell me where it is?"

"Because I don't have it."

"And who does… Ah. I see. You left it with Samara."

"What do you want with the eel venom, anyway?"

"I want to end the secrets. I want to end the fighting. And it's time for Lyasanna to get what she deserves."

"It's true?"

"Do you think I made that up?"

"I think you made up many things, particularly when it had to do with Sam."

"Only to keep that boy safe. What choice did I have, especially when Lyasanna wanted him dead and the gods only knew what his father would do. Where is he?"

Alec frowned. Didn't Marin know? How was it possible that she didn't?

Would it matter if he shared with her? Now that he realized what she was after, maybe it didn't. Maybe telling her that Tray was out of the city would be a way of getting her to leave, and maybe to leave him alone.

"He left. Escaped, really. And took Ralun with him, probably to learn more about what he is and what Ralun might be to him."

"That fool. What was he thinking taking that man off with him?"

"He's probably thinking that he wants to understand his father. It's no different from Sam wanting to understand her mother, and you are the reason that she doesn't."

"You know so little about what took place," Marin said. "You know so little about how I offered a different type of protection. And it doesn't matter what you think. All that matters is that I find Tray and keep him safe from Lyasanna."

"If she really is his mother, why would she hurt him? Why would she do anything that would bring harm to him?"

"You don't understand the Anders," Marin said. "You don't understand the reason they are here, holed up in the city, hidden within the palace. If you did, maybe, but no. You *can't* understand."

She came around the table and grabbed him, jerking him to his feet with the strength he'd learned to expect from her. "Come. If Samara has the eel venom, that is where we are going."

"Why? What does it matter who has the eel venom?"

"It matters because few have managed to extract it. It matters because the venom is the key to many things."

"The easar paper?"

"Easar paper? Is that what you think is the only reason to care about it?" She shook her head. "No. Now, you are going to come with me."

She dragged him out of the tavern and into the darkened street. It was late enough that there wasn't anyone out, and Alec didn't have any hope of finding anyone here. Bastan's men had abandoned this section in their attempt to rescue him.

"Why do you want to hurt her so much?" Alec asked.

"Hurt her? If I wanted to hurt Sam, I would have done so long ago."

"Then why are you doing this?"

"She has to know. She has to be exposed to the truths. She has to see it. Because she is in a better position to change it than I ever was."

"I don't understand."

"No. Because you're a Scribe."

She said it was such derision that Alec paused. Wasn't Master Jessup her Scribe? Didn't she have someone who she worked with?

They crossed the canal, and Alec wasn't surprised to see that there were no guards. At this time, this late hour, there wouldn't be, not any that cared whether people got out of Caster. She dragged him through the streets, taking a straight line toward the Hosd section.

"You were working with Ryn?" he asked.

"Ryn. Others like him. It's time the safety of the palace is squeezed."

"The people in these sections won't attack the palace."

"No, not at first, but with enough pressure, the palace will no longer be the safe haven that the Anders have found it to be over the years. With enough pressure, they will be forced to step outside of their walls, and then—"

"Do you really think that you'll be around long enough to take vengeance on them?"

"This isn't about vengeance. This is about doing what is right. I've waited long enough, sitting on the side, watching. I thought it wouldn't matter, and that I could help guide Samara and Tray, but events prompted me to take action."

"You were responsible for many of those events."

"I wasn't responsible for bringing the Thelns into the city. They came after Lyasanna on their own after the Kavers made the mistake of reengaging with the Thelns."

He fell silent as she dragged him along the street. Alec couldn't think of anything to ask or say, but felt a burgeoning sense of unease rolling through him at their steady pace. Eventually, she would get him into the Hosd section, and when she did, he feared he would be forced into something he wanted no part of.

Every so often, he would attempt to jerk his arm free, but to no avail.

When they reached the crossing that would take them over to Hosd, Alec decided he had to take one last chance.

He yanked on his sleeve and managed to pry himself free of Marin's grip.

Surprise filled him, but he turned and ran, heading into the city and away from her. He cast a glance over his shoulder, fearing she would chase him, but she did not. Instead, she headed across the canal, away from him.

And over to Sam.

Without augmentations, there wasn't anything he could do to help her. He needed easar paper, and there was only one place where he could go to get it.

Could he reach the university fast enough?

Alec ran through the streets, moving as quickly as he ever had. Everything blurred past, and his mind raced nearly as fast. He needed to get there before Marin reached Sam. He needed to get to Master Helen and a supply of easar paper. That would be his only way of helping Sam.

He lost track of how long it took him to reach the university. When he crossed into that section, he briefly nodded at the guards, fearing they might stop him at this time of night. He no longer had the sigil that Sam had given him, the sigil that would grant him access to the palace grounds.

Once inside the university, he raced into the hospital ward. Hopefully, Master Helen had gone there, using the knowledge that he had gained about the eel venom to help those who were injured, but he saw only a few junior physickers, no one else. He hurried over to one of them, a fat man by the name of Fenwick.

"Have you seen Master Helen?"

Fenwick frowned at him. "It's late, Physicker Stross."

"I understand that it's late. But have you seen Master Helen?"

His brow furrowed. "No. Master Helen has not been here, Physicker Stross."

Alec scanned the room. He saw his father lying motionless, and his gaze darted to Beckah near him, and even to Kara. He could help all of them, but first, he needed easar paper. Now that he knew—really knew—that they were injured by eel venom, he could help them.

"If you see Master Helen, tell her I'm looking for her."

Alec raced up to his room. The door was slightly ajar, and he entered carefully. He had always been careful about closing it, but maybe Master Helen and Sam had come here when they were looking for him.

He had a scrap—nothing more than that—and he dug through his supplies, coming to a journal near the bottom of the stack that was older than many of the rest.

Stuffed between the pages was a partial page of easar paper.

Alec threw it on to his desk and rummaged through drawers until he came upon a vial of his and Sam's blood. It was old—possibly weeks old—and he didn't know how effective it would be. Did its age matter?

He had to try. He sat down at the desk and started writing.

31

BROTHERS AND A BATTLE

Sam reached a door at the back of the building and ripped it open. She had augmentations that allowed her to do so with much more force than she normally would, and it practically came off the frame, much as the door had when she had been captured by Jessup. This time, it wasn't anything about Alec's augmentations, it was more about what she had managed to do on her own.

Marin had been right about that.

Sam could hardly believe she had told her the truth. But there was no denying it, not anymore.

It had first worked when she was attempting to rescue Alec, and now that she had tried it again while working for Bastan, it had been even more apparent.

If Marin had been telling the truth about that, could she have been telling the truth about Tray?

If so, it meant Lyasanna was guilty.

It meant the people Sam had been working for—and

on behalf of—weren't the people she should have been working for.

There was another room on the side, and several men were startled by her sudden appearance.

Sam glared at them.

She knew that her short stature was not intimidating —not in the slightest—but she swung her staff and leapt forward, spinning toward the men and dropping them as quickly as she could. They didn't have a chance to even react.

There was another door behind the first, and Sam pulled that one open. Surprisingly, her augmentation didn't seem to be fading, not as it did when Alec used the easar paper. Maybe when she applied her own augmentation, there was no failure to it.

Sam hurried through that room and into another. This one was as large as the first, nearly as large as Ryn's tavern, but was not decorated nearly as well. It was sparse, very few things here at all, nothing other than a chair with shackles.

This was where they had kept Bastan.

Sam hurried forward.

There were two doors on the other side of the room. Sam hesitated. If she chose the wrong door, she risked delaying her response for Bastan. He needed her to choose correctly. If she didn't, then… Would Ryn escape? Was he taking Bastan with him?

She wasn't going to let that happen.

Sam hurried to the first door and kicked it open. There was nothing there but a storeroom.

She made her way to the other and kicked it open.

With her augmentations, the door splintered, and when it opened, it smacked a man who had been on the other side. She darted forward, slamming her staff into his chest and throwing him to the ground. She raced past him, meeting a line of people, and unscrewed the ends of her staff as she hurried through the hall.

She moved as she never had before, knocking the men down, enhanced in a way that felt surprisingly natural.

She reached the end of the hallway, and there was another door.

She tested the handle and found it locked, so she kicked it open, screwing the ends of her canal staff back together. It was a better weapon that way.

Ryn waited. Two men stood behind him on either side of Bastan, holding him in place.

Ryn had a knife to Bastan's throat.

"Now that you're here, let's see what choice you might make."

"Why are you doing this?" she asked.

"Why? When he decided to press his influence, I decided it was time for me to press mine."

"He only did it for—"

Bastan shook his head slightly, barely any movement.

"I know why he did it," Ryn said.

"You don't know anything, not nearly what you think you do," Bastan said. He remained incredibly calm despite the fact that he was held in place and there was a knife up to his throat.

"Really? I seem to know that I have captured you without very much difficulty."

"Very much difficulty? How long have you been at it?

How long have you been trying to chase me down?" Bastan laughed bitterly. "You wouldn't even have managed what you have had it not been for me. Were it not for my connections, you would know nothing about the venom."

"Just because I wouldn't have discovered it as quickly doesn't mean I wouldn't have learned anything," Ryn said.

Sam took a step forward, and Ryn shook his head, warning her back.

"I think that would be a bad idea, Samara."

He said her name in a knowing way. Had Bastan revealed her name? Or had it been the "she" Ryn had referred to earlier? Someone who was supposedly "concerned" about her.

"What?" Sam asked. "Do you want me to believe that you would actually kill your brother?"

"My brother? He hasn't been my brother for decades. Ever since he decided that he didn't need me. He discarded me, the same way he will discard everyone else he cares for—or, he pretends to care for."

"I didn't discard you. Your violence separated us."

"Violence? I find that amusing coming from you, Bastan."

Sam's mind raced. Did she have enough augmentation to hurry forward and strike before Ryn managed to cut Bastan's throat? If she did, she would have to hit him in such a way that threw him away from Bastan.

Maybe Bastan could help.

It wasn't that he was weak. The gods knew he was strong and had always seemed strong for someone his age. Sam had always felt that way about Bastan.

That left her trusting her augmentations.

It meant trusting that she could reach him in time and before Ryn had a chance to slaughter him.

"Why do you even care?" she asked, trying to distract Ryn. "What does it matter what Bastan did all those years ago? All that matters is that the two of you—"

"All that matters is that the two of us are competing for our place in the city. And with Bastan gone, and with my special connection, the rest of the city will fall into line."

"You have no special connection," Bastan said.

"I don't? I find that interesting, especially considering how well she seemed to know you."

"Marin?" Sam asked. Her gaze drifted to Bastan and his brow furrowed. "Is that who you're talking about?"

"The mistress has not provided me her name. She hasn't needed to, especially given that everything she has promised has come to fruition. She promised she would provide me with a way to expand my influence. She promised she would help eliminate those who might interfere. And she promised to bring my brother to me."

Bastan tensed. Sam could see it from where she stood and knew that if he were to lunge, if he were to make the mistake of trying to attack, all it would take would be a short slip of Ryn's knife.

She needed to act before he made a mistake.

At least she understood why everything seemed to be connected. It was because it was. Marin had used her influence to reveal the true nature of the eel venom. Had she been the one to use it against Alec's father?

Could she be the reason Sam hadn't been given augmentations from Alec?

Kyza!

She had to end this and get back to Caster, so she could determine what exactly had happened. She wouldn't put it past Marin to have been involved.

She nodded. "Bastan?"

"I am fine, Samara."

"I wanted you to know…" She swallowed. She needed to get this out, especially if something happened before she rescued him. She had to tell him how she felt before there was no chance to do so.

"Samara," he started, but the two men jerked on his arms.

Bastan tensed. She had seen that angry, clenched jaw expression from him before.

Ryn watched her. "You think you might say something that would somehow rescue him? Lower your staff."

"All I wanted to tell him was that he's been a father to me, especially since I didn't have a father, either. I wanted him to know before…"

"Before what?" Ryn asked.

"Before I take you down."

Sam jumped.

Her augmentation flowed through her, and it gave her strength, helping carry her forward. She swung her staff around toward Ryn's chest, wanting to keep him from jabbing forward with the knife.

She was too slow.

The knife slashed.

Bastan jerked his head backward, and there was a

gentle spray of blood. He slammed into the two men behind him, and they went crashing to the ground.

Sam swung her staff around, anger pulsing through her as she hit Ryn. He collapsed and stopped moving.

She vaulted and landed next to one of the men, stabbing down with her staff. She flipped again, coming to land near the other man, and kicked him in the head.

Another man was reaching for Bastan, and using her augmented strength, she jerked Bastan free.

Blood covered his face.

She had been too late. Even with augmentations, she had been too late.

Her hand went to his neck.

"I'm sorry, Bastan. I wasn't fast enough."

"You were fast enough, Samara."

"No. Let me see your neck. Let's see if we can't—"

Bastan shook her away. "He didn't do anything more than graze me," Bastan said.

He moved his hand, and she saw that there was a deep gash, but it didn't seem to spurt blood, not as she had expected.

"You… You're going to be okay?"

"I don't know. I would never have expected him to take such steps," Bastan said, wiping his hands on his pants as he looked over at Ryn, who lay motionless.

"I thought you said you didn't know what happened to your brother?"

"I didn't. As far as I knew, he left the city."

"You hadn't heard anything of Rynance Vold?"

"I've heard the name, but that's not my brother. He went by a different name, though at the time, so did I."

There was a thunderous crash and the sound of shouting, and Bastan looked over Sam's shoulder. She released her grip on him and stood, preparing to fight, but a line of men appeared, led by Tanis.

"You did this?" he asked Sam.

"You taught me well," she said. "You taught me to look out for those I care about. I couldn't just leave you here, not when there was something I could do about it."

Bastan smiled. Sam had never seen him smile—not a real smile. This was a flash of true emotion, and it reached his eyes in a way that other emotions from Bastan did not. "Thank you," Bastan said.

"It's not over," Sam said.

"No. It never is."

"It's about Marin."

"That is what I understand."

"But… I can't kill her. I can't even turn her over to someone who might."

"And why is that?" Bastan asked softly.

"Because she knows something that matters. She might have acted wrongly, but I'm not entirely convinced that her motivations were terrible."

"She allowed Ryn to pursue me. If it were up to Marin, she would have killed me," Bastan said.

"But she didn't," Sam said.

"Samara—"

Sam shook her head. "Please, Bastan. I don't want to fight with you over this. I need to have a chance to find Marin, and then…" And then she would use her. Sam understood why Marin had stayed in the city, now. She had believed that Tray was still here.

"What do you need from me?"

She didn't know quite how to respond. Bastan hadn't questioned her. He simply had asked what she needed from him. There was a time when that would never have happened, a time when he would have challenged her, but had so much changed between them?

"I'm afraid something might happen to Alec. He was in Caster, and remained behind, to help me… To give me strength," she said, choosing her words carefully. Now that others were in the room, she needed to be more careful. She didn't want to reveal too much, regardless of whether these others worked with Bastan. They might be his family, but she hadn't decided whether they were hers. "Bastan, he's my family."

Bastan took a deep breath. "I have a hunch this is how it feels when a father has to let his daughter move on."

Sam laughed. "Just because I told you that you were something of a father figure to me doesn't mean that you get to act all paternal."

"I think I get to decide how I will act," Bastan said.

"Will you help?"

"He's your family. Which means that he is mine."

AFTER MARIN

Ryn was heavier than he looked, and Sam dragged him from the room, keeping his hands bound behind his back. Bastan looked ridiculous with a bandage tied around his neck, wearing it as if it were nothing more than a scarf, but he leaned occasionally on Tanis, admitting to Sam that he was more injured than he let on.

"You should go back to the tavern and rest," she said.

"Not until this is done."

"You're no good to me if you're dead."

"Is that right?"

"I don't mean it like that. All I'm trying to say is that—"

"I understand what you're trying to say." They stepped out of Ryn's tavern and into the night air. All of a sudden, Sam realized that she was exhausted. Fatigue set in, and it was nothing like fatigue she had felt before. When she had used augmentations with Alec, she had often been tired after them. This was something quite a bit different. This was fatigue that seemed to settle deep within her, and she wasn't sure she would be able to go after Marin. It might be that she needed to rest.

There was a soft splashing nearby.

The swamp.

Those stupid eels within the swamp were splashing around.

"Bastan—"

She cut off when she realized the splashing couldn't be the eels. It was too rhythmic. It was the sound of a...

Kyza!

"Take Ryn. Get back to Caster," she said to Bastan.

"Why? What's happening?"

Sam looked out into the night, staring out over the swamp. There was a strange reflective glow over the swamp. "Nothing you can handle."

"Samara."

She turned back to him. "No. Not with this. With this, I have to take care of it. If I allow her to get too close to the rest of you, there's a chance that someone else will get hurt. I can't have that." She stepped over to him and gave him a quick hug. It felt strange hugging Bastan, but at the same time, there was something reassuring about it. He was strong, and he was able to protect her most of the time, but this was a time when she would have to protect him. "Please, Bastan."

"Don't get yourself killed."

"I won't."

She reached into her pocket and dipped the pen into the eel venom. If she was left with no other option, she may have to use it. She didn't like that idea, much as she didn't like the idea of losing Marin before she had the answers she wanted, but she wasn't going to let her hurt anyone else.

Sam flipped out into the night.

When she landed, she perched on her staff, looking around. The steady splashing was out there, near the shore, but not so near that she could see where Marin was coming from.

She focused on augmentations.

She needed to augment her strength and her speed, but right now, sight would be the most beneficial. She thought about what Alec might write, thinking about the way he would disparage her normally weak eyesight, and use some combination of enhancing medicines that would give her better sight. She tried to think about the sense of cold that would wash through her.

Were she not so tired, she wondered if it would be easier.

It came.

Slowly—ever so slowly—the sense of the augmentation washed over her.

With it, everything seemed to lighten.

In the distance, she saw another staff, and Marin perched on it. She was probably two hundred yards away, far enough that she may not even see Sam, not without enhancements of her own. Did Marin know enough to add visual enhancements?

Of course she did. After all, Marin was the one who had told her how to enhance herself.

Sam had to believe that Marin didn't want to hurt her. Or maybe she did, but more than anything, Marin's primary interest was Tray. He had been her focus all along.

Sam had to use that.

Tray was *her* focus too.

She flipped out into the swamp, trying to land softly so she didn't make too much of a splash. She didn't want to draw Marin's attention before she had a chance to get close enough to counter her.

Sam watched, and Marin started toward the shore again.

Was there any way she could head her off?

It would take a significant jump—and strength she didn't have without an augmentation.

Could she add another augmentation, or was she already pushing the limits of her strength?

Sam took a deep breath and focused on strength. With it, as she often did, she wanted speed, but she decided that strength might be the most important this time.

Even more slowly than before, the sense of the augmentation washed over her, and she jumped.

When she landed, she was directly in front of Marin.

Sam kicked, thinking she could disrupt Marin, but the woman was quick, and she grabbed Sam's leg, trying to pull her off her staff. Sam jerked her leg free, the augmentation granting her enough strength to do so.

"Your Scribe must have found more paper."

"Did you hurt him?"

"Hurt him? Why would I hurt him?"

"You don't have to do this, Marin. Tray isn't even in the city."

"Ah, I know that now. Your Scribe told me. Much as he told me that you have the remainder of the eel venom."

Sam tapped her pocket, perched on her staff as she was, just far enough away that she couldn't be attacked where she stood. Marin would have to leap at her with an augmented jump.

"Why do you want the eel venom?"

"There are things that need to be done, Samara."

"Like poisoning Lyasanna?"

"You say that as if she doesn't deserve it."

"I don't know what she deserves. I don't even know if I can trust what you've told me she did. All I know is that you claim Lyasanna wanted Tray dead when he was born. All I know is that you used the Book of Maladies on me to steal my memories because of something that my mother did."

"It wasn't all about your mother," Marin said. She jumped and swung around with her staff, and it nearly cracked into Sam's head. She moved fast—much faster than what Sam could counter, even with her strength augmentation. She needed speed, but she didn't have it— not yet. She wasn't sure she would be able to focus on that augmentation while facing Marin.

"You could have been skilled," Marin said. "And it is a shame that there isn't more that I can do to explain my actions, but know that Tray is my primary focus."

"Why just Tray? You used me for some reason. There was something about my connection to him that was important."

"I thought there was, but now that your mother has gotten to you…"

Marin jumped again, and she swung her staff around.

The movement was so quick that even as Sam tried to push off, Marin's staff collided with hers, and Sam went down.

She would hit the water. There was no way to avoid it, not now, and when she did…

Then the eels would attack.

She plunged into the foul-smelling water, holding tightly to her staff. As soon as she went down, she tried to push her staff into the muddy bottom of the swamp, so she could climb back up, but it wouldn't gain purchase. It was her body weight and movement that typically allowed it to push deep into the muck. She continued to work at it, floundering underneath the water, and then she felt movement near her.

Kyza!

Was this going to be how she would die?

Alec had explained the barbed tale of the eel, and she had seen men die from the poison, and she wanted nothing to do with it. The eels seemed drawn to her, especially the way they continued to attack her staff when she was out in the swamp. There was no way she would avoid them.

Cold washed over her.

Was that the water, or was that her augmentation fading? Something bumped up against her.

She pushed, and with a heave of strength, she managed to clear the water. When she did, something clamped on to her leg.

An eel.

It was clamped on, but it wasn't piercing her skin.

How was that possible?

Could Alec have actually found easar paper? Was that the reason?

She grabbed the eel and pulled it off her leg and flung it at Marin.

The other woman tried to move, but the eel arced, twisting toward her, and the mouth clamped on to her foot.

Marin jumped, flipping into the air, and when she landed, Sam saw the spiked tail swing around. She wasn't even sure whether it was intentional or not. It might have simply been Marin's movement that forced the tail into her thigh.

Marin screamed and slipped off of her staff.

Kyza!

She didn't want to help Marin, but at the same time, she didn't want to lose her and lose the possibility of answers.

Sam flipped forward and landed near where Marin had gone underwater. The woman's canal staff drifted away, floating across the surface of the water.

She prayed softly that Alec's augmentations continued to hold. If they didn't, she would be once again vulnerable should the eels attack.

Taking a deep breath, she dived beneath the surface. It was no more pleasant than above. She found Marin and jerked her free, and then pushed off with a massive heave of her staff, flipping forward. Reaching the shore would be difficult, and she didn't know if her augmentation would last long enough, and so far, it didn't seem as if

Alec had given her any other augmentation other than the impermeable skin.

Cold started to drain away from her.

This time, she knew it was the augmentation fading.

The shore was only ten feet away.

Sam pushed off and threw herself forward.

As she did, the rest of her augmentation failed.

She splashed down only a few feet from shore.

She kept Marin wrapped around her, hoping the augmentation Alec had placed would hold, and felt an immediate flurry of eels swarming around her, attempting to grab at her legs. She kicked, afraid to stop moving, afraid that one of their tails might stab into her.

And then hands grabbed her and pulled her out of the water.

She rested on the shore, taking a deep, gasping breath. Bastan looked down at her.

"You were supposed to go back to Caster," she said looking up at him.

"And you were supposed to stay out of the water."

Sam rolled over. She was exhausted. It was the kind of exhaustion that she hadn't felt in quite some time. It was the kind of exhaustion that would take a long time to recover from.

And yet, she had Marin. Whatever else happened, she had Marin.

But for how long? if she did nothing, the woman would die.

She reached into Marin's pockets and found soggy pages of easar paper. They would be useless now. There was the jar that Alec had filled with the strange milky white fluid, and she opened it.

"Are you going to tell me what you're doing?" Bastan asked.

"Look at her leg," Sam said.

Bastan glanced to Marin's legs, and then he pulled back the fabric of her pants, revealing the deep puncture wound. The skin around the wound had blackened, and it was already starting to work up toward her chest.

"There's nothing that can stop this, Samara. Without the apothecary—"

With a surge of inspiration, she jabbed the pen into the jar of milky liquid and then stabbed it into Marin's leg.

"Samara?"

"Alec thinks these two venoms will counter each other," she said.

"And if they don't?"

"Then Marin dies, and with her, so does any chance that I can really understand what happened to me and get answers as to why she used me in her plan with Tray."

Bastan frowned and settled himself down on the ground. He looked worse than Sam felt. How badly had he been beaten by Ryn's men?

"Samara, even if she doesn't come around, you understand that the answers you seek may not be the answers that you need."

"Fatherly advice now?"

"General advice. I've seen plenty of men who go in search of something and when they find it, it's nothing quite like they had hoped it would be."

Sam breathed out in a heavy sigh. Perhaps Bastan was

right. Perhaps any answer that she might get would not matter. And perhaps all she needed was to focus on the people around her that she could trust and that she cared about.

"But I might need her," she said.

"Why?" There seemed to be hurt in his voice, and she owed it to Bastan to explain.

"Because, whatever else, I have to go after Tray. Marin might be the only one who can teach me what I need to know."

"You don't think your mother can teach you?"

"I think Marin knows things that my mother does not."

Bastan just nodded. He sat next to Sam, neither of them saying anything, watching Marin. Sam didn't know how long it would take to see if the antivenom worked, but as time passed, stretching out into long moments, she began to think the worst.

And then, Marin took a gasping breath.

Sam looked over to Bastan. "I… I think I'm too tired to hold her."

"Don't worry. You don't have to hold her."

"Somebody does, Bastan. Marin doesn't need to be augmented to have her abilities."

Bastan looked at Marin, and the same intensity came to his eyes that she had seen before. "With this, I think I am able to ensure that she does not escape. Maybe I put her and Ryn together."

"Bastan," Sam started, "you really can be a bastard."

He laughed.

"But you're *my* bastard."

HEALING

Sam found Alec at the university.

"You... You're still alive," Alec said.

Sam glanced over her shoulder and waved to the two men Bastan had sent with her to ensure that she made it here safely. This was where she needed to come, mostly because if there was anything she could do to help Alec, she needed to be here. If it was about easar paper, the pages she had taken back from Marin should be enough to help with those at the university who were poisoned by the eel venom.

"I think because of you," Sam said.

"I managed to find a scrap of easar paper. I don't have much, and the"—he lowered his voice and leaned toward her as they made their way through the halls of the university—"blood that I have is old, so I wasn't sure whether it would work."

He started to guide her up the stairs and toward his

quarters, but she shook her head. "We need to go and help your father and the others."

"Sam, we don't have easar paper. I can't find Master Helen or any of the other Scribes, and I don't have my sigil to get over to the palace."

"I don't know that it matters," she said.

"What? Finding Master Helen or the other Scribes? They can help us, especially if it is about having easar paper."

Sam shook her head. "I don't know that I can go back to the palace, not yet."

"Why?" Alec looked at her with a deep expression of concern.

"I'm not sure I can trust them. I don't know how much of what Marin has told me is the truth."

"You know, you could just go and ask the princess."

"I don't know that I can." Even if she went to Lyasanna, would she tell Sam the truth? Sam wasn't sure Lyasanna had told her anything that was true. And what reason would she have to be truthful with her?

"Come on, let's go down to your father. I have some easar paper that I rescued from Marin. It's a little wet, but…"

Alec took the paper from her when she pulled it from her pocket, and smoothed it out, rubbing it against his chest. "This should be more than enough."

He hurriedly guided them down to the hospital ward, and they reached the cot with his father lying on it. There was another physicker standing next to him, and he had a vial of some liquid in his hands that he was trying to administer to Alec's father.

"What are you doing?" Alec asked.

"He started to tremble," the physicker said.

"What are you using on him?"

Alec didn't wait and grabbed the vial from the other man.

"This won't work. Didn't you learn anything from the other patient? Go. Leave me with him."

The man hurried off, glaring at Alec.

"I get the sense that not everyone is thrilled with your promotion."

Alec glanced up and his gaze shifted briefly to the other physicker. "Maybe not," he said. "But if they knew how to handle treatments better, it wouldn't matter."

Sam liked this Alec, the confident one. He had every reason to be confident in his abilities and his knowledge, and too often, he was not.

She held her hand out, and he glanced at it before making a small cut in the center of her palm. He did the same on himself and hurriedly began to write. She watched the words as they formed on the first page of the easar paper and waited.

Within a few moments, the trembling stopped. Another moment later, his father awoke.

"Alec?" His father's voice was weak.

Alec leaned toward his father and wrapped his arms around him in a hug. "Father? It worked." Tears welled in his eyes.

"What… What did you do?"

"It's the easar paper. We—"

His father shook his head weakly. "The easar paper

won't work on this. It will be temporary. You need to find the…"

His father faded.

Alec's eyes went wide. "I don't understand it. The easar paper has always worked."

"Maybe it's the paper." When Alec looked up at her, she shrugged. "Both Marin and Helen seem to think the eel venom is tied to the paper. Maybe the poisoning can't be countered with the paper."

Alex dropped onto the floor. "If that's true, then the only way to help them would be by harvesting more eels. That will take too long," Alec said. "And considering that he has started to have the same seizures as Kara, I don't know how long we have."

Sam reached into her pocket and pulled out the two jars of eel venom. "Then use these."

Alec's eyes widened. "You have them? Marin had taken the one I had, and I thought—"

"I got it back from her."

"I don't even know if it will work," Alec said. "It needs to be tested before we try, or we might end up—"

"It works. Marin was attacked by an eel, and I used the antivenom on her. You were right about this," Sam said, taking his hand.

Alec took a deep breath. He grabbed the milky venom and spooned a small amount into his father's mouth. "What if this ends up killing him?"

"It won't. Trust me."

They waited. Moments passed without anything changing.

Had it been too long since Aelus had been poisoned? Could it be that the antivenom *wouldn't* work now?

Alec just shook his head and let out a mournful sound. "It's not working. And if the easar paper won't work, then—"

Sam looked at the other jar. The combination was what was important, but what if they'd tried the wrong one? Maybe his father had been poisoned with the milky venom and needed the other one now. "Try this one."

"This is the venom," Alec said.

"You said it was all about the combination, right? Does it matter the order?"

Alec watched her and then started laughing. "You might be right. Even if it doesn't work, he's already dying."

Alec picked up he jar of yellowish liquid and put a small amount on the spoon, and Sam noticed that he held his breath when he dipped it into his father's mouth.

They waited.

A few moments passed, and then a few more.

Sam was convinced that their treatment would be ineffective, but then, surprisingly, Alec's father opened his eyes.

"Alec?"

"It's me," he said.

"The paper won't work. It will be temporary. You need to use the—"

"I need to use the antivenom."

His father frowned. "Antivenom? No. It would be the venom."

Alec frowned. "Why do you think that?"

"Because I know what was used. It was a combination of the flesh with the fluid at the incisor."

Alec glanced over to Sam. "Are you saying you made that?"

"You don't understand."

"What don't I understand, Father? Have you… Have you been making poisons?"

His father kept his gaze. "There has to be some way to fund my work, Alec."

"I thought you did what you did because it was the right thing."

"It is the right thing to heal those that we can. It is right to offer our services to those who need it."

"And what about offering services to those who would hurt someone else?"

"Alec, everything isn't black and white. There are shades of gray that you need to be aware of."

Alec stared at his father for a moment before shaking his head. "Just when I think I have come to understand you, you do something like this. Do you know how many have been hurt because of what you did? Do you know how many were poisoned because of you?"

"Nobody else should have been affected."

"No one? There were others—many others. And all because of your desire to do what?" Alec took a step toward his father and rested his hands on either side of the bed. "There continue to be things that you conceal from me," he said. "How much more haven't you shared?"

"Alec, there are things that I've been trying to protect you from."

"Protect me from? I've gotten more involved because you hid things from me. And now…" Alec shook his head.

Sam grabbed him and pulled him away. "I think it's better to just take a step back," she said. "We can talk with him more later."

"I don't know that I have anything to talk to him about," Alec said.

"You don't mean that," Sam said. "This is your father."

Alec studied her for a moment. "Come on. We need to help the others."

She nodded, not sure what to say. She'd not seen Alec this angry before. She understood it, but it still surprised her.

They stopped at Beckah's cot, where she lay still motionless. Alec worked quickly preparing the eel venom. Sam still didn't understand what had happened or how the venoms had worked, only that Aelus had concocted something different from what even Alec had thought. He placed a few drops of venom into Beckah's mouth and looked up.

"Bastan needs to know so he can help Kevin," he said. "And you need to have him find Tanis. I healed him using easar paper. He needs the venom, too, or he'll relapse and die."

"I'll send word," Sam said.

"And when were done, then it's time for us to go after Tray," Alec said.

"Are you sure that's a good idea? Think about what Master Helen and the others have said about the temptation for you in the Thelns lands."

"You don't think I can withstand the temptation?"

"I'm sure you can, it's just…"

Alec looked back to where his father lay and let out a heavy breath. "I need to do this with you, Sam. I need to understand myself just as much as you need to understand yourself. If that means going to the Thelns lands and seeing what they can teach me about what it means for me to be a Scribe, then that is what I need to do."

Sam could only nod. Alec deserve answers just as much as she deserved to understand why Marin had stolen her memories, and why she had used Sam with Tray.

"I intend to bring Marin with me."

As Beckah began to stir, he looked up at her. "And I think my father will need to come with us."

Grab the penultimate volume in The Book of Maladies: Amnesia

Deception runs deeper than the canals in Verdholm.

Taveling to the Theln lands will be dangerous and possibly deadly, forcing Sam to ask for help from an unlikely ally. What she learns reveals how she is woefully underprepared for the journey, but she doesn't dare wait any longer. Her brother's life might depend upon her ability to reach him.

While Sam prepares, Alec uses the newly discovered secret of the canal eels to try and understand the key to making easar paper. A visit with his father reveals that his deception runs deeper than Alec had ever imagined and that his mother might hold the key to what he's searching for.

Just as Sam and Alec think they understand what must be done, a shocking revelation proves another deception, one that threatens not only the safety of the city, but of the ruling Anders family. Somehow, they are the only ones able to challenge a foe who has planned an attack for a decade or longer, leaving them to question everything they have learned about themselves.

People:

- Aelus Stross: An apothecary and skilled healer. Alec's father
- Alec Stross: a physicker
- Bastan: a thief who essentially runs Caster
- Elaine: Sam's mother. Kaver.
- Hyp: a moneylender in the Arrend section who frequents Aelus's shop
- Kevin: Bastan's employee
- Lyassana Anders: Princess, Scribe to Elaine
- Mags: a painter with a unique talent
- Marcella Rubbles: owner of a stationary store in Arrend
- Marin: a Kaver who had a dangerous assignment
- Master Carl: Master Physicker, unpleasant to Alec

- Master Eckerd: Master Physicker, mentor to Alec
- Master Helen: Master Physicker
- Ralun: A Theln
- Rynance Vold: A dangerous man
- Samara (Sam) Elseth: a thief
- Trayson (Tray) Elseth: Sam's brother

Places and Terms:

- Arrend section: a merchant section
- Balan Day: a day to celebrate the festival god
- canal eels: possibly mythical creatures living in the canals
- Callesh section: a merchant section
- Caster section: a lowborn outer section of the city
- Central Canal: the canal that separates the lowborn sections from the merchants and highborns
- Drash section: a merchant section
- easar paper: magical paper
- Farnum section: a merchant section
- Highborn: a term for the wealthier living in the center of the city
- Hosd section: a lowborn section near the swamp
- Jaku section: a highborn section where easar paper was found.

- Kyza: one of the many gods worshipped in Verdholm
- Lostin section: a merchant section
- Lowborn: a term for people living in the outer sections of the city
- Lycithan: a southern nation. Known for their skilled artisans.
- Narvin Plains: east of the city, thin stretch of land
- Physicker: healers with specialized training at the university
- Piare River: connects to Ralan Bay and the canals
- Ralan Bay: a trading hub along the coast of Verdholm
- Sacred Alms: the healing religion Alec follows
- Sornum: Bastan's tavern
- Thelns: dangerous brutes
- Valun: a country known for various artifacts, including the stout rope Sam uses
- Verdholm: an isolated city situated near the coast with canals running through it separating it into different sections
- Yisl: one of the many gods worshipped in Verdholm

The Dark Ability

The Heartstone Blade

The Tower of Venass

Blood of the Watcher

The Shadowsteel Forge

The Guild Secret

Rise of the Elder

The Sighted Assassin

The Binders Game

The Forgotten

Assassin's End

The Teralin Sword

Soldier Son

Soldier Sword

Soldier Sworn

Soldier Saved

Soldier Scarred

Printed in Great Britain
by Amazon